Was it an accident—
or deliberate cruelty?

"Oh, Lord," Clint said when he and Blair entered the barn and found Black Magic, the champion stallion, lying on the floor. Clint examined the horse, then moved one of its front legs.

"It's broken," Clint announced. "How the hell did this happen?"

"I don't suppose we could save him," Blair murmured doubtfully.

"The bone is shattered. We don't have any choice."

She remained silent, realizing that he was right.

Suddenly Clint remembered the Thoroughbred on the neighboring farm who'd broken a leg in much the same manner three months ago. Perhaps it was only a coincidence. Then again …

"This is looking damn suspicious," he growled.

"You're not suggesting …"

"That someone purposely broke Black Magic's leg? That's precisely what I *am* suggesting. Someone wants to destroy Clearwater Hills Farm!"

RISKY PLEASURE

JoANN ROSS

Harlequin Books

TORONTO • NEW YORK • LONDON
AMSTERDAM • PARIS • SYDNEY • HAMBURG
STOCKHOLM • ATHENS • TOKYO • MILAN

To my niece,
Barbara Elliott, with love,
and to Star Helmer,
whose idea it was to bring Brandy and Ryan's book to life.

———————————————

Harlequin Intrigue edition published October 1985

ISBN 0-373-22027-8

Chapter One

Jason Langley was dead.

The thought struck as harshly as the intense California sun flooding Clint Hollister's bedroom. Seconds later, the dull throbbing in his head reminded him of last night. At least he'd sent the old man off in style. Squeezing his eyes shut against the blinding morning light, Clint reached out, unerringly locating the glass of bourbon resting on the bedside table. He propped himself up on one elbow and downed the fiery liquor in long, thirsty swallows.

Clint's mouth felt as if Patton's entire army had marched through it on the way to liberate Paris. Today was going to be rough enough without his having to face it with the granddaddy of all hangovers.

The ringing of the phone shattered his bleak thoughts, and he dispensed with amenities as he growled "Yeah?" into the mouthpiece.

"Hollister?" The cultured male voice on the other end displayed a moment of confusion.

Clint groaned. *When it rains, it pours.* "It's me, Blackwood," he confirmed. "What do you want now?"

"I was calling to remind you of the reading of the will this morning. You are planning to attend, aren't you?"

Clint shook his head, regretting the motion as rocks tumbled about in his brain. He flung away the sheet and swung his legs to the floor, slumping on the edge of the mattress.

"Look," he suggested, "why don't you just call me this afternoon and give me a rundown? After all, the whole deal is pretty cut-and-dried. Blair MacKenzie is the old man's only living relative. So she inherits the ranch, sells it to the highest bidder, and goes back to New York City, where she belongs."

He bent down, groping for the crumpled pack of cigarettes on the floor. He pulled out a cigarette and tapped it absently on the bedside table before sticking it between tightly set lips.

"That's a tidy little scenario you're painting, Hollister," Ramsey Blackwood allowed. "But you may be in for a surprise."

Clint lit the cigarette, inhaling the smoke deep into his lungs, willing his mind and body to forgive last night's abuse and come to life.

"No way. Jason left Clearwater Hills Farm to his granddaughter, and she's the last person in the world who'd want to hang around a horse farm."

"You seem very certain of that."

"I should be. I was with him last month when he turned down an offer to sell the place. He said he was paying off some old debts by leaving the place to our exotic Ms. Tigress Perfume...although what a woman like that would want with a horse farm is beyond me."

"Jason built a very profitable stable."

"It's only profitable if the owner knows what he's doing," Clint muttered. "If by any stretch of the imagination the woman did decide to stay on, she'd run the place into the ground in six months."

Jason Langley's attorney refrained from answering that accusation. "You *will* be here, won't you, Hollister? After all, you are the trainer for Clearwater Hills Farm. The old man specifically requested that you attend."

If he hadn't had enough trouble lately, Clint considered bleakly, now he was expected to spend an afternoon with Ramsey Blackwood and an empty-headed model who was about to destroy everything he'd worked for. Just what he needed. Clint couldn't remember the last time he'd ever refused the cantankerous old man anything. Lord knew, he was probably the closest thing to a friend that Jason Langley had ever had. But this was above and beyond the call of friendship.

"I've still got to pack."

"You're not staying on?"

Clint ground the cigarette out in an ashtray overflowing with butts. "Hell, no. I've worked too hard building this place up to watch some underdressed female flush it down the tubes."

Dispensing with politeness, he hung up the phone and made his way into the bathroom for a well-needed shower. He wondered idly how much Tigress perfume Jason's cover-girl granddaughter would have to wear to overcome his aroma of stale sweat, bourbon and cigarette smoke.

BLAIR MACKENZIE SAT ALONE in the backseat of the gray Mercedes, lost in thought. She was vaguely aware of Marni's flirtatious chatter, designed to charm Jason Langley's attorney, but the words were only a dull buzz in her ears. Her gaze was directed out the tinted window, her tawny brown eyes drinking in the vastness of the rolling grasslands. Blair was unable to believe the whole place was hers now. She felt like pinching herself. A lifetime dream had suddenly been dumped in her lap

She hadn't wanted to come to the farm today; she still didn't know why she just hadn't ignored the cable in the first place. Blair assured herself that it had been curiosity and not any sense of misplaced responsibility that had caused her to arrive at Clearwater Hills Farm four days after her grandfather's heart attack. The man meant nothing to her. He'd never seen fit to acknowledge her existence while he was alive, and Blair was damned if she would get all misty-eyed and pretend that she cared about his passing.

She would admit to feeling a tinge of guilt for having wanted to dance a jig when Ramsey Blackwood had informed her that she'd inherited the farm. After all, no matter how she felt about Jason Langley personally, he *had* just died; she had no business feeling as if Christmas had arrived nine months early.

That thought brought up one nagging little problem. Clint Hollister. Her entire future lay in the hands of a man she'd never met. Blair sighed, hoping he wouldn't prove difficult. She glanced over at the rearview mirror and saw the dazed look in Ramsey Blackwood's eyes as the attorney fell predictably under Marni's seductive spell. Perhaps she should just let Marni propose the idea to Mr. Hollister, Blair mused. There wasn't a man alive who could remain impervious to her best friend's charms for very long.

As enticing an idea as that was, Blair knew she could never do it. She'd been fighting her own battles all her life, and she wasn't about to back down now. Besides, she might be borrowing trouble. There was no reason to believe that Clint Hollister wouldn't jump at her offer. Especially when she was dangling such sweet bait.

The man Blair was thinking about cursed under his breath as he viewed the cloud of dust billowing up from the road. Moments later the gunmetal-gray Mercedes pulled up to a stop in front of the sprawling ranch house.

"Here, Jerry, you'd better take over," Clint said, handing the bucket of spring-water laced with baby oil to the young groom standing beside him. He patted the chestnut filly's neck. "Unless my luck has changed, your new owner has just shown up," he muttered to the horse with a frustrated sigh.

Ramsey Blackwood emerged from the driver's seat of the Mercedes, his navy-blue suit looking out of place in the rural surroundings. The two women also exited from the car. All three watched Clint cross the expanse of gravel to meet them.

"We missed you," the attorney began without preamble. Clint had been acquainted with Ramsey Blackwood long enough to know it was only the presence of the women that kept the man from professing his irritation in more graphic terms.

"I was busy."

"So I see. Isn't it a waste of the farm's expenses to have the trainer bathe a horse?"

"I would suppose that's up to the new owner to decide," Clint countered brusquely, his gaze moving to the two women.

He had to force himself not to stare at the lithe brunette standing next to the car. This was the Tigress perfume woman? No way. He'd checked out the advertisement again that morning, not that he didn't have the wildly erotic vision emblazoned on every memory cell of his brain.

The ad had shown her skimpily clad in a tiger-striped bikini, lounging beside a jungle pool, her parted lips moist, the open sexual invitation gleaming in her hooded, golden-brown eyes. Masses of thick dark hair had tumbled over bare shoulders, arranged in what he knew to be an exacting portrayal of casual disarray. She was the type of woman every man fantasized getting into his bed.

This woman was an impostor. Her dark hair was tucked demurely into a navy fedora. Her matching suit was relieved only by a simple white silk blouse and a triangle of crimson tucked into the breast pocket of the tailored navy jacket. Safely hidden behind his dark aviator glasses, Clint's eyes traveled down the long, slender legs, clad in dark stockings, to her pumps. If it hadn't been for those unforgettable legs, he'd have thought this woman was an associate of Ramsey's. She certainly resembled an attorney more than she did one of America's most popular models.

He forced himself to look at her companion and recognized her immediately. Long blond hair fell over deeply tanned bare, shoulders. Her body was poured into a strapless camisole and white designer jeans that looked as if they'd been spray-painted on her. Marni Roberts's face and figure were every bit as celebrated as Blair MacKenzie's, yet Clint noticed with detached interest that even though Marni was dressed in that revealing outfit, she didn't affect him with the same jolt as the Tigress Woman did. He turned his gaze back to the new owner of Clearwater Hills Farm.

As his eyes locked onto her face, Blair MacKenzie felt her breath catch in her throat. She couldn't remember ever having seen a more rawly masculine man. The effect he had on her went beyond his looks—although his thick silver hair, wide shoulders and broad chest were definitely impressive. The sleeves of his blue work shirt were rolled above his elbows, and his wet denim jeans clung to long, well-muscled legs.

His eyes were shielded by dark lenses, and Blair found herself guessing their color. A very good-looking man, she acknowledged, but in her business she knew plenty of good-looking men.

No, what this man possessed was an impression of explosive strength that boded ill for anyone who might be foolish enough to cross him. "Dangerous"—that was the only word that came to mind.

Blair nervously shifted her gaze to the raw-boned chestnut horse that had surprised skeptics by sweeping the New York Racing Association's Triple Crown for fillies. "She's magnificent."

Clint took a cigarette pack from his shirt pocket, ignoring Ramsey's irritated expression as he tapped the cigarette on the roof of the car.

"I've heard a lot of descriptions of Risky Pleasure over the past three years, but that's a new one." Clint knew that most people saw only the filly's admittedly less-than-noble frame at first glance.

"I saw her run last year at the Meadowlands. Except 'run' is a poor choice of words. She flew. It was the most magnificent thing I've ever seen!"

Clint fought down the pleasure that Blair's softly issued words brought him. Shrugging with feigned disinterest, he forced his voice into a short, gruff tone as he said, "Well, she's all yours now."

"Not exactly," the dapper attorney broke in. "That's why I wanted you at my office today, Hollister. Jason Langley left Clearwater Hills Farm and all its inventory to his only living heir, Ms. MacKenzie...with the exception of Risky Pleasure. You both share a fifty percent interest in the filly."

"What? Jason never mentioned anything about that!"

Ramsey Blackwood cleared his throat, his pale blue eyes moving significantly from Clint to Blair and back again. His expression was definitely superior. "It isn't necessary for someone to disclose his final wishes, Hollister—especially to a hired hand."

Blair noticed that the younger man curled his hand into a fist, and she realized there was no love lost between the two. The attorney's attitude had been distinctly condescending, but after the way Clint had glared at her, she had little sympathy for him.

Ramsey cleared his throat again. "I believe I've been remiss in my duties. Ms. MacKenzie, Ms. Roberts, may I introduce Clearwater Hills Farm's manager and head trainer, Clint Hollister. Hollister, this is Jason's long-lost granddaughter, Blair MacKenzie, and her friend, Marni Roberts."

Accustomed to male scrutiny as she was, Blair was inexplicably unnerved by Clint Hollister's silent study. She nodded politely, holding out her hand. "Mr. Hollister, it's an honor to meet you. Your name is a legend in racing circles, but of course you know that already."

Clint ignored Blair's extended hand. Instead, he pulled off his sunglasses, meeting her friendly gaze with a bland look of his own. "Your reputation precedes you, too, Ms. MacKenzie. In fact, you're far from long-lost. It's impossible to pick up a magazine or turn on the television these days without seeing the Tigress Woman."

Gray, Blair considered silently, even as she fought to control her quicksilver temper at the accusing innuendo in his tone. His eyes were a rich, lustrous pewter. She forced a light laugh, dropping her hand back to her side.

"I've also portrayed a lady executive demonstrating the advantages of a computer in the marketplace. Why doesn't anyone ever remember that campaign?"

Clint's hangover made him more reckless and far more uncaring of her feelings than he otherwise might have been. "Simple," he drawled insolently. "If you want a man to concentrate on your mind, Ms. MacKenzie, you shouldn't drape yourself all over billboards in outfits that call out to his primitive instincts."

His tone flailed like a well-aimed whip. Blair stood up a little straighter, prepared to take on this male chauvinist who'd never understand how much she would have given to change places with him. Even to working with Jason Langley.

Blair had long ago decided that for Clint Hollister to have worked with her grandfather all those years, he would have had to be either a saint or every bit as cold and unfeeling as his employer. After years of speculation, the puzzle was finally solved. This man leaning against the fender of the gray Mercedes was definitely no saint.

"Well, *I* cetainly don't mind a man remembering me for my body," Marni Roberts offered, her blue eyes bright with interest. "Hello, Clint. Blair goes on and on about you all the time." Clint was not allowed to dwell on those surprising words as Marni's thick lashes fluttered exaggeratedly. "It's a pleasure to meet you...up close and personal, as they say."

Blair could cheerfully have strangled Marni for giving Clint Hollister that little bit of information. The man already had the advantage; there was no point in helping him stack the deck. Her mind went into high gear, trying to come up with a casual explanation.

"Now that the necessary introductions are over," Ramsey intervened smoothly, "I believe Ms. MacKenzie has an offer to make to you, Hollister."

Clint felt a fist twisting his stomach and knew it was more than a reaction to last night's binge. Blair's next words confirmed his gut reaction.

"I'm hoping you'll agree to stay on at Clearwater Hills Farm as trainer, Mr. Hollister."

"I'm afraid that's out of the question."

She arched a delicate eyebrow. "Oh? Won't you work with a woman?"

She said "with" and not "for", he noticed with some interest. It crossed Clint's mind that there were several things he'd like to do with the Tigress Woman. But training racehorses sure as hell wasn't one of them.

"I don't work with amateurs who consider owning a stable of racehorses a lark, along the lines of a skiing weekend at St. Moritz."

It took all of Blair's inner strength not to flinch at his gritty, censorious tone. She forced herself to appear coolly self-assured, relying on skills honed during long hours playing poker with the crew while on location. Blair MacKenzie never folded her hand this easily; she could bluff with the best of them.

"I can understand your reservations, Mr. Hollister. Suppose I assure you that I take the entire enterprise more seriously than I've taken anything in my life?"

He almost laughed at that one. What did this pampered creature know about serious enterprises? He leaned toward her, jamming his hands into the back pockets of his jeans.

"Look, lady, I'm one of the few trainers on the circuit who doesn't have an ulcer, and I don't intend to get one by having to listen to inane remarks from a woman whose only claim to fame is that she fills a bikini admirably."

Marni gasped, but Blair reminded herself that at this moment she needed Clint Hollister more than he needed her. Fortunately, her grandfather had left her one ace.

Clint unwillingly gave the woman points for composure. Only a fleeting flash of fire in those tawny brown eyes hinted at her anger.

"I see. And what do you suggest we do with Risky Pleasure?"

"Since she's half mine, I'll continue to train her."

Blair smiled sweetly, laying all her cards on the table. "I'm relieved to hear that because it would be difficult to find a trainer with your skills at this late date in the season. And of course, since she's half mine, she'll be stabled at Clearwater Hills Farm."

Blair paused, then folded her arms across her breasts, vowing not to falter as she watched the pewter-gray of his eyes turn to cold steel. She only hoped she wasn't overplaying her hand.

"And since you'll be training Risky Pleasure," she continued silkily, "it shouldn't be that much of a burden to work once in a while with the other horses, should it?"

Damn her! Clint dragged his gaze out across the rolling grass fields ablaze with poppies and blue lupine. She'd boxed him into a very neat corner without a blink of those dark sable lashes. He recognized the technique, having seen it in action over the years. Jason Langley had been a master at the art of manipulation, so why should Clint be surprised that the old man's granddaughter seemed to have inherited the trait? Stifling a deep sigh, Clint realized he was probably about to make the worst mistake of his career.

He turned his attention back to Blair, who appeared irritatingly calm as she awaited his answer. "You really are Jason Langley's granddaughter, aren't you?" he muttered.

"So I've been told."

"I expected you to sell," he admitted.

"Ms. MacKenzie refused that suggestion immediately." While the attorney's expression gave nothing away, his clipped tones could not hide his displeasure.

"Do you actually believe you can run a racing stable without any experience?" Clint asked her.

"I've more experience than you realize, Mr. Hollister. And yes, I believe I can, with your help. After all, we both want what's best for Risky Pleasure, don't we?" she coaxed, her level gaze holding his without the slightest hint of feminine guile.

Clint folded his hand, deciding that the booze from last night must have killed every brain cell he possessed. Even attempting to work with this woman would be pure folly. Still, if that was what it would take to fulfill his plans for Risky Pleasure, he'd forge a partnership with the devil.

Blair watched Clint make his decision. She'd been waiting her entire life for the chance to work with a filly like Risky Pleasure; at this point she'd agree to sign the devil on as trainer. She put out her hand once again. "Do we have a deal?"

This time Clint couldn't refuse taking her slender hand in his. He tried not to notice how smooth her skin was or how she trembled slightly at his touch. "Just for this season," he warned. "Then we're going to have to work out a compromise concerning Risky Pleasure."

Ramsey entered the conversation. "There's always the possibility of selling the filly," he said, a hopeful ring to his voice.

"Never!"

"Not on your life!"

Blair and Clint both spoke at the same time, rejecting the attorney's suggestion instantly. They exchanged a long, appraising look.

"I suppose you want the grand tour," Clint said. It was more a reluctant statement of fact than an invitation.

"I'd love it," she agreed, her face lighting up with the first real smile she'd granted him. Clint stared, momentarily bemused by the brilliance of that smile.

"Can't we get unpacked first?" Marni complained crankily. "My clothes have been smothered in these suitcases for hours, Blair."

Blair knew that her roommate had no real interest in Clearwater Hills Farm. Marni had come along in search of greener pastures, but horses had nothing to do with it. Suffering from a disastrous end to a longtime affair, she had been uncharacteristically depressed lately. Blair had suggested that California might be a nice change for her, and from the way Marni's wide blue eyes had lit up at the sight of two eligible men in just a few short hours, Blair realized she was on the road to recovery.

"I suppose that's a good idea," Blair said with a definite lack of enthusiasm.

"Why don't I help Ms. Roberts get settled in?" Ramsey suggested smoothly. "And Hollister can show you around the farm."

Blair's questioning gaze moved to Marni, who nodded. "That's a marvelous idea," she agreed, slipping her hand through the attorney's arm. "And please, call me Marni. I have the feeling we're going to be very good friends."

Blair shook her head with resignation as she watched the two leave, hoping Marni wasn't jumping right out of the frying pan into the fire.

"Your friend doesn't waste any time," Clint offered with an extra dose of scorn.

"We all have to get over pain in our own way, Mr. Hollister."

The pounding in his head reminded him once again of last night, and although he agreed with her observation, he didn't respond to it.

"I can't take off all day," he said firmly. "There's a lot to be done around a farm, Ms. MacKenzie. It's a little different from lying around on bearskin rugs all day."

"Tiger skin," she murmured.

He arched a brow, inviting elaboration.

"The rug is tiger skin. But the bikini is one hundred percent polyester."

"Fascinating," Clint drawled sarcastically. "I can't wait to see the Tigress perfume woman mucking out a stall. We could probably sell tickets and pay the feed bill for an entire year."

Blair felt her inner tension building. "You know, Mr. Hollister, I'm going to love watching you eat those words."

"Don't hold your breath."

Despite his gritty tone, Blair experienced a rush of anticipation at his challenge. Over the years she'd proved to more than one doubting male that she was hardly an empty-headed Barbie doll. But she couldn't recall any apology for impulsive typecasting that she had savored as much as she would Clint Hollister's.

This will never work, Clint told himself as they headed toward the training barns. *Never in a million years.* The voluptuous scent of Tigress perfume filled his nostrils, and he allowed himself a brief fantasy as he imagined Blair MacKenzie's proper navy suit giving way to a tiger-skin bikini. *You're a fool even to try it,* he warned himself one last time.

This will never work, Blair told herself. In their brief acquaintance, the man had shown himself to be cold, opinionated and obviously a class A chauvinist. *You're a fool even to try it.*

THE AIR IN THE OFFICE overlooking San Diego Bay was rife with tension. The ashtray on the desk was filled with red-tipped cigarette filters, and the woman seated behind the expanse of mahogany had been tapping her fingernails impatiently on the polished surface for the last half hour.

"Well?" she asked finally. "When will we know?"

The question had been directed at the tall man gazing unseeingly out the window at the merchant ships in the harbor. "Hollister's with the MacKenzie woman now; he's supposed to call me as soon as things are settled."

"Here? Is that wise?"

"The call's being forwarded so no one will be the wiser."

"Good. I wouldn't want to take any unnecessary risks at this late date."

"I told you not to worry. It's going to be a piece of cake."

The woman lit yet another cigarette. "I hope you're right."

"I have been so far, haven't I?"

"You have," she allowed, eyeing the tense stance of the man at the window. "But don't forget, without Clear-water Hills Farm, everything we've accomplished will go right down the drain.

The man spun around, shooting a furious glare across the room. "You'll have the damn farm!"

"I hope so," she said smoothly. "Because if you end up blowing things, you'll be the one facing a homicide charge."

"I told you, it was an accident!"

She viewed him through a thin veil of blue smoke. "And such a fortuitous accident it was, darling," she purred. "I just hope you never have to convince the police of that."

The shared acrimony became a living, breathing thing, swirling about the two participants to the highly charged moment, as each tried to stare the other down. Finally, a silent truce was forged. The man threw himself into a chair, and they both returned their attention to the damnably silent telephone.

Chapter Two

Clint's head was throbbing with an unholy pain as he walked with Blair across the paddock. Already regretting his decision, he wasn't in the mood for small talk.

Blair finally broke the heavy silence. "I know you hate me, Mr. Hollister, but we are stuck with each other, whether we like it or not."

"What makes you think I hate you?" Clint glanced over at her, but she was suddenly pretending an avid interest in the rows of black Kentucky-style fences.

"Because of the will, of course," she murmured.

"The will?"

"After all, you're the one who made Clearwater Hills Farm what it is."

"Your grandfather's money is what built this farm," he corrected her brusquely. "So by rights it's yours, Ms. MacKenzie, even if you never did care enough to come home while the old man was alive."

"A lot you know about my family," she shot back.

"I know that you're just as stubborn and self-centered as your mother."

That was a low blow, even from a man who had yet to show her an ounce of welcome. Blair stiffened. "Don't you ever dare to talk that way about my mother again," she retorted in a blaze of anger, "or I'll...I'll..."

"You'll what?" he inquired dryly. "Dock my wages?"

Her tawny eyes were as hard as agates. "Just don't make cracks about a woman you never even knew."

He shrugged. "I know enough."

"Then you know that Jason Langley was a horrid man who forced his daughter to leave home so she could be with the man she loved." Blair's tone was cold with resentment.

"I know Jason didn't believe that marriage would be right for them. She was the lady of the manor, don't forget, and David MacKenzie was nothing but a hired hand. Jason was only thinking of her own good."

"Oh, he thought a great deal of her," Blair spat out sarcastically. "So much so that when I sent him a telegram informing him she had died, his only response was an expensive funeral wreath. Without any card, Mr. Hollister," Blair tacked on pointedly.

"If you're so down on the guy, why did you bother to show up today? As if I couldn't figure it out for myself."

"I've been asking myself the same question for the past two days," she admitted.

"And?"

"Curiosity," she said after a thoughtful pause. "The stables are legendary, and I guess I wanted to see everything just once. Never in my wildest imaginings did I expect to inherit the farm. It's still difficult for me to believe I own fifty percent of the best filly that's racing today."

"She's the best horse, period."

"I agree with you. But you'll never really prove that, will you?"

Clint didn't answer, feeling that this was not the time to bring up his plans for Risky Pleasure. "Your grandfather didn't want me to buy her," he said instead. "We had one helluva argument when I came home with that big-boned filly.''

"My mother said he was a cruel man." Blair waited for Clint to deny the obvious question in her voice.

He only shrugged. "I can't comment on that. He was never cruel to me."

"Then you always got along with him?"

Clint exploded into harsh, unrestrained laughter. "Hell, nobody *always* got along with Jason Langley! I figured that if we had fewer than fifty arguments during a twenty-four-hour period, we were having a good day."

"Yet you stayed, when you could have worked anywhere in the world."

He nodded, his laughter stopping as abruptly as it had begun. "Yeah, I stayed."

They fell silent, and Blair looked out at the rolling hillsides abloom with fragrant color. "It's absolutely beautiful," she murmured.

"It's colorful now," he told her, "but we had a dry winter. All that color will be brown in another month."

"It'll still be lovely. I'll admit I was surprised to see so much commercial development on the drive up here from San Diego. Whoever's in charge of zoning around these parts should be horsewhipped."

That earned a laugh, and Blair fought against the way her body responded to the deep, rumbling sound.

"Yep, you are definitely Jason's granddaughter. He's been hollering about the encroaching development for the past five years."

Blair didn't miss Clint's use of the present tense when he talked about her grandfather. "You and my grandfather must have been very close."

Clint's hands tightened into fists as he reminded himself that Jason was indeed gone. He wondered how long he'd suffer this empty feeling.

"I suppose we were. As close as anyone could be to Jason Langley, anyway. He wasn't an easy man to get to know."

They reached the smaller of the two training barns. Blair inhaled the sweet, fragrant scent of hay and thought how different all this was from her apartment in Manhattan.

"We don't live a jet-set existence out here," Clint stated, as if reading her mind.

There it was again. Blair was growing extremely tired of Clint Hollister's typecasting. "I don't live a jet-set existence in New York, either."

He slanted her a disbelieving glance. "Oh, no? Swimsuit layouts in the Carribean, designer fashions in Paris, Tigress perfume ads at the Taj Mahal and in Sri Lanka— that's what you call laid back?"

"It's harder than it looks," she defended herself. "Besides, I'm not as young as I used to be; I can't be out late at night and still look presentable for a morning shoot."

She neglected to tell him that she was usually up at dawn, working at Aqueduct for Ben Winters, a trainer almost as renowned as Clint Hollister and who paid her the minimum wage. Clint would never believe it anyway. Not until she'd proved to him that she knew her way around.

"Yeah, you're absolutely ancient. Let's see, according to Jason, your mother ran off with David MacKenzie the year Moonglow won the Belmont Stakes. And you were born—"

"Six months later," Blair finished abruptly. "So not only do you know that I'll be thirty on my next birthday, but you also know that I'm what is euphemistically referred to as a 'love child.'"

He glanced over at her, unreasonably disturbed by the paling of her complexion. He wasn't usually so rough on women. Especially not on women who were capable of stimulating lustful fantasies.

"Did they?"

"Did they what?"

"Love each other?"

Her expression softened, her eyes gleaming with golden lights that had Clint thrusting his hands into his pockets. He suddenly wanted to yank that ridiculous hat off her head and let loose the Tigress Woman's flowing mane of dark chestnut hair.

"Immensely. I think that's why Mom had her heart attack six months after Daddy's accident. After twenty-five years, she didn't want to live without him."

"That's rare—a marriage lasting that long in this day and age."

Blair couldn't miss the edge to Clint's voice. "Are you married?" she asked suddenly.

His expression grew inscrutable, only the cold glitter in his gray eyes revealing any emotion. "Do I look like a married man?"

Blair turned toward him, one pink fingernail tapping on a white front tooth as she submitted him to a prolonged study. His hair was obviously prematurely gray, but it was no run-of-the-mill salt-and-pepper. Instead, it was a lush, gleaming silver. His forehead was broad and deeply tanned; his eyebrows, in a disconcerting contrast to his hair, were dark. They framed eyes that were a rich pewter-gray, but she'd seen them turn just as quickly to cold steel. At the moment they held a challenging glint.

His nose was aquiline, as unforgivably sharp as a well-honed Toledo blade, directing her gaze down to his full masculine lips. His jaw was broad, and so far, she'd seen that well-cut chin directed her way far too many times already.

"Well?"

Because of his tenseness and the fact that she assumed he was in his late thirties, Blair ventured an educated guess. "You were married when you were younger. But it didn't work out."

A muscle jerked in his harsh jawline, and Blair considered once again that this man represented more danger than she'd ever faced living in New York City.

"Very good," he grated out. "What else did your crystal ball tell you about me?"

Unable to determine what she'd said wrong now, Blair decided to opt for humor and play along. "Oh, everything," she replied blithely. "Madame Tigress's crystal ball sees all, knows all. Cross my palm with silver, and we shall look far back into the murky shadows of your past," she droned in a deep, melodramatic accent.

"What the hell." He dug into a front pocket, extracting a handful of coins. Blair tried not to be affected by the way the gesture pulled the material tight against his thighs. "Here you go, Madame Tigress. Now what do you see?"

She pressed her fingertips against her temples, closing her eyes for effect. "I see a handsome young man... moderately handsome...at least not ugly enough to make babies cry," she tacked on wickedly as she caught his self-assured look through her lowered lashes.

"I preferred the 'handsome' before you added the qualifiers. So what else does the famed Madame Tigress see?"

"I see horses. Many horses. And a woman. A lovely, lonely woman who resents playing second fiddle to a stable of Thoroughbreds." It was a shot in the dark, but it was obvious she'd hit the bull's-eye.

"I think we've played this game long enough," Clint said abruptly, turning toward the door of the barn.

"I'm sorry," she said softly. "I'm divorced myself, so I know how long it can take to get over something like that."

She could also understand why the man wasn't eager to discuss his ill-fated marriage. Her own, which she'd entered into with high hopes, was certainly not her favorite topic of conversation. She'd married Keith Taylor when she was a young model just starting out and he was a struggling photographer. After her career had taken off like a skyrocket, Keith had given up his work to act as her manager and agent.

The only problem, she thought back sadly, was that Keith had lacked self-confidence. In order to show the world that it was he, not Blair, who was responsible for her success, he'd developed an increasingly abrasive attitude that nearly ruined her career. No one in the industry wanted to work with him. Blair was eventually forced to hire another agent, but in an attempt to soften the blow to Keith's delicate ego, she kept him on as her business manager.

Five years later, when she couldn't take his abusive behavior any longer, Blair had gotten a divorce. At the same time she discovered that his foolish investments and obsessive gambling habit had left her without a cent. She had nothing to show for her five years of hard work, and her dream of purchasing a horse farm that year remained just a dream. Never one to dwell on the negative, Blair had picked herself up, dusted herself off and again started saving toward her goal.

"I'm not divorced."

"I thought you said you weren't married any longer."

His granite face could have been carved onto the side of Mount Rushmore. "You said I wasn't married any longer," he reminded her.

He was right. Blair told herself that jumping to conclusions usually made for uncomfortable landings. Before she could apologize, his words sliced through the air.

"Heather died several years ago."

"I'm sorry." Without thinking, she put her hand on his arm.

Clint stared down at the slim, feminine hand as if attempting to figure out exactly whom it belonged to. In reality, he was wondering how such a gentle touch could burn his skin, but he was damned if he'd let her in on that little secret.

It was bad enough she'd come so close in her silly guesses about Heather. Would Blair MacKenzie still want him working here—living here—if she knew the truth behind his wife's death? He was determined that she would not find out. At least not until Risky Pleasure had proved herself. Then Blair could toss him out on his ear; by that time his decision to purchase the raw-boned filly would be vindicated.

"Don't worry about it," he said gruffly. "It was a long time ago."

Blair nodded, deciding that Clint Hollister must have loved his wife a great deal. That obviously explained his unwillingness to discuss the subject further. She remained silent as she followed him into the barn, her heart swelling at the realization that after all these years of working to earn enough money to buy herself a small farm, she had become—overnight—the owner of one of the top breeding and racing stables in the country.

A thrill coursed through Blair while she explored the place, reading the famous names on the door of each stall.

The training barn was immaculate, not a straw askew, which told her what she had already suspected—that Clint Hollister ran a very tight operation. But one thing did surprise her, and although she knew that he would not easily take suggestions from a woman, she felt obliged to bring the matter up.'

"You store the hay in the loft?"

He arched a brow. "Something wrong with that? Historically, that's the way it's been done."

Blair's only outward sign of discomfort was that her hands suddenly brushed at nonexistent wrinkles on her skirt. Well, she'd opened Pandora's box; she might as well continue.

"In the first place, it's a lot of extra work, putting up the hay and taking it down. A separate, single-story hay shed is more desirable."

"No one around Clearwater Hills Farm has ever been afraid of a little extra work, Ms. MacKenzie."

She decided to ignore the challenge. "And dust," she went on. "Surely you've read the reports that suggest that dust in the air of barns and stables leads to heaves."

Clint remembered that he and Jason had argued about that very subject when Karma's Lady had come down with chronic obstructive pulmonary disease. While there was no hard research data to confirm that the ever-present dust from hay led to respiratory disease in horses, Clint had made his position quite clear. He wasn't quite prepared to tell this to Blair MacKenzie, however.

' "I've read them," he mumbled.

Reminding herself once again how important Clint Hollister was to Clearwater Hills Farm, Blair bit her tongue. "What about fire?" she asked with feigned patience.

"The barns are made of concrete blocks," he pointed out.

"Still," she persisted, "from a purely economic aspect, if we kept the hay storage separate from the stalls, our insurance costs would be bound to be lower."

Clint understood all her arguments, having stated them himself over and over to Jason. But he was surprised to hear them come from this woman's lush red lips and wondered where she'd gotten her information.

"Is that an order?"

Blair met his challenging gaze head-on. "Merely a suggestion, Mr. Hollister."

"I'll keep it in mind," he allowed.

She nodded. "Fine."

As she toured the barn, Blair could find no other problems. The oak-wainscoted stalls were light, clean and dry, and her discerning eye recognized the cut-and-bleached rye straw used for bedding. The adjoining paddocks allowed a full acre and a half for each horse, giving them sufficient room to run.

"It's all wonderful," she murmured.

Clint shrugged. "Jason always alleged that proper management is the key to success."

Her brown eyes were admiring as she looked up at him. "And he obviously found the perfect manager. I'm glad you're staying, Mr. Hollister."

Why did her soft statement make him feel as if one of his horses had just won the Triple Crown? Clint tamped down the rush of pleasure instilled by Blair's words.

"Risky Pleasure's down here," he muttered, striding off before he succumbed to Blair's natural charms.

She shook her head with inner frustration at his remote attitude and followed him. When they arrived at Risky

Pleasure's stall, she ran her palm over the white star emblazoned on the filly's forehead.

"Hello, sweetheart. How's my favorite New York Triple Crown winner?"

Clint was honestly surprised. "You really do know about her, don't you?"

She nodded. "As well as about the rest of them: Wind Song, Black Magic, Matador, all the others. You can give me a written test later if you like, Mr. Hollister. I'll bet I'd pass with flying colors."

"I think you just might. Although I'll admit to a certain curiosity as to how a model could know so much about Clearwater Hills Farm."

His tone let Blair know exactly what he thought of her profession. Previous profession, she corrected. The past few years had merely been a steppingstone on the way to a lifelong goal.

"I'm surprised you're willing to stay on as trainer, since you think I'm such an empty-headed bubble brain."

"I'm Risky Pleasure's trainer," he reminded her. "It was your idea for me to continue working with the others."

Blair suddenly felt her blood turn to ice. "You will, won't you?"

His answer was a careless shrug.

"Mr. Hollister, it's only fair for you to let me in on your intentions. Are you going to train the rest of the stable or not?"

"What if I don't?" he countered, more out of curiosity than anything else."

"Then I suppose I'll have to train them myself."

"That statement demonstrates about as much intelligence as I'd expect from the Tigress Woman."

"And yours demonstrates about as much ignorance as I'd expect from a raving male chauvinist. I suppose you're one of those purists who don't believe women belong out on the track as jockeys, either.''

His eyes moved with wicked insinuation over her slender curves. "Thinking about becoming a jockey, Ms. MacKenzie? If you are, I feel obliged to point out that you're about seven inches too tall and twenty pounds too heavy. You'd have to ride a Clydesdale.''

She glared at him. "At least all my muscle isn't between my ears.''

His gaze dropped to her breasts, which were rising and falling beneath the white silk blouse as she fought to keep her temper in check. "Now, *that* I'm forced to agree with.''

Blair's palm itched to slap the arrogant man's face, but she curbed the impulse with every ounce of self-restraint she possessed.

"Why don't we just wait until tomorrow morning,'' she suggested, folding her arms across her chest, "when you can see me ride before you make a decision as to my qualifications.''

"You're not riding any of these horses tomorrow morning.''

"Why not?''

"Because I don't even know if you've ever had that well-photographed fanny in a saddle.''

"I ride all the time in New York.''

He made a harsh, derisive sound. "These horses are a helluva lot different from lazy, old stable bums. And these hills aren't exactly Central Park, Ms. MacKenzie. No, you're sticking to motorized horsepower until I say otherwise.''

"It's my farm. And they're my horses,'' she reminded him acidly. This man certainly knew how to bring out the worst in her.

He nodded, his expression grim. "I was waiting for that one. Do you know, in all the years I worked for him, Jason pointed that out only once?" His gaze was definitely accusing. "You can get dressed up in all the proper, ladylike outfits you want, sweetheart, but you're definitely proof that money can't buy class."

Even as he said it, Clint realized his statement was far harsher than it needed to be. But during their short acquaintance, Blair MacKenzie was proving to be the most frustrating woman he'd ever met, and he didn't see any point in retracting his rash words.

Blair had the grace to blush. He was right, she determined miserably. She was behaving like a petulant, spoiled child. She wanted to apologize, but she reminded herself that his attitude was not above reproach.

"When was that?" she asked instead.

"When was what?"

"When did he say that to you?"

There was a hint of a smile in Clint's eyes as he answered. "The day I came home from a sale with Risky Pleasure."

"You were serious about his not wanting her?" Blair wondered how a man who had the reputation for horseflesh that her grandfather had could have made such a mistake. True, the filly didn't look like anyone's idea of a winning racehorse, but she had proved a legion of doubting Thomases wrong.

"Dead serious," he acknowledged. "The old guy hit the roof and didn't come down for three days. He fired me at least a dozen times that week."

"But you didn't leave."

"I had a new horse to train," he reminded her. "Besides, Jason needed me."

So do I, she admitted inwardly, vowing not to be so quick to fight with him. If Clint Hollister packed up and left Clearwater Hills Farm before the end of the season, she might as well allow Ramsey Blackwood to bring in his real estate experts. Because then there wouldn't be anything worth salvaging. While Blair had trained long and hard, she knew her experience couldn't begin to compare to Clint's. She needed him, pure and simple. The money brought in by race winnings was nice, but the real support of the stables came from breeding fees. If a horse started losing races, its value plummeted.

"I can't believe a man with his knowledge of horses couldn't see her potential."

"Oh, he knew enough to look beyond her less-than-beautiful exterior," Clint agreed. "But he screamed bloody murder when he looked at her pasterns."

"They *are* set too high," she agreed, studying the filly's long legs. "I can see where a lot of people might worry about her going lame."

"The only thing lame was the judgment of the fools who let her go for twenty thousand dollars. They all forgot the key thing to look for in a racehorse."

"Heart," she murmured, more to herself than to him.

Clint's glance in her direction held surprise. "That's right. How the hell did you know that?"

She smiled. "Don't forget, I'm the offspring of a horse breeder's daughter and a trainer. Dad was darn good at his job, even if he never moved in the circles you do. He always told me never to bet against any horse with heart, because it would win every time."

Clint had put the sunglasses back on, and Blair couldn't read his expression as he eyed her for a long, silent time. "You may be the daughter of a damn good trainer, but

I've never heard that horse sense is genetic. You're jumping in over your head, Ms. MacKenzie,'' he warned.

"Don't you think it's time you removed that chip from your shoulder, Mr. Hollister? If it grows any larger, you'll tip over."

She was right, but Clint was damned if he would admit it. She might be the boss on paper, but they'd have to come to an understanding about whose word was law around here. And when it came to the horses, that word was going to be his.

She'd turned away, her hand rubbing Risky Pleasure's nose while she murmured under her breath to the filly. The horse displayed instant acceptance of her new owner, nuzzling her head against the white silk blouse. Clint was suddenly and inexplicably jealous of the filly. What he wouldn't give to be able to get away with that!

"If you're going to insist on staying, you'll have to make some changes in your wardrobe," he said abruptly, his gaze raking Blair's navy-blue suit. "That isn't exactly the appropriate attire to wear around a farm."

"I realize that," she responded levelly, refusing to rise to his baiting tone. "I was just anxious to meet Risky Pleasure. Why don't I change and meet you in a few minutes?"

Clint shook his head. "Mildred will have dinner ready soon."

"Mildred?"

"Jason's housekeeper. You'll probably want her to stay on." His expression indicated that he expected the total sum of Blair MacKenzie's domestic skills to be little more than the ability to boil water.

"I probably will," Blair agreed, thinking how much of her time would probably be spent in the stables. While she was an adequate cook, Marni was an absolute disaster in the kitchen. Not that her roommate ate enough to feed a dieting canary, anyway. "What time does she usually serve dinner?"

"Five o'clock. I realize that's an unfashionable hour, but we do get up before the sun around here."

"That's fine," she murmured. "I can see the rest of the farm tomorrow morning. However, after dinner I would like to sit down with you and go over the day-to-day operation."

"I'll be up to the house around six."

Her dark eyebrows rose. "Don't you live in the house?"

"No. I've got my own place here on the property."

"Oh. I thought you said dinner was served at five o'clock."

"That's right."

"But you'll be at the house at six."

"Bulls-eye. Give the lady a Kewpie doll."

"I suppose this is your way of telling me that you're not having dinner with me," she guessed correctly.

"Hired hands don't eat with the owner, ma'am," he stated in an exaggerated drawl.

"Oh, come off that hired-cowpoke routine," she snapped. "I'll bet you ate with Jason."

"Jason was my friend."

Blair nodded thoughtfully. "I see. And I am..."

"The boss. *La jefa*," he repeated in Spanish. "Any more questions?"

"Just one," she said, turning to walk toward the door of the barn.

"And that is?"

"As the boss, I'm entitled to set down a few rules, aren't I?"

"You are. Just as I'm entitled to ignore them." His gray eyes were as hard and unyielding as forged steel.

Blair decided they were getting nowhere this way. She softened her tone. "I'd like you to eat with me tonight, Mr. Hollister."

Clint didn't like the soft touch of her hand on his arm, just as he didn't want to hear her silky, seductive tone coaxing acquiescence. It was obvious Blair MacKenzie was a woman who was used to getting her own way with men, and from the way his body was responding instinctively to her nearness, Clint could understand why.

"I've a date for dinner this evening, Ms. MacKenzie. Even the hired hand is entitled to an evening off."

"You said you'd be up at the house at six."

"That's right. I'm a fast eater."

"What about your date?"

He shrugged. "She can amuse herself for an hour or so while I go over the books with you."

"She won't mind?"

"I'll just explain that the new boss is a dragon lady who insists on my working at all hours, day and night."

"You paint such an attractive picture," Blair murmured. "So you think that'll keep you in the lady's good graces?"

"Don't you worry about my love life, Ms. MacKenzie," he instructed brusquely, "and I won't worry about yours. Besides, I'll make it up to her after you and I finish our business."

"You've no idea how that relieves my mind, Mr. Hollister," Blair drawled on a deep, throaty tone, refusing to let him see that her exhilaration was fading fast. Even though she was admittedly a perennial optimist, Clint Hollister's attitude was less than encouraging.

As they exited the barn, Blair stopped in the doorway. "Do you wish I'd agreed to sell the farm?"

At her forthright question, Clint rubbed his jaw thoughtfully. While he'd never wanted Jason to sell out, despite Ramsey Blackwood's urgings, he didn't believe this woman could make a go of it. You had to be a combination of tough-minded pragmatist and incurable dreamer to run a Thoroughbred racing stable. Blair MacKenzie seemed to know something about horses, and he had no doubt she was a dreamer, but he didn't believe she was strong enough to pull this stunt off.

"I still think it's a dumb idea, but I'm beginning to suspect that Jason Langley's stubborn blood is definitely flowing in your veins, Ms. MacKenzie."

She grinned. "How about that? We finally agree on something."

He shook his head. "I don't know which of us is crazier, you for thinking you can run this place or for me staying on to help you."

"I'm not as inexperienced as you think."

"I don't have a single doubt about that."

Blair knew they were talking about two entirely different things, but before she could answer, Clint cursed harshly and flung her to the ground. A moment later she was pinned under him.

Blair looked up into his gray eyes, her own flare of anger extinguished as she saw his expresion of honest concern. And something else that was too expertly guarded for her to read.

"Are you all right?" he asked on a gritty tone.

"I will be as soon as you get off me," she protested, her hands pushing at his chest as she wiggled underneath him, trying to free herself.

"I was trying to save your damn neck!"

"You mean you were trying to break it," she corrected acidly. "It's amazing to what extremes some people will go to run off a new owner."

To her surprise, Clint abruptly jumped up and ran back into the barn. She heard the harsh sound of his boots as he climbed the ladder to the hayloft, letting lose a string of epithets that turned the air blue. Blair sat up, pulling her skirt back over her knees, and waited curiously for Clint Hollister to stop acting like a madman.

"Some of those horses are far too young to be hearing such language," Blair stated as Clint strode back to her.

He squatted down beside her, his strong fingers cupping her chin as he jerked her head toward the door of the barn.

"Look over there. Where you were standing a minute ago," he instructed tersely.

Blair's confused gaze swept the area. Her eyes came to rest on the pitchfork lying on the ground, and she felt the blood leave her head.

Chapter Three

"Where did that come from?"

"Obviously from overhead. And I don't think it was any accident, either."

"Because a pitchfork slips out of a bale of hay?" she argued. "That's not so unusual."

"It is in *my* training barn. Tell me, did you see one piece of straw out of place in there?"

She shook her head.

"The kids know that if they ever did a dumb stunt like leave a pitchfork where it could fall on someone, I'd can them so fast they wouldn't know what hit them."

"Perhaps someone forgot," she murmured.

"Yeah. Perhaps." His tone didn't sound convincing.

Before Blair could ask Clint what he meant by that inscrutable statement, he stood up again, towering over her.

"I've got a telephone call to make," he said, his eyes unreadable behind the dark glasses.

Blair nodded. "Fine. I'll see you at six."

"Six," he agreed curtly, turning on a booted heel and marching off.

Blair rose wearily, brushing the dust and straw off her navy skirt. Working with Clint Hollister wasn't going to be any bed of roses, she determined. Perhaps she should just come out and lay her credentials on the table and let the man see that she wasn't totally unqualified to be running Clearwater Hills Farm.

But then she'd be cheated out of watching the amazement on his face when he realized she knew a lot more than he'd given her credit for. And that, Blair considered with a small grin as she made her way back to the house, she wouldn't miss for the world.

So lost was she in her own pleasant little fantasy, Blair neglected to notice the solitary figure standing in the shadows of the barn, watching her with unwavering interest.

THE MAN CAUGHT the telephone receiver on the first ring. "I've been waiting for your call," he said as soon as the individual on the other end of the line had identified himself. "How did it go?"

The watching woman puffed nervously on her cigarette as her companion paced the floor, stopping when he ran out of telephone cord.

"She's what? You gotta be kidding!" He slumped into a chair and stretched his legs out in front of him. "Couldn't you talk her out of it?" He made a motion with his hand. The woman rose and lit a cigarette, which she then placed between the man's taut lips. "That's one hell of a surprise," he stated, once the explanations had been dispensed with. "Yeah, I'll bet it was to you, too," he agreed. "Well, good luck."

He hung up and leaned his head back against the chair, blowing a chain of smoke rings up toward the ceiling.

"Well?"

"She isn't going to sell."

The woman expelled a harsh, unfeminine oath. "That's ridiculous. She *has* to sell."

"And if she doesn't?"

"Then she'll simply have to be dealt with in some other way."

The threat in her cold voice was infinitely clear.

MARNI MET BLAIR at the front door, her blue eyes dancing with excitement.

"Blair, this place is simply incredible! Do you realize we could put our entire apartment in this room alone? My God, you must be filthy rich!"

Blair's eyes circled the living room, taking in the adobe walls, panels of carved stone and wood. A cathedral ceiling of cedar planks gave a feeling of spaciousness, while the wood contributed a warmth that was echoed in the earth tones of the furnishings.

"It *is* lovely," she said. "And large."

"Ramsey told me those sections of the walls are rare portions of old monasteries. The old man might have been a bastard, but he sure knew how to spend his money."

Blair inwardly agreed, but something else caught her attention. "Ramsey?"

Marni managed a slight smile. "You think I'm doing it again."

Blair sighed, then sat down on a leather-upholstered sofa. "What do you think?"

Her roommate wrinkled her nose. "Now you sound just like my shrink. He never answers a direct question, either."

"Don't you think Ramsey Blackwood bears a striking resemblance to Christopher Adams?"

"Of course," Marni answered promptly. "That's probably why I'm attracted to him. If it's one thing I have a knack for, it's picking out men who'll make me believe the only thing I've got going for me is great looks."

"You know you've got a lot more than that," Blair argued. "Damn it, Marni, we've been through this before. It's as if you go out of your way to find condescending men who won't accept the fact that you're also a warm, loving, intelligent woman."

"Speaking of that, how did you make out with that scowling hunk of a trainer?" Marni inquired, deftly sidetracking the conversation they'd had too many times.

"He is a hunk, isn't he?" Blair admitted. "I noticed that didn't escape your attention, despite the fact you tend more toward the stuffy, professional types."

"I'd throw myself in front of the man's horse if I thought it would get his attention." Marni grinned. "But he'd probably be so busy watching you, he'd gallop right over me."

"That's ridiculous. The man doesn't even like me."

"Oh, I think what's bothering our Mr. Macho is that he doesn't like the fact that he likes you."

Blair laughed. "Your reasoning gets more convoluted every day." She glanced over at the grandfather clock. "We're eating early tonight," she said, suddenly realizing she'd been remiss in not seeking out Jason's housekeeper immediately.

Marni looked decidedly uncomfortable. "I'm afraid I won't be eating with you tonight."

"Why not?"

"Well, in the first place, I wandered into the kitchen…and guess what the woman's cooking?"

"I give up."

"Spaghetti. And ravioli with meatballs!"

Personally, Blair thought that sounded delicious, but she knew Marni's Spartan eating habits. "So…you can pop those vitamins and keep me company while I pig out."

"Uh, there's something else."

"You're going out to dinner with Ramsey Blackwood."

Marni appeared decidedly defensive. "You're the one who's always telling me to quit moping around about Chris and go out with other men," she reminded Blair.

"I didn't mean for you to go out and find yourself a carbon copy of the guy who not so long ago had you wanting to stick your head in the oven!"

Marni managed a crooked grin. "I probably would have, but electricity doesn't have very lethal fumes. More than likely I would've ended up with split ends."

Blair rose wearily, giving up the battle. "Just be careful," she warned.

"Aren't I always?" Marni replied with false brightness.

Blair refrained from answering, but as she sought out the kitchen, it crossed her mind that Marni's romantic instincts definitely resembled the actions of a kamikaze pilot. Following the delicious aroma, Blair found the kitchen without any trouble. She was prepared to introduce herself to the woman standing at the stove, but that proved unnecessary.

"My goodness, child, you look just like your mama!"

"You knew my mother?"

"Sure did. Oh, I'm Mildred Kent, but I was Mildred Harris when Kate and I were going to school together. We were as close as sisters, inseparable. I spent more time over here with Kate and Jason than I did at my own house."

"My mother didn't talk about many good times," Blair said by way of apologizing for never having heard of Kate Langley's best friend.

The older woman shook her head, heaving a deep, regretful sigh. "I can understand that. Once Kate met David, everything just kind of went crazy.... For the first few years, she'd write every so often. Then it dwindled down to Chrismas cards, and finally I just lost track of her altogether.''

"We moved around a lot," Blair admitted.

"I hope she was happy."

"She was. But although she never came right out and told me, I think she missed the farm.''

The auburn head laced with silver strands nodded. "I'm glad things worked out for her and David. I have to tell you, child, your grandfather sure missed her. He was really torn up when she died."

"I could tell," Blair said dryly.

Mildred shook her head and gave an unladylike snort. "Just like your mama. Really, the poor man's heart started hopping around like a Mexican jumping bean. The doctor had to put him in the hospital for observation."

"That may have explained why he didn't come to the funeral," Blair pointed out. "But he still could have called. Or sent a card."

Mildred gave her a long, pointed look. "Kate wasn't the only one who bore a grievance from those days. They were two hardheaded, foolish people. I'm guessing you've got a fair streak of stubbornness in yourself, girl, from the fact you're staying on here to try to make a go of it. But don't let that trait ruin your life. Like it did for Jason and Kate."

With that advice she took off her apron, pulled on a bright red sweater and picked up her purse. "The ravioli is in the warming oven. I've left the spaghetti sauce on the stove. Would you mind boiling the pasta?"

"Of course not," Blair answered immediately, not used to such service in the first place.

"My youngest is playing in a high school basketball tournament over at UCSD, and I promised I'd be there to cheer him on."

"Wish him luck for me," Blair offered.

"I will. He's the last of the brood, so pretty soon I can retire my pom-poms."

"You have a large family?" Blair plopped down onto a kitchen bar stool.

The woman grinned. "Large enough. Six kids, and Jimmy's the youngest. And what a surprise he was, too, let me tell you. He was born the same day as my first grandchild."

"In the same hospital?"

"Yep. You know, I realize people are going in for smaller families these days, but myself, I kind of like the warmth you get from so many people loving one another."

"It must be nice," Blair agreed wistfully.

"See you in the morning," Mildred said, heading toward the kitchen door.

"In the morning," Blair repeated absently, her mind still on the housekeeper's words. "Good night, Mildred."

"Good night, Blair. Be sure to lock the house up after I leave."

"Out here?" Blair's Manhattan apartment boasted three sturdy locks, but there was nothing here, for miles around except rolling grasslands.

"I know it sounds overly cautious, but some weird things have been happening around here lately. If they hadn't started before Jason died, I'd think the place was haunted."

"Haunted! Surely you don't believe that, Mildred." Blair's tone revealed her skepticism.

The woman shrugged well-padded shoulders. "Lock the doors," she ordered firmly.

"Yes, ma'am," Blair said with uncommon meekness, sliding off the stool to comply.

She locked the door, suddenly unnerved by the quietness of the rambling ranch house. "This is ridiculous," she scolded herself, going off in search of Marni. "You've lived in New York for years without being afraid of anything. A few minutes listening to a woman who believes in ghosts and you turn into a nervous Nellie."

Blair found Marni preparing for her dinner date, and she settled down on the queen-sized bed to watch. Her friend's black silk dress hugged her body like a second skin, the dark color a striking foil for her light complexion.

"When is Mr. Wonderful picking you up?"

"Don't be so snippy," Marni complained, digging through the vast depths of her jewelry box. "What do you think?" she asked, trying on a pair of dangling rhinestone earrings. "I usually wear these, but perhaps they're too flamboyant for San Diego."

"Since when do you worry about that?"

Marni ws busily rooting through the jewelry again. "I don't want to embarrass Ramsey," she said under her breath.

"For Pete's sake, you're not going to eat with your fingers or tuck your napkin in your neckline or get roaring drunk," Blair said on an exasperated breath. "What could you possibly do to embarrass the man? He should be damned glad you agreed to go out with him in the first place. He looks about as exciting as a slice of white bread."

"To each her own," Marni murmured, giving up the search as a car horn blared outside the house. "Gotta go."

Blair rose instantly from the bed. "He honked the horn for you? Like some teenager?"

Flushing, Marni hurried toward the door with Blair on her heels. "Uh-uh. That's the taxi."

"A taxi?" Blair's voice rose several octaves. "He's not even bothering to pick you up himself?" She couldn't believe that Marni would let her bad habits control her again so quickly.

"It's a long drive up here from the city," Marni answered defensively.

"It's a long drive for you, too."

"I've already got one mother who drives me crazy, Blair. I don't need another."

Blair gave up, knowing she was licked. "Have a good time," she offered, trying to put some enthusiasm into her voice.

Marni gave her a quick peck on the cheek. "Thanks, hon. Don't wait up." With that she was out the door, leaving a trail of Shalimar floating behind her.

Blair sighed, then decided to take a shower before dinner, hoping she would feel more enthusiastic about everything once she'd washed her hair and changed her clothes.

As her footsteps echoed loudly on the Mexican tile flooring of the hallway, the shower she'd planned seemed far less inviting.

"Don't be a ninny. You're perfectly safe," she muttered, pulling an emerald-green terry-cloth robe from her closet. Feeling incredibly foolish, she locked the bathroom door before undressing.

She stood under the shower and allowed the pelting water to soothe the stiffness in her muscles that she knew was due to stress. While today would go down as one of the red-letter days of her life, it had also held a few low spots. One was her concern about Marni. And then there was Clint Hollister's attitude.

As she massaged the shampoo through her hair, with her eyes closed, she wasn't particularly surprised to find that she had no trouble conjuring up the face of the ill-mannered Thoroughbred trainer. That he did not want her at Clearwater Hills Farm was obvious. He'd let her know that as far as he was concerned, she was nothing but a member of the idle class—a lotus-eater.

Her fingers rubbed her scalp with more strength when she recalled the way he'd behaved as if she knew nothing at all about horses. He was probably safe in assuming that, she admitted, standing under the streaming warm water, and rinsing out the fragrant suds. She vowed that she'd sit down with Clint Hollister after dinner and have a serious talk about the future of the farm. At least they had that interest in common.

Just then Blair thought she heard a sound outside the bathroom door. Her hands froze at the back of her head. *Ridiculous,* she scolded herself firmly. *You've seen* Psycho *too many times, that's all. It's simply the house settling, dummy.*

Convinced, but still uncomfortable, Blair hurried through the rest of the shower, feeling unreasonably safe once she'd slipped into her robe. She ran a wide-toothed comb through her wet hair and decided she was too tired to blow it dry. Jet lag had begun to catch up with her, as well as the fact that she hadn't eaten all day. She returned to the kitchen, realizing she was absolutely starving.

Her eyes widened when she saw Clint standing at the stove. "What are you doing here?"

"Are you always this hospitable? Or do I just bring out your good side?"

"I locked that door, Mr. Hollister."

His back was to her as he lowered a handful of pasta into a kettle of steaming water. "Why don't you call me Clint? I did save your life this afternoon, remember? I'd say that puts us on a first-name basis. As for your locking the door, I have a key."

"How convenient," she said, wondering exactly how to go about asking for it back.

"I think so," he agreed.

"What are you doing here?" she asked again.

He turned toward her, his pupils flaring ever so slightly at the sight of her. God, she was lovely! Her curves were easily visible under the green robe, her hair was curling into wild waves about her oval face, and her tawny eyes dazzled with golden sparks. He still hadn't witnessed the Tigress Woman, but this one wasn't half bad.

"You're even less domestic than I would have guessed if you can't tell I'm making spaghetti."

Unnerved by the way Clint was looking at her, Blair crossed her arms firmly over her chest. "I can tell that," she snapped. "I just don't understand why you're boiling my spaghetti in my house."

"Simple. I was invited to dinner, remember?"

"I thought you had a date."

"I changed my plans. On the way over here, I ran into Mildred and she told me she was going to Jimmy's basketball game. Since even someone used to a swinging New York life-style would be slowing down after the day you've had, I thought I'd come over and give you a hand." His expression held absolutely no guile that Blair could see. "The time difference should be catching up with you about now."

She nodded, her smile of appreciation unfeigned. "It is. You'd think with all the traveling I've been doing over the years, I'd learn to conquer jet lag, wouldn't you?"

His eyes took on a hard gleam. "Ah, the painful sacrifices of the jet set," he drawled. "I can tell you're going to love getting up at three-thirty."

"I'll manage," she promised briskly, sitting down on the stool and crossing her legs in a smooth, fluid gesture that did not go unnoticed by Clint.

He turned his back on her, busying himself with the dinner preparations. Blair shifted uncomfortably. "I suppose you think I'm terrible for missing my grandfather's funeral," she said softly.

Clint took out a cigarette and tapped it on the counter. "Your grandfather didn't have a funeral."

"He didn't? But Mr. Blackwood said everything was already taken care of. I thought..." She tried to make some sense out of the two men's contradictory statements.

Clint lit the cigarette, taking his time to answer. "Jason was cremated yesterday without any fuss. Or without any relatives standing by to shed any false tears." He eyed her blandly. "Feeling guilty that you bothered to show up only to collect the farm, Blair?"

Why did he do this, he wondered, regretting his words as Blair shoved her slightly trembling hands into the pockets of her robe. Clint knew he kept baiting her; he just couldn't figure out why.

"I was out of the country, Mr. Hollister. It took the cable two days to catch up with me. I came as soon as I could."

"You don't have to apologize to me."

Blair didn't like the way his tone suggested just the opposite. "Well, perhaps we should have a memorial service. Could you give me a list of his friends?"

"Jason didn't have many friends."

That information didn't come as much of a surprise to her. "I see." Her smooth forehead furrowed suddenly. "Do you know what religion my grandfather was?"

"He didn't attend any church."

"Oh. Then I suppose a secular service—"

His hand sliced through the air. "No, Jason was adamant about that. No service of any kind."

Blair didn't know whether to feel relieved or distraught. After all, she hadn't even known her mother's father, and nothing she'd ever heard about the man had

made her want to know him. However, he had granted
Blair her most heartfelt wish, so some recognition seemed
to be in order.

"I feel I should do something," she murmured, more to
herself than to him.

Clint knew exactly how she felt. That was the reason for
last night's drunk. It hadn't seemed right—one minute the
old man was there; the next, he was gone without a trace.

"There's something you can do," he suggested, his tone
softening at the sight of her beautiful, distressed features.

"What's that?" she whispered, her gaze suddenly trapped by his intense gray eyes. An odd warmth spiraled out
from her innermost core, and Blair wondered what kind of
woman she could possibly be to experience desire while
discussing death.

Clint reminded himself that this woman represented
more trouble than he wanted or needed in his life. What he
had to concentrate on was Risky Pleasure—and not the
luscious body of the filly's other owner. He jerked his eyes
away, busying himself by setting the table.

"Clint?"

He did not miss the fact that she'd called him by his first
name, and as he turned, Clint steeled himself against her
confused gaze.

"What can I do? All this has happened so suddenly, I
feel..."

"Win." He repeated it with more vigor, as if reassur-
ring himself as well as Blair. "Win every damn race you
can this season. Because that's what the old man really
cared about. Winning."

The look of gratitude Blair gave him made Clint feel
oddly guilty for the rough time he'd given her. "Win," she
agreed slowly. "That's exactly what I intend to do. We'll
make this the best season ever."

It sure won't be boring, he thought. Even dressed in those prim and proper clothes she'd worn this afternoon, Blair had struck a nerve deep within him that was a first. Not even Heather had affected him that way, and Lord knew the woman had possessed more than her share of sex appeal. And had known how to use it.

Oh, yes, Clint decided, it was not only going to be an interesting season, it was also going to be a very long one.

Chapter Four

Blair could not miss the gleam of desire in Clint Hollister's steady gaze. But what was even more unnerving was the way his warm gray eyes triggered an answering response deep inside her.

Dangerous, she reminded herself, not for the first time. She'd have to remember that.

"I'll be right back," she said suddenly, realizing that to sit in this intimate kitchen with the man, dressed as she was, was just asking for trouble.

"Running away?" he asked, his tone laced with amusement.

Blair shook her head. "I'm going to change."

His eyes took a slow, leisurely tour of her skimpily clad body. "Don't bother on my account," he drawled.

"Look," she warned, suddenly serious, "I don't know what type of arrangement you thought I was offering this afternoon, but it was strictly business, Mr. Hollister. I think we need to get that straight."

If she wanted to believe that, Clint mused, it wouldn't hurt. For now. It was going to be a long season, and he was a patient man.

"Agreed," he said simply.

Blair hesitated a moment before leaving the room, not quite trusting his easy acquiescence. Then, deciding not to push her luck, she nodded briskly and escaped to the privacy of her own room, where she changed into a pair of cream-colored jeans and a red sweater.

Clint greeted her with an admiring glance as she reentered the kitchen. "That didn't take long," he said, handing her a tall stemmed glass of burgundy. "Here. It's not champagne, but it should go nicely with spaghetti."

"Why, thank you, Mr. Hollister. That's very nice of you."

"Clint," he corrected absently, his head inside the huge refrigerator. "And I'm just trying to get in good with the boss."

He pulled out a bowl of salad and placed it on the table. Blair sipped her wine and watched him pour the dressing over the fresh greens.

"Where's your friend?" Clint asked as he took a copper colander down from a hook on the wall.

"Out." Blair's slight sigh told her feeling about that subject.

Steam rose like one of Mildred's ghosts as he emptied the pot of spaghetti into the copper strainer. "Then I guess it's just you and me tonight, huh?" He looked at Blair over his shoulder, his eyes filled with devilment.

Suddenly Blair felt as if she would have been safer if it *had* been Norman Bates of *Psycho* fame who'd come in while she was showering. She slid off the stool and refilled her wineglass.

"Don't get any ideas about this," she warned. "You're going back to your own house right after we discuss the farm."

"Wrong again."

"Exactly what does that mean?"

"In case you've forgotten, someone aimed a pitchfork at that silly little hat today. I'm moving in until I'm certain that you're safe."

"That was an accident."

"Prove it," he countered.

"I can't prove it was an accident any more than you can prove it was intentional."

"Then we'll play it my way until one of us is proved wrong. Don't worry, Blair, it's a big house. I'll be so inconspicuous you won't even know I'm around."

Suddenly too tired to argue any longer, Blair fell silent, watching as he piled the strands of pasta onto a platter that joined the salad bowl in the center of the table. She sat down in the chair Clint held out for her, but refused to allow this one gentlemanly act to make up for all the cracks he'd aimed at her that day.

He filled two plates with the homemade ravioli, meatballs and spaghetti, then offered her a thick slice of French bread. When she accepted, he appeared surprised.

"I thought all you high-fashion models lived on rabbit food," he said, his eyes skimming over her slender curves.

"This is the first thing I've eaten today," she admitted. "Besides, *this* high-fashion model is a heretic. I can resist everything except temptation," Blair added with a grin.

"I'll keep that in mind."

"Don't get any wrong ideas—we're talking about Italian food here, mister. Besides, I'm retiring. I can eat anything and everything I want."

"Retiring?"

"Retiring."

"What about the Tigress campaign?"

"I'm calling my agent Monday morning and telling him to do whatever's necessary to get me out of that contract."

"He's bound to be thrilled."

She grinned again, and Clint tried not to be affected by the way her breathtaking smile seemed to light up the room. "He'll hit the roof," she agreed happily.

"You know," Clint said thoughtfully, "it's not always wise to burn your bridges."

"It is if you're sure you're staying on the other side." Her expression turned serious. "We're going to make this work, Clint. I know we will."

"Heaven protect me from cockeyed optimists," he muttered, digging into his spaghetti. His tone, however, was not harsh, and there was a ghost of a smile at the corners of his lips.

A temporary truce settled over the kitchen as they enjoyed the excellent fare Mildred had prepared.

Blair knew the truce was too good to last. Watching her refill her glass, Clint advised, "I'd go easy on that; considering the jet lag and that you didn't eat anything all day, the wine is bound to go right to your head."

"A few glasses are not going to make me roaring drunk."

"Too bad," he murmured. "It could only be an improvement."

"If you're hoping to take advantage of me while I'm plastered, Mr. Hollister, don't hold your breath. I'd have to be dead drunk before you got that lucky."

"You know, you remind me of that princess in the fairy tale," Clint said suddenly.

"There are a lot of princesses in a lot of fairy tales," Blair pointed out. "Which one are you talking about?"

"The beautiful one."

"I believe they're all beautiful."

He nodded. "That's true. The one I was thinking of, though, is the one with the exceptionally lovely mouth."

His eyes focused on her lips, and Blair's fingers curled tightly around her fork. If she was still capable of breathing, it would be a miracle, for such was the strength of his warm gaze.

"It's just too bad all those snakes and toads popped up every time she talked," he added, turning his attention to his ravioli.

Blair was speechless with rage, and it didn't help any when Clint glanced up and stated blandly, "Close your mouth, Ms. MacKenzie. Otherwise you'll draw flies."

She debated throwing her wine in his face, but that would have been a distinct waste of good California grapes. Instead, she took a calming slip of the excellent burgundy. While she'd never admit it to Clint, Blair realized her head was spinning just a little. The idea that he might be right about the combination of jet lag and alcohol only served to irritate her further.

Clint observed her push away the wineglass and nodded. "That's better," he stated approvingly. "Believe me, it's hell getting up at dawn and working all day with a hangover."

"I'm perfectly capable of hard work, and for your information, I've never had a hangover in my life," Blair snapped back. "I think you ought to remember who's boss around here."

Something flickered in the depths of his gray eyes, but it was gone before Blair could read it. "Such a lovely mouth," he murmured, "to be home to such a viper's tongue."

"You're pretty charming yourself," she retorted. "The way you strut that magnificent body around this place, one would think you possessed some divine right of kings."

Clint felt a burst of masculine satisfaction at her words. "Did you say what I thought you did?"

She blinked. "I don't know. What did I think you said? I mean, what did I say that you thought?" Her smooth brow puckered with labored thought. "Wait a minute," she said, holding up her hand. "I'll get it.... What did you say that I thought?"

A brilliant smile lit her face, altering her features, and Clint found himself staring, momentarily bewitched.

"Now I've forgotten."

Her look of distress was real. "Don't make me try to say that again," she begged.

He reached out, tracing the full-blown line of her lips with his fingertip. "Absolutely lovely," he murmured, his pewter eyes growing lustrous as he held her gaze. "You are the most beautiful woman I've ever seen."

"As beautiful as a woman can be with reptiles leaping out of her mouth, right?"

"I apologize for that. I should be used to it, living with your grandfather all those years." His eyes looked deep into hers, searching out a hidden message.

"I'm not my grandfather."

It was barely a whisper, but Clint heard it in the sudden stillness of the room. The only sounds were the ticking of the copper teakettle clock and the wild thudding of his heart.

"Oh, sweetheart, you don't have to point that out to me."

Pushing back his chair, he rose slowly and came around the side of the table. As he took her hands and lifted her to her feet, Blair's words of protest were suddenly lodged in her throat.

She watched the gleaming gray eyes, the strong nose, the chiseled lips approach as long as possible before allowing her eyes to drift closed. When his lips brushed hers, Blair sighed lightly, her breath mingling with his in a scented cloud. There was nothing tentative in the way Clint's mouth moved on hers, nor was it a kiss of hungry passion. His lips caressed hers in tender exploration—teasing, tantalizing, tasting—leisurely sampling what Blair was so willing to offer.

The man might drive her up a wall with his arrogant attitude, but he was one heck of a kisser, she decided as his tongue lightly stroked the flesh of her lower lip, feeling like a flickering flame against her skin.

"Mmm," he murmured, his lips plucking gently at hers. "You taste very good, Ms. MacKenzie."

Blair's body was rapidly warming to a temperature that made the California spring weather seem downright Siberian in contrast.

"So do you, Mr. Hollister. So do you."

"Clint," he corrected, his breath a gentle breeze against her flaming skin. "I saved your life, remember?"

"You and Mildred are both really paranoid, do you know that? Your wild imagination is even getting to me. When I was in the shower, I kept expecting Norman Bates to show up."

"I should have been there to protect you."

"Ah, but who would have protected me from you?"

"Would you have honestly wanted protection?"

How could she answer that truthfully, Blair agonized through her swirling senses. While that little voice of reason in the back of her mind was trying to make itself heard, her body was giving her an entirely different message.

At her silence, Clint looked down into her flushed, lovely face. No woman responded as willingly as Blair had just done without possessing some measure of trust for the man. He wondered fleetingly if, given a little time, he could convince her to sell the farm. After all, he'd only be moving the timetable up. Blair would have to sell eventually. Then, thinking he'd be damned if he would do Ramsey Blackwood's dirty work for him, Clint forced himself to back away from the all-too-tempting situation.

"No toads," he said in a voice that was still husky with unsatiated desire.

Blair struggled to return to reality. "Toads?" she whispered.

"I was wrong. Your mouth is a virtual treasure trove of sweetness. Nary a toad or a snake in residence."

She suddenly became aware that her fingers were entangled in Clint's hair, and she pulled her hands away. "That never should have happened."

"I think it was inevitable," he responded with a shrug.

"Well, it isn't going to happen again," she pledged.

He arched an argumentative brow. "Isn't it?"

"You're forgetting—"

Clint sighed. "I know—exactly who's boss. I always knew I'd hate working for a female."

"Chauvinist. May I point out that Risky Pleasure is a female?"

He began to take the dishes from the table. "You can point it out, but all that proves is that even female horses are smarter than women."

"I resent that, in the name of all of my sex!" Blair's flare of anger drained her, and she realized that the events of the day had caught up with her. She stifled a huge yawn.

"Now that's a great idea." He grinned over his shoulder at her. "Why don't you just keep that pretty little hand over that sharp little mouth for the next few months and we might just survive the season without one of us killing the other."

"Stop teasing me," she demanded, feeling like an out-of-sorts two-year-old as she stamped her foot.

"Very good. I once saw a horse on the Carson show that could do multiplication tables. But, of course, that was a gelding. A male horse," he added, as if Blair might not know the term.

"I know that," she replied airily, tossing her head. "In fact, I'll bet I know more than you do about horses, old Clint Know-it-all Hollister."

He turned away from the sink, wiping his hands on a dish towel. "I should teach you not to make such rash statements, Ms. MacKenzie, and take you up on that bet. But there's a certain code of honor about not taking advantage of a lady when she's smashed."

"Smashed! That's ridiculous."

"Whatever you say," he agreed, spanning the distance between them in two strikes. "However, you are decidedly tipsy, lady." He put his hand on her shoulders, turning her in the direction of the kitchen door.

"What are you doing?"

"Putting you to bed before you pass out."

"I've never passed out in my life. And I've never been drunk in my life, either," she argued, nevertheless allowing him to direct her down the long hallway.

"Which room?"

"What?"

It was very difficult for her to concentrate, since his face kept going in and out of focus. Blair might not be smashed, but she had to admit she was feeling a bit tipsy, not to mention very exhausted."

"Which room are you in?"

"Oh...a big one. Third door on the left."

Clint flinched momentarily, remembering when he and Heather had shared that same room. After their marriage, she'd refused to live in his smaller but comfortable house, and Jason had invited them to live here. At least the room had been redecorated, expunging some of the old memories.

He sat Blair down on the bed and went over to the dresser. After opening the top drawer, he pulled out a red nightshirt that had a big orange cat covering the front of it.

"Do you actually wear this thing?" he asked.

She folded her arms over her chest. "Got something against Garfield?"

"No. I just figured you'd wear something a little..."

"Sexier?"

"That's it," he admitted.

She rose, swaying slightly as she held her hand out for the nightshirt. "You're stereotyping again, Mr. Hollister," she stated firmly.

"You may be right. Want some help getting into it?"

"Even if I were as dumb as you seem to think, I'd never be stupid enough to take you up on that offer." With that she marched into the bathroom and closed the door loudly behind her.

When she came out several minutes later, Clint experienced that now familiar surge of desire. "I was wrong," he said.

Her eyes widened. "Clint Hollister admitting he'd made a mistake? Did you call the papers and tell them to stop the presses? The world must be coming to an end."

He ignored her sarcasm. "You look sexy as hell in that outfit. All of a sudden I find myself envying Garfield."

She ran her hands nervously down the front of the nightshirt. "I think I should go to bed now."

Clint knew she had not been unaffected by the sensual aura suddenly surrounding them once again. "That's probably a good idea."

He'd pulled down the comforter, and as she slid between the sheets, he was treated to a flash of slender thigh.

Even though he'd seen almost every inch of the Tigress Woman's body in those advertisements, Clint found himself very much wanting to see more of Blair MacKenzie. He was beginning to believe the two women were very different.

While the Tigress female inspired lust, Blair herself stimulated more protective feelings. Oh, he still wanted to make love to her, but he wanted it to be a leisurely experience; he wanted to pleasure her as no other man had ever done before.

"Good night, Ms. MacKenzie."

"Blair," she said softly. "My name is Blair."

"Good night, Blair," he repeated, loving the sound of her name on his lips. "Go to sleep," he instructed with a mock gruffness. "We've got a big day tomorrow and we start a lot earlier than you're used to."

Blair shook her head, trying to clear away the fog that made thought so difficult. "That's what you think," she murmured, burrowing into the soft down pillow. "I'm going to surprise you, Clint Hollister. Just you wait and see."

You already have, Blair MacKenzie, he answered silently. *You already have.*

HE WAS SITTING in the darkened den, smoking a cigarette, when the phone rang. Knowing instinctively who would be calling, he heaved a weary sigh as he picked up the receiver. "Hello, Blackwood."

There was a momentary silence on the other end of the line. "How did you know it was me?" the attorney inquired.

"Didn't you know? I've gotten psychic in my old age." Clint braced the receiver against his shoulder while he poured a tall glass of bourbon.

"Very funny." The dry tone indicated that Ramsey Blackwood found nothing humorous about their situation. "There was no answer at your place."

"You're an intelligent man; obviously you figured out I wasn't home."

"What are you doing up at the house?"

"Smoking a cigarette and talking to you."

"What about later?" the attorney questioned.

"Later I'll probably get a little drunk, then go to bed. Alone," he tacked on pointedly.

"I had dinner with her friend tonight."

"I figured that much out all by myself."

"She's an amazing asset, considering how things turned out."

"Turned out?" Clint decided there was no point in making things any easier for the lawyer. He'd known Ramsey Blackwood a long time, and not one moment of that acquaintance had given Clint any pleasure.

"Well, we both expected her to sell immediately."

Clint shrugged. "Hell, she'll probably be begging to sign those papers by the end of the week, once she sees what she's gotten into."

"What do you mean by that?"

Clint didn't miss the strain in the man's usually modulated tones. "Once she disovers how much work is involved in running this place. What did you think I meant?"

"I didn't know."

"Blackwood, so help me God, if you're behind the problems I've been having, I'll break every bone in your body."

"I've already told you, Hollister, that your accusation was ridiculous the first time you brought it up, and it still is."

Clint's only response was a muffled grunt. He took a long drink of the bourbon.

"There's something about the woman we didn't know, something that might change things," the voice on the other end warned.

Clint had already discovered that for himself. He'd never expected her to be so strong, so feisty, all the while maintaining a tantalizing femininity. That morning he had dreaded Blair's arrival; tonight, sitting alone in the den, he'd been pondering how he could keep her here.

"She's been working for Ben Winters. In fact, Marni told me she'd been helping train horses since she was a kid."

Suddenly Clint understood both Blair's knowledge of his horses and her irritation at his dismissive attitude. He wondered why she hadn't just told him straight out that she'd been working for Winters. Then he realized she'd been planning to surprise him. Hell, he thought, he could go along and play her little game. What would it hurt?

"Well?" Blackwood asked.

"Well, what?"

"She might not sell so easily."

"Might not," Clint agreed, knowing that his behavior would only irritate the lawyer even more.

"You could talk her into it."

Clint decided that Ramsey Blackwood's inability to understand human nature prevented him from realizing that Clint would rather be dragged behind one of the horses than help the attorney in any way. He crushed out his cigarette in a ceramic ashtray and immediately lit another.

"What are you suggesting?"

"You're an attractive-enough man, Hollister, in an earthy sort of way. I know Heather certainly thought so, and—"

"I don't want to talk about her!"

There was a pregnant silence on the other end of the phone. "Of course," Ramsey said smoothly. "I can understand how that might be the case. Considering the way she died, and all."

Clint's jaw tensed as he fought down the anger and pain created by Ramsey Blackwood's words.

"Go to hell, Blackwood."

"We need to talk."

"I don't think so," Clint countered abruptly. "As a matter of fact, why don't you just go peddle those legal papers somewhere else?" Ignoring the man's spluttered protests, he hung up on him.

"Was that for me?" Blair stood in the doorway. She couldn't think of anyone who'd be calling her here. But it was now her phone. And her house. And her farm and stables. She'd had to pinch herself to make herself believe she wasn't dreaming.

Clint tried not to be affected by the vision she presented, her sleep-tumbled hair a dark cloud about her shoulders.

No," he replied, thinking fast. "It was simply a friend, calling to offer condolences. I'm sorry it woke you up."

"Oh." Blair stared at him for a long, silent time. His expression was shuttered, giving away nothing.

"Well, good night."

"Yes. Good night," she murmured. She'd turned away when something occurred to her. "Clint?"

"Yeah?"

"I just realized that Marni doesn't have a key."

"No problem. I'll stay up and let her in."

"She could be very late."

"I don't think so," he replied, knowing that Marni must already be on her way back to the farm. Blackwood wouldn't have taken the chance to call, otherwise.

"What gives you that idea?" Blair had lived with Marni Roberts for three years, so she knew that a date could last anywhere from an hour to a week, depending on whether Marni considered the guy a real loser or if he happened to have a Lear jet and a condo in the Bahamas. Blair had long ago given up expecting her roommate to be in at a reasonable hour.

"Hey, Madame Tigress isn't the only one around here with a crystal ball. I'll bet she's home before you get back to your dreams."

"Just make sure you get some sleep," Blair instructed briskly. "We've got a busy day tomorrow."

Clint gave her a snappy salute. "Yes, ma'am."

Blair's light laughter followed her as she headed back down the hall.

Chapter Five

It was still dark when Blair's clock radio came on. She lay in bed, listening to the unfamiliar voice, momentarily confused by her strange environment. Then it all came back to her and she stretched happily, a smile wreathing her face.

She was at Clearwater Hills Farm, and it was time to feed the horses. Her horses. Despite an uncharacteristic headache, she'd never felt better in her life. She washed her face, brushed her teeth and dressed in record time, braiding her hair as she tiptoed down the long hallway.

Marni's door was shut; Blair wondered what time her friend had gotten in. She hoped Clint hadn't had to wait up too long. She was determined to start over with her temperamental trainer, and one thing she didn't need was for him to be in a bad mood at four o'clock in the morning.

She went in search of Clint, stopping to ask a young groom where she might find him.

"He's in training barn A," the young man said, pointing toward the smaller barn that housed the fillies and geldings.

"Thanks. You're Jerry Graham, right? Risky Pleasure's groom."

"That's right," he replied, looking pleased that she knew his name.

"I'm Blair MacKenzie," she introduced herself.

"I know," he said, putting down a small plastic bucket to shake her hand. "Welcome to Clearwater Hills Farm, Ms. MacKenzie."

"Call me Blair," she said. "Tell me, Jerry, isn't it unusual for a horse to have its own groom?"

"The other grooms have three horses each," he informed her. "But Clint knows how much I love that filly, so he lets me work just with her." His blue eyes brightened. "She's the greatest horse in the whole world!"

"You won't get any argument from me on that score." Blair's gaze moved to the bucket Jerry had placed on the ground. "Is that her feed?"

"Yeah. I was just going in there."

"Would you mind very much if I fed her today?"

"Of course not, ma'am," he answered instantly. "After all, you're the boss." Despite his deferential tone, his eyes displayed concern.

Blair smiled reassuringly. "Don't worry, Jerry, I'm not going to change your assignment. I'd just like to get to know Risky Pleasure a little better, and feeding her is a good way to start, don't you think?"

"Sure," he agreed, handing her the plastic bucket.

"What's in here?"

"It's a special mix that Clint had developed by some guy up at the University of California, Davis. Bran, vitamins, trace minerals and oats. Plus an extra helping of clover hay."

Blair arched an eyebrow. "Isn't that a little fattening?"

"She seems to run it off," Jerry assured her. "There's nothing that filly likes to do better than run."

"I could tell when I saw her at the track," Blair said with a smile, turning in the direction of the training barn. "Thanks a lot, Jerry."

"You're welcome, ma'am. Uh, Blair, I mean," he corrected himself.

At the barn doorway, Blair watched Clint as he greeted each horse with a warm, individual welcome.

"Good morning!" she said cheerily, determined to start the day off on a friendly note.

Clint turned at her words, his eyes narrowing at this latest version of Blair MacKenzie. If he'd had a hard time earlier to picture her as the Tigress perfume model, now it was an impossibility.

"You look about seventeen," he responded honestly with the first thought that had entered his head.

She ran her hands self-consciously down her faded denim jeans. She always wore them when working at the track, so why did she suddenly feel like Little Orphan Annie?

"That bad, huh?"

His eyes glinted dangerously. "Turn around."

"You're making me uncomfortable," Blair complained.

"I don't know why," Clint drawled. "You've certainly displayed your body in a lot less." He gave her a devastatingly attractive smile. "Humor me," he suggested quietly.

Unwilling to admit that no one had ever caused her body to glow with such a radiant heat, Blair shrugged with what she hoped was an uncaring gesture. Holding out her arms, she turned slowly, watching Clint's reaction over her shoulder.

The tight denim jeans hugged every curve, each one more lushly rounded than he thought professional models were allowed. Her cotton shirt was open at the neck, her skin glowing in the vee framed by the madras plaid fabric.

Her face was scrubbed free of makeup, but the lashes framing her dark eyes were thick and naturally dark. A high flush rose on her cheeks as his prolonged study became intensely personal. When she unconsciously licked her suddenly dry lips, Clint had to stifle a groan.

"It's your hair," he said finally.

"My hair?"

He drew nearer, picking up the thick plait and laying it across his palm, as if testing its weight. "It's a crime the way you keep tying it up; you should always wear it loose."

"Ah, yet another male seeking the Tigress Woman."

"Is that so bad?" He lifted the braid and brushed the fan of freed hair against her throat.

Her pulse leaped at the tantalizing touch, but as much as she wanted to, she couldn't move away. "Perhaps I'd like to be appreciated for myself, not for some image created by Madison Avenue."

"Oh, you're appreciated, Blair, for every little bit of yourself."

Blair backed up, her retreat stopped by the door of a stall. "I don't think we understand each other, Mr. Hollister."

"I think we understand each other perfectly, Blair." Clint held her gaze with the sheer strength of his will, daring her to deny the shared physical attraction. "The chemistry has been going crazy between us since you arrived yesterday. You can't deny that."

She couldn't. But that didn't mean she was in the habit of jumping into bed with every man she was attracted to. Not that there were that many; in her business, all the men she seemed to meet were either happily married or gay. Once in a while, she came across an interesting photographer, or a male model in some foreign, romantic locale. But all too often either the photographer was more interested in taking pictures of her or the model was unduly concerned that she might be the slightest bit more attractive than he. As it was, Blair's spare time was usually devoted to horses. At least that was one species of animal she could understand.

"I told you yesterday, our arrangement is strictly business," she protested.

"You did," he agreed amiably. "But you also have to admit you gave me just the opposite message last night."

"I said that was a mistake!" She marched over to Risky Pleasure, determined to get to work before this conversation became any more uncomfortable.

"How do you know what mix she gets?" he asked, catching up with her.

"I ran into Jerry on the way here and he gave me her feed. *He* seems to like the idea of working for a woman."

"Damn, I won't get anything out of him all day now that he's seen you."

She looked back over her shoulder, eyeing Clint questioningly.

"He's a nice kid and he adores Risky Pleasure. In fact, he insists on sleeping with her whenever she races out of town. But his hormones seem to be stuck in high. I guarantee that if we went outside right now, he'd still be standing there with a glazed look on his face."

"I wish you'd stop exaggerating," Blair complained.

"I'm not, believe me, sweetheart. If you didn't have a devastating effect on the entire male population of this place, I wouldn't be running behind schedule this morning. Mildred will have our breakfast ready before we finish feeding this crew."

"Do you personally feed all the horses?" Blair found that surprising.

"No, just the ones in training. I like to keep an eye on things."

"So you're actually up this early every day?"

"Worried about getting your money's worth?"

Blair glared at him, all her good intentions dissolving like sugar in hot tea. "Of course not. I just thought it must limit your—uh—social life."

Clint leaned back against the door of Risky Pleasure's stall, folding his arms over his chest. "Why, Blair, are you by any chance digging for personal information?"

"Not at all," Blair lied quickly. "I was just wondering how your lady friend was going to take your living under the same roof with me."

"I told you yesterday, don't worry about my love life."

Well, then, Blair thought, she wouldn't. After all, he certainly didn't seem to take it seriously. The shared kiss, which she had not been able to get out of her mind, probably hadn't meant a thing to him. She was determined not to let Clint Hollister come within kissing distance again.

They worked comfortably, Blair taking one side of the barn, Clint the other. She'd just reached Matador, a bay gelding, when Jerry burst into the training barn.

"Clint, come quick! It's Black Magic—he can't stand up!"

Hay scattered unheeded to the barn floor as Clint took off on a run in the direction of training barn B. Blair was right behind him.

She had special feelings for Black Magic, a coal-black stallion that was one of the stable's home-grown prodigies. Sired by Magic Moments, the stallion was out of Illusion, both champions trained by Clint at Clearwater Hills Farm. The mare, Illusion, had been sired by Irish Rover, a Derby winner named and trained by Blair's father during his tenure at the farm.

"Oh, Lord," Clint said on a sigh.

Black Magic was lying down, his velvet brown eyes alert as Clint examined each leg. Blair squatted down beside the stallion's head, stroking his sweat-dampened neck while she crooned encouraging words in a trembling voice.

Clint moved the front leg, and the horse shuddered. "It's broken," he announced grimly. "How the hell did this happen?"

Blair had trouble forcing the words past the lump in her throat. "I don't suppose we could save him?" She was a professional herself; she knew better. But the softhearted woman in her asked the question anyway.

"It's a little difficult to keep a horse in bed while the bone heals. The pastern's shot, Blair. Even if I wanted to risk gut troubles by keeping him in a sling for several weeks, the corporation wouldn't allow it. They'd be better off collecting the insurance."

"You're thinking of this as a business decision?" Hot tears sprung to her eyes, and even though Blair knew she was being irrational, she was still furious.

"He's not my horse, honey," Clint said in a low, soothing voice. His eyes displayed his own misery at the situation.

"Well, he's mine," Blair argued.

Clint shook his head. "Your grandfather syndicated Black Magic for three million dollars after he won the Derby and the Belmont. What you and I want doesn't have a damn thing to do with it."

Blair turned her head away, unwilling to allow Clint to see her cry. In doing so, she missed seeing a similar moisture brighten his own eyes.

Clint decided to try again. "Blair, you know as well as I do that even if Black Magic could survive the weeks it would take for the bone to mend, he'd never be the same. Besides, he was born to run; he could die from inactivity.''

"But surely the syndicate could recoup its racing losses with breeding fees," she countered weakly.

He took her hand in his, bringing it to the injured stallion's leg. "Feel that," he instructed gruffly. "The bone is shattered. Believe me, it'd take all the king's horses and all the king's men to put this leg together again just so he could stand. We don't have any choice."

Feeling the shattered bone under her probing fingertips, Blair realized Clint was right. She remained silent, her grief threatening to overwhelm her.

"Jerry," Clint called softly to the silent groom.

"Yes, Clint?"

"Go call the vet."

The young man left the barn, his slender shoulders drooping.

As she sat there, stroking Black Magic's sweat-drenched flanks, Blair thought back to how happy she'd been when she'd awakened that morning. That feeling certainly hadn't lasted long, she considered grimly. She wondered if anything about this enterprise would turn out the way she'd always imagined it in her daydreams.

"Blair?" Clint reached out, brushing away some errant tears with his knuckles. "I am sorry. I love this horse. I was there in the middle of the night when he came into the world. We won a lot of races together, Black Magic and I. If there was anything I could do..."

Blair put her hand over his. "I believe you, Clint," she whispered.

His bleak gaze held hers. "Truce?"

She tried a smile that failed miserably. "Truce," she agreed.

"Want to try for friends?"

Black Magic's dark eyes turned to her at that point, and it was almost as if the horse were encouraging Blair to drop her combative stance.

"I'd like that," she admitted, thinking that right now she needed all the friends she could get.

Ramsey Blackwood seemed to view the farm simply as an investment. Marni obviously considered it a resort. Only she and Clint shared a common bond—their love of horses and the thrill of watching those horses run, the wind blowing through their manes as they pounded around the track. Right now, she determined, Clint was the only friend who'd understand how much she was suffering.

She didn't know how long they sat there, trying to comfort the weak Thoroughbred. The sun was creeping above the hills when the vet walked in the barn door, carrying a black bag.

"Damn sorry about this, Clint," he said. He stopped at the stall door and looked down at Blair. "You must be Kate's daughter."

Clint introduced them. "Bill Collins, this is Blair MacKenzie, new owner of Clearwater Hills Farm. Blair, this is the best racing vet in the business."

"I should be," Collins said without a show of false modesty. "I put myself through college and vet school by working for your grandfather. He wasn't easy to work for, but I sure learned a lot."

"You must have known my mother."

"I was madly in love with the girl," he announced with a grin. "I kept thinking if I stuck it out, she'd see what she was missing. But then David showed up, and that was that."

"I'm sorry," Blair murmured, wondering why she should be apologizing because her mother fell in love with her father.

"Hey, David was a great guy. I was happy when I ran into him one day at Hialeah and found out they were happy. They were both nice people and deserved some good times."

Bill Collins's expression turned sober as he knelt beside the injured stallion, his deft fingers probing the shattered bone. "Perhaps you'd better leave now, Ms. Mac-Kenzie," he suggested.

Blair shook her head. "I'm staying."

"I don't know if that's such a good idea."

"Blair knows what she's doing," Clint broke in, giving her a weak but encouraging smile.

She was holding Black Magic's head on her lap, and now she bent over to press a kiss against his nose, closing her eyes when she felt the man beside her insert the hypodermic needle into the stallion.

"Well, that's that," he said.

Blair rubbed her free-falling tears unselfconsciously with the back of her hands. While neither man was crying, neither looked at all comfortable with the state of affairs.

"This is one part of my job I always hate," Bill muttered. "I was hoping, after I had to put Northern Lights away, that he'd be the last one for the year."

Clint muttered an oath, banging one fist into his palm. In his despair, he'd forgotten the ill-fated Thoroughbred on the neighboring farm who'd broken a leg in much the same manner three months earlier. Perhaps it was only a coincidence. Then again, perhaps not.

"Suddenly this looks damn suspicious."

Blair reached out and put a trembling hand on his arm. "You're not suggesting..." The idea was too horrible to state aloud.

"That someone purposely broke Black Magic's leg?" Clint questioned harshly. "That's precisely what I am suggesting."

The older man's expression revealed both surprise and disbelief. "That's a strong accusation, Clint. Who'd do something like that?"

"Someone who wants to destroy Clearwater Hills Farm. It's not the first thing that's happened around here, Bill. Yesterday someone tried to deck Blair with a pitchfork."

"You've got to be mistaken!" The vet's green eyes widened. "It must have been an accident."

"That's what I tried to tell him," Blair offered, her tone not as certain as when she had said that last evening. "Besides," she continued, trying to come up with a logical reason that wasn't so distressing, "it's always possible that Black Magic was on his back and kicked out too hard. Horses have been known to jam their legs into a corner, Clint."

"If it was an isolated incident, I might tend to believe that. But I think it goes a lot deeper."

"Wait just one minute," the vet urged. "If it's somebody who wants to destroy you, why would he break Northern Lights' leg?"

"I don't know," Clint admitted. "But you can be damn sure I'm going to call Matt Bradshaw and see if we can come up with a common thread."

"I'll send someone by for the—uh—for Black Magic," Collins said, packing up his bag. Blair knew he'd edited his words for her benefit, and she tried to give him a smile to show her appreciation.

Clint's arm was around her shoulder as they stood in the doorway of the barn, watching Bill Collins drive away.

"Oh, Clint," she said sadly, "I feel as if I'm a hundred years old."

"I know. I've had to do it only a few times, but it never gets any easier." He squeezed her shoulder. "You were quite a trooper, lady. I'm impressed."

Well, Blair considered miserably, that was something. "Then you think I can make a go of it?"

"Do you still want to try? After this?" He jerked his silver head in the direction of the stall.

Blair met his questioning gaze with a level one of her own. "If it's an accident, I'll take it as such and carry on. If it was done to scare me away from Clearwater Hills Farm, it isn't going to work. I'm staying."

"Just like your grandfather," he murmured. "And I mean that in the very best way."

THE MAN SAT ALONE in the gray dawn, wondering how much bourbon he'd have to drink before reaching oblivion. The level of liquid in the bottle had lowered considerably during the past few hours, but he was still miserably aware of the pain infusing every cell of his body.

How the hell had this gotten so damn complicated? It had all seemed so easy in the beginning. But first there had been Jason Langley to contend with. And now there was his granddaughter, who was showing signs of being just as stubborn as the old man.

The phone rang and he reached for it blindly, knowing instinctively who was on the other end. Only one person would call him at this ungodly hour of the morning.

"Is it done?" the feminine voice asked.

He took a long drink of bourbon.

"Well? I'm waiting for an answer."

"Since I haven't heard otherwise, I assume everything went as planned."

"Good."

The pleasure in her voice grated on his nerves. "Don't you care about anything?" he asked brusquely.

"Of course I do. I care a great deal about money. And about you." This last was said in a silky, seductive tone that never failed to strike a responsive chord in him, despite his better judgment.

"And Black Magic?"

"He was only a horse, darling," she cooed reassuringly.

"A great horse," he muttered, tossing off the bourbon.

Her deep sigh came over the wire. "Excuse me if I can't get as excited about those dumb animals as you do, sweetheart. May I point out that they never brought you a world of wealth?"

She didn't understand, and no amount of explanation would make it any clearer. "I need some sleep," he decided. "I'll talk to you later."

"Fine," she agreed instantly. "I'll be expecting your call."

"Sure," he mumbled, "but don't worry. If this doesn't work, I've a second surprise planned that's bound to have her packing her suitcases."

"You'd better, darling," the woman warned. "Or Black Magic's little accident will look like child's play."

He stared at the telephone for a long time after hanging up. Then, heaving a weary sigh, he staggered down the hall to the bedroom, hoping the bourbon would provide sufficient anesthetization to allow him a few hours of untortured sleep.

Chapter Six

Mildred met them in the doorway, her grim expression revealing that she'd heard the news. "Jerry told me, Clint. It's a damn shame."

"Yeah."

"The coffee will be ready in a minute," she offered.

"Thanks."

"Are hotcakes okay for breakfast?"

He shrugged. "Sure."

The conversation was going nowhere. The housekeeper turned to Blair. "Good morning, dear. Don't you look nice."

"Good morning, Mildred. Thank you."

"Are hotcakes all right with you?"

"Fine, thank you."

"Is Bill coming in for breakfast?" Mildred glanced out the kitchen window, looking for the veterinarian's truck.

"He's gone," Clint answered.

Since it was obvious that no one was in a chatty mood, Mildred busied herself by mixing the batter. Clint slumped into a chair at the table. Blair took a chair across from him. Both remained silent, staring into the depths of steaming black coffee Mildred had placed in front of them.

"I'm calling Matt," Clint said abruptly, the legs of his chair scraping across the floor as he stood up.

Remembering how edgy Mildred had appeared last night, Blair followed Clint into the den, wanting to talk in private.

"Who's Matt Bradshaw?" she asked.

"He owns the neighboring farm. And he used to own Northern Lights, before the stallion had the misfortune to break his leg three months ago."

"Do you really believe Black Magic's leg was broken intentionally?"

"I do." He gave her a challenging look, as if expecting an argument.

"Why? It's such a dreadful thing for anyone to do."

"I don't know," he admitted, sitting on the edge of the desk, the telephone receiver in his hand. "When all this stuff first started happening, I thought we were simply having a rash of bad luck."

"But you've changed your mind."

"Accidents happen, even around the best-run farms. So far, taken one at a time, everything could have been a coincidence. But when you add them all up, there's a disturbing pattern."

"What's that?"

"They keep getting worse. The first few incidents weren't so bad, just irritating little aggravations. A stone in a shoe right before a race, broken fences, broken stall latches. That sort of thing."

"But nothing dangerous," she murmured, recalling yesterday's pitchfork. Her skin broke out in goose bumps as she began to wonder if Clint wasn't exaggerating the seriousness of that "accident," after all.

He shook his head. "Not really. We did have a few rough minutes last week. Do you remember Star Dancer?"

"Of course." She knew that the experts had not given the Cal-bred horse a chance against the Kentucky and Florida entries, but two years ago the roan had proved them wrong, making his Triple Crown win look easy. "I was always amazed at how calm he looked before the gate opened. Then he'd come out of that thing as if someone had shot him from a cannon."

"He was about the most docile horse we ever had around here," Clint agreed. "Except perhaps for Irish Rover, but I wasn't around during his racing days."

No, Blair thought sadly, her father had trained Irish Rover. The horse had helped Clearwater Hills Farm become what it was today. After a long and successful career on the track, he'd been retired to stud. She'd always felt proud that many of his almost four hundred offspring had gone on to become champions. The thought of Irish Rover brought back the tragedy with Black Magic and caused her eyes to mist.

"You were telling me about Star Dancer," she said into the heavy silence.

Clint's gray eyes were the color of a stormy winter morning, proving that his thoughts were running along the same dreary lines. "Yeah, I was, wasn't I?" He raked his fingers through his hair, and it didn't escape Blair's notice that his hand was shaking.

He took out a cigarette, tapping it absently on the desk as he spoke. "Something happened when we bred him the first time. We all figured he'd be real shy, but damned if he didn't catch on right away. Since then, he's been aggressive and overly excitable if there's a mare anywhere around. We tie him up when we're breeding other horses, but he got loose a couple of weeks ago and just about tore the place apart."

"I'd never have believed that about Star Dancer!"

"You never know," Clint said, lighting the cigarette. "He turned out to be a real eager beaver, while Apache Son has to be introduced twice to a mare before he shows any interest."

"But Apache Son practically crawled out of his coat on the racetrack," she protested.

Clint shrugged, drawing on the cigarette. "As I said, you never know." He exhaled, eyeing her through a veil of blue smoke. "But the way I read things, there's a pattern to these 'accidents.' And they're getting worse every day."

"Did my grandfather have any enemies?"

His harsh laughter held no humor. "Hell, more than you could count. But most of them were horsemen who'd be incapable of doing what I believe someone did to Black Magic." He paused, his expression thoughtful. "Although there probably would have been a waiting list for the opportunity to break Jason's leg."

He began to dial Bradshaw's number.

Blair became aware that the slight headache she'd awakened with had increased, no doubt because of the morning's disaster. She left the den to search for some aspirin. Marni's door, she noticed, was still closed. After she had found the aspirin in the bathroom, she passed by the pantry on her return to the kitchen and managed a weak smile for Mildred, who was rummaging through the cans on an upper shelf.

"Matt will be over here after the morning exercise runs," Clint informed Blair as he entered the kitchen and joined her at the table.

She slowly lowered her coffee cup. "If you're right about all this, do you have any idea why these things are happening?"

"One," he muttered, thinking immediately of Jason's attorney. If Ramsey Blackwood was involved, he'd break the man's leg himself.

"Well?" she inquired finally. "Are you going to let me in on it or keep it to yourself? And whatever the reason, shouldn't we call the police?"

"No!" He punctuated his outburst with a slam of his coffee mug down onto the table.

Blair watched in wary fascination as a stream of coffee zigzagged its way along the clean surface. There had been an amazing amount of barely restrained violence in Clint's gesture, and once again it crossed her mind that he was the most potentially dangerous man she'd ever met.

"Don't look that way," he said suddenly, a shadow moving over his stormy eyes.

"What way?" she inquired on a weak thread of sound.

"As if I'm going to go berserk and kill you with my bare hands at any minute." Although his voice was low, the tone was harsh.

Her eyes widened. "I wasn't thinking that at all," she protested, telling the truth.

Actually, Blair had been considering that Clint possessed an amazing capacity for explosive passion. If she ever allowed herself to fall prey to his expert seduction techniques, she'd be a goner.

His gray eyes studied her wide golden ones, as if probing to the depths of her soul. Finally his stony epxression softened. "Truthfully, you are driving me crazy, Blair. But wringing your lovely neck is not at all what I had in mind." He put his hand over hers.

She allowed herself a fleeting moment of pleasure before tugging her hand away. "We agreed to be friends, Clint, not lovers."

"Any reason friends can't be lovers, too?"

Oh, it was so easy for him, she thought with a burst of irritation. All he had to do was turn on the charm and women fell at his feet.

"Have you ever noticed how some people seem to resemble animals?" she asked suddenly, appearing to change the subject.

"Yes," he answered instantly, thinking of the seductive Tigress Woman.

"You're beginning to remind me of Star Dancer," she murmured. "Tell me, did your wife have to tie you up to keep you from roaming into strange pastures?"

Blair was unprepared for the thundercloud that moved across Clint's face. Before she could say another word, he stormed out of the kitchen, slamming the door behind him.

"Oh, dear," Mildred sighed as she returned with a bottle of maple syrup. "And his breakfast is all ready. What on earth were you two talking about? There's only one subject I know of that could get Clint so riled up."

"I mentioned his wife," Blair admitted, not wanting to discuss the intimate nature of the conversation. Belatedly, she remembered how painful that particular subject had seemed to him yesterday. *Dummy,* she lambasted herself. *Just when it looked as if you might be able to work together.*

Mildred's harsh intake of breath caught her attention. "Oh, Blair, you didn't! And after all the time it took Clint to put that mess behind him."

"Mess?" Blair attempted to restrain her curiosity, telling herself that his marriage was none of her business. But she was becoming more and more intrigued by this complex man. Blair assured herself it was only in the interest of the farm that she wanted to understand him.

The housekeeper's face shuttered. "I'm sorry, dear. It's not for me to tell you. But I will tell you this. There's nothing you could have said that could hurt Clint more. I think you owe him an apology, even if what you said was inadvertent."

As Blair rose from the table, she wondered again if anything about Clearwater Hills Farm was as it appeared. She felt just like Alice after her passage through the looking glass.

"I'll be back."

Mildred nodded approvingly. "I'll keep both your breakfasts warm."

It didn't take Blair long to find him; he was in the training barn, brushing Risky Pleasure. As she stood in the doorway and heard him talk to the filly under his breath, she had a vague feeling that the horse was more than a source of pride for him. Risky Pleasure seemed to serve as a source of comfort as well.

"I'm sorry," she said simply, leaning her arms on the door of the stall.

He merely shrugged and continued brushing the horse's long mane.

She tried again. "You were right about the toads. Sometimes I have a tendency to talk without thinking first."

He lifted his gaze to her lips, making Blair incredibly nervous as his gray eyes studied them for a long, silent time. "Forget it. Besides, we've already proved I was wrong about the toads, remember?"

Remember? How could she forget? Even now she felt her skin warming at the memory.

He shook his head, a faint smile on his lips. "Do you have any idea what it does to me when you look at me like that?" he inquired softly.

"Like what?" she whispered.

"As if you want me as badly as I want you."

Oh, yes, screamed her impulsive, sensual self. That woman was steamrollered over by the strict, no-nonsense side of her personality that had enabled Blair to establish her name in the modeling profession while spending every free waking hour learning how to train Thoroughbreds.

"Mildred's keeping your breakfast warm" she said, trying to drag her eyes away from his.

"I know what I'm hungry for, Blair. And it sure as hell isn't Mildred's sourdough hotcakes."

Blair knew the feeling. Very well. "Clint, we have to talk about this," she protested softly. "I'll admit I'm not nearly as self-assured as I've been trying to behave. I'm quite honestly scared to death that I don't have the knowledge to run a farm this size. And if you're right about the accidents, then I've got even more to worry about.

"I can't make a go of it without you," she admitted on a low tone, tracing circles in the dust with the toe of her boot. "But I can't work with you if I have to keep dodging these passes you're making."

"You already admitted you're attracted to me," he reminded her, putting down the currycomb. Reaching across the door of the stall, he cupped his fingers around her shoulders. Blair knew he could feel her slight tremor at his touch.

"That doesn't change things. I can't work with you all day after sharing your bed at night."

"Afraid the hired hand will refuse to take orders once he's found out how soft you really are?" he asked with a provocatively sensual smile.

Blair didn't return the smile; her expression remained grave. "You're more than a hired hand, Clint. You're what keeps Clearwater Hills Farm alive."

As soon as she heard herself say those words, Blair knew what she had to do. The idea was so obvious, she couldn't understand why she hadn't thought of it right away.

Clint wondered if, despite her words, Blair didn't honestly consider him beneath her, now that she was sole owner of the farm. After all, Jason had never apologized for his feelings about David MacKenzie and Kate Langley. He'd always believed Kate had no business marrying a mere trainer when she had every young man in San Diego County trailing after her. Rules were made to keep order, Jason had always insisted, and by eloping, Kate and David had broken those inviolate social tenets.

Clint asked himself what in the hell he was doing spending so much time worrying about this woman's feelings toward him when he had far more important things to be concerned about. He decided that Blair had a point; they couldn't go on this way.

"All right," he agreed reluctantly. "I promise to be on my best behavior. If we make love, Blair, you're going to have to ask me."

She could live with that. "I'm glad we understand each other."

"Me, too. Ready for breakfast?"

"I'm not very hungry." Black Magic's tragedy had dulled her usually strong appetite.

"Me neither," he said, leaving the stall to walk back to the house with her. "But Mildred equates food with love. It'll hurt her feelings if we don't eat her hotcakes."

Blair murmured an agreement, thinking it was sweet of him to consider the housekeeper's feelings. When Clint Hollister put his mind to it, he could be a very nice man.

Her spirits buoyed slightly by the idea that had come to her moments ago, Blair didn't want to wait for Ramsey Blackwood's office to open. He'd written his home number on the back of his business card in case she needed anything after office hours. Excusing herself, she slipped away into her bedroom to make the call.

The attorney's voice was muffled, his words coming slowly, and Blair realized she'd obviously awakened him. She could, however, hear him snapping to life when she told him what she wanted him to do.

"Ms. MacKenzie, you can't be serious!"

"Perfectly."

"Do you realize what you're giving away?"

"Not giving it away, Mr. Blackwood. I'm making an investment. If Clint Hollister owns fifty percent of Clearwater Hills Farm, he won't leave to work somewhere else. Let's face it, the man *is* the farm. Without him, I might as well close up shop."

"That's not such a bad idea," the attorney offered instantly. "I'm certain I could find a buyer who'd be willing to take the farm off your hands."

She shook her head, the gesture ineffective over the telephone line. "That's not what I want," she stated firmly. "I want to deed Clint a half interest in the farm."

"If that's what you want, Ms. MacKenzie," the attorney sighed his acquiescence, apparently recognizing the Langley stubbornness. "I'll draw up the papers and bring them out to the farm this afternoon for you to sign."

Blair smiled. "Thank you, Mr. Blackwood. I'll see you then. Oh, I'm sorry I woke you up."

"That's all right, Ms. MacKenzie," he said dryly. "In another hour or so I'll be able to watch the sun rise."

She hung up then, returning to the kitchen. Clint was busy eating. As Mildred set a plate in front of her, Blair found that her appetite was suddenly restored. She dug into her meal, ignoring Clint's amazed stare as she single-handedly made the entire stack of hotcakes, as well as two fried eggs and four pieces of bacon, disappear.

"Good Lord," he murmured after Mildred had cleared the table. "Where do you put it all?"

"Good metabolism. And daily exercise."

"That's going to be a welcome addition to the schedule around here."

"What?" She took a last sip of coffee.

"Watching you dressed in a skimpy little leotard, bending and twisting to rock music. It still isn't vintage Tigress Woman, but it'll come closer to anything else I've seen so far."

"Sorry. I'm not into aerobics," Blair stated blandly.

"Oh." His face actually fell at the news. "Swimming?" he asked hopefully.

"Nope. Sorry."

"*She's* sorry," he mumbled, thinking of the tiger-skin bikini. "What do you do to keep that dynamite shape, then?"

Blair knew he'd only laugh if she told him. "One of these days, when I can trust your discretion, I'll let you know," she promised. "Right now, don't you have morning workouts scheduled?"

"Yeah," he answered without enthusiasm, his mind on the puzzle she'd dangled in front of him. "Tennis?" he asked as they left the house.

"Uh-uh."

Jerry walked by, leading Risky Pleasure along for her workout. He kept his eyes to the ground, and his demeanor was unsually sober.

"Poor Jerry," Blair murmured. "He's taking Black Magic's accident really hard. Perhaps we should give him the rest of the day off."

It didn't miss Clint's attention that she'd said "we" and not "I." So far, except for a few instances of feminine pique, she hadn't thrown her weight around as he'd suspected she would.

"It's always hard," he agreed. "But Jerry has to learn that life does go on.... Come on," he suggested. "You're going to watch a real champion."

He put his arm around her shoulder as they walked out to the practice track, but Blair didn't feel threatened, since his touch was more a friend's than a lover's. She smiled inwardly, thinking how surprised he'd be that afternoon.

"Racquetball?" He started in on the quiz again.

"Nope."

"Surfing?"

"In Manhattan?" she asked incredulously.

He laughed. "Sorry, I forgot." His eyes held a fond message as they looked down into hers. "For a moment there, it seemed as if you'd lived here forever."

Blair had certainly dreamed of the farm enough times while she was growing up to feel the same way. "I know," she said softly, sharing a smile.

A pink glow tinted the clouds as the sun rose over the hills, bathing them in a pearly light. The meadows perfumed the cool morning air with the scents of many blossoms.

Blair joined Clint next to the fence ringing the oval exercise track. "There aren't any other horses here," she remarked with surprise.

"That's part of the reason for the early hours," he explained. "I like to get Risky Pleasure out here before any of the others."

"Why, Clint Hollister, are you by any chance showing favoritism?"

"Of course not. It's just her damn penchant for galloping. We found if there are other horses running past her, she just takes off. In fact, if you don't take a long hold on her, with that high knee action she tends to climb, and that isn't good for those pasterns."

At that moment the filly came onto the track, the exercise jockey walking her in a clockwise direction. Blair noticed that the jockey was a woman, and she felt a tinge of regret for her hastily issued words about Clint's apparent chauvinism.

"Risky Pleasure may be a terrific runner," Blair murmured, "but she's not real good at directions. Isn't she headed the wrong way?"

Jerry had just joined them, and he broke in before Clint could answer. "Clint likes to break the pattern every day," he explained, his admiration for the trainer evident. "We've found if we vary her workout, running her clockwise one day, counterclockwise the next, it keeps her guessing all the time and takes her mind off arguing with Annie and trying to run away with her."

"That's very clever," Blair acknowledged, knowing horses to be creatures of habit.

"Thank you, ma'am," Clint said with a grin. "I like to think so."

"Clint's the best," Jerry agreed, his mood seeming to pick up as he watched the big-boned filly.

Clint laughed. "If you're bucking for a raise, you're soft-soaping the wrong guy. This lady signs the paychecks now."

Blair thought she'd detected a hint of annoyance in Clint's tone, but before she could dwell on it, he'd turned the conversation back to Risky Pleasure.

"You know, she's stronger than most fillies. If she had an easier gallop, I'd let her go two miles every day. But wait until you see this up close."

Blair waited, watching as the exercise jockey jogged Risky Pleasure clockwise around the track for approximately three eighths of a mile. Even with Clint's precautions, she could tell that the young woman was having difficulty in keeping the horse from breaking into a full gallop.

Then Risky Pleasure was given her head, and Blair gasped at the sheer power the filly exhibited. The dark head was down, the ears were up. and the hooves hit the ground as if she were driving nails. She tore past, a streak of flowing mane and tail. The filly had gone a quarter of a mile before the rider could bring her to a stop.

"Well?" Clint looked at Blair, an inscrutable expression on his face.

Blair's gaze was fixed on the horse; she was stunned to see that Risky Pleasure wasn't even breathing hard. "You're right. She's not just the best filly. She's the best Thoroughbred racing today. Period."

"I'd like to prove that."

"So would I, but how on earth would you ever do it?"

"I want to race her against Cimarron."

Blair stared. "You can't be serious!"

"Of course I am. Don't you think she can win?"

Blair had seen Cimarron run only twice, the previous fall at Aqueduct. The two-year-old had shown signs of being a contender when the field of three-year-olds started narrowing for the Spring Classic—The Triple Crown. Everything she'd read about the stallion acclaimed him to be the greatest horse since Secretariat.

"Even if she could," Blair argued, "it would be too much of a risk. Don't forget what happened to Ruffian when they ran her against a stallion. She had to be destroyed, Clint.''

"This horse is older than Ruffian was; and has a lot more experience. Besides, as great as that filly was, I think Risky Pleasure's even greater.'' His expression became intense. "Blair, believe me, she's the best horse I've ever trained. They just don't come with any more natural ability.''

"Or with worse pasterns,'' she pointed out.

Jerry seemed to sense the impending battle. "I'd better get back to work,'' he said quickly. Both Clint and Blair remained silent, watching him leave.

"You're against the idea,'' Clint said finally.

"Of course I am! My God, did my grandfather know about this crazy scheme of yours?''

"Yes.''

"And?''

"He was against it,'' Clint admitted.

"There, you see.'' Blair turned away as if the matter were ended.

"I don't see anything except you're as shortsighted as he was. Don't forget, Jason Langley didn't want to spend a lousy twenty thousand bucks on a horse that earned well over half a million dollars as a three-year-old. Her earnings this year will top that easily.''

"All the more reason not to risk her going lame in some stupid match race!''

"She's half my horse, Blair,'' he said quietly.

"And half mine,'' she felt the need to point out, wondering if her impulsive behavior earlier that morning had been the right thing to do. If they could argue over a single race for a single horse, how in the world could they ever hope to run the farm together?

They both fell silent, as the jockey began to jog the filly around the track once again.

"What do you suggest we do?" Clint asked.

At that moment, Risky Pleasure broke into a run, and Blair felt her breath stop in her throat at the display of raw power.

"Do you think beating Cimarron will be easy?" she asked, her gaze directed out to the five eighths of a mile practice track.

Clint tried to keep the excitement from his voice when he realized that Blair was beginning to consider the idea seriously. "No," he answered honestly. "But do you know anything in life that's easy?"

She turned, leaning against the fence and crossing her arms over her breasts. "No, I don't." She glanced back at the filly for a long, silent moment. "Let me think about it, okay?"

Clint fought to keep the breakaway grin from claiming his face. "Sure," he managed to answer casually. "Take your time."

Blair fought down her irritation as she watched the victory flags waving in his gray eyes. It was an intriguing idea, she admitted to herself. And exciting. But like so many other things around Clearwater Hills Farms, it was potentially dangerous. She remained quiet during the remainder of the workout, only responding to Clint's observations with murmured monosyllables.

FROM THE ICY atmosphere in the kitchen as Blair entered after Risky Pleasure's workout, she knew that Marni and Mildred had argued about breakfast.

"Hi," Blair greeted them, taking the fresh cup of coffee Mildred extended. "Um, nice. Thanks a lot, Mildred. You're an absolute doll."

She turned to Marni. "Hi. How was your date?"

"Okay," Marni mumbled, after swallowing her morning ration of vitamin pills. "But it's a little hard on a girl's ego when a guy takes her out and spends the entire evening talking about some other woman."

"I wouldn't think Ramsey Blackwood would be the type," Blair commented, sitting down at the table.

"You made quite an impression." Marni's voice held a sulky tone.

"Me? You talked about me?"

"All evening," Marni said. "And it got really odd, too, let me tell you. First, he told me about how hard it was to run a horse farm, and how it was no place for a novice. So I told him all about your working with Ben Winters and that you know everything in the world about horses."

"I don't know everything."

"Well, you know a lot more than I do. It's all I can do to find my way to the betting windows."

"I'm sorry you had a bad evening."

Marni shrugged. "It wasn't that bad. You should see his house, Blair. It's the most amazing thing I've ever seen! It makes this place look like a slum."

"Where did that taxi take you last night? Buckingham Palace?"

"Better." Marni leaned forward, her blue eyes sparkling like sapphires. "The house is in La Jolla, and it has an audiovisual center, two wet bars, and a two-bath master suite that takes up the entire second floor."

"Nice," Blair murmured, forcing her tone to remain neutral.

Marni bristled. "For Pete's sake, he was only showing me around. I didn't go to bed with the guy."

"I didn't say you had."

"No, but you thought it just the same."

Blair had the good grace to blush.

"Hey, I may be crazy, but I'm not dumb enough to fall in the sack with any guy who can't quit talking about my best friend," Marni assured her. "Anyway, let me tell you about his house. The lower level has a huge party room that opens onto an oceanfront dance floor. And get this—there's a pool that comes right up to the edge of the cliff-side terrace. You can float in the pool and look right out over the ocean. Isn't that about the neatest thing you've ever heard of?"

"It sounds pretty marvelous," Blair admitted.

"Wait until you hear this." Marni had a smug look on her face as she got up to refill her coffee cup. "The house next door is for sale. And it's just as terrific."

"So?"

"So why don't you buy it?"

"Me? What on earth for? I've got a farm to run."

"You could always sell the farm," Marni advised casually.

"Marni! I thought you were my friend," Blair protested.

"Of course I am."

"Then how could you suggest such a thing? After all, you know how long I've dreamed about having my own stable, my own colors."

"I know." Marni observed her gravely over the top of her cup. "But it's not going to be easy Blair, running this place all alone."

"I've got Clint to help."

"That's another thing."

"What's another thing?"

Marni cast a surreptitious look at Mildred, who was cleaning off the kitchen counters. "Come with me."

Once they were behind her closed bedroom door, Marni didn't waste any time. "Ramsey's worried about your being alone all the way out here with that trainer of yours."

"I'm certainly not all alone. There are tons of people working here. Besides, what could he be worried about?"

"Your safety."

"My safety?"

Marni reached out and took Blair's hands in her own. "Honey, the man's been in prison."

The morning sun was shining through the window, but Blair heard the thunderclap just the same. "Prison?" she said, trying to keep her voice steady. "I don't believe it."

"It's true," her friend insisted. "Ramsey showed me an old newspaper story.... Blair, the man was convicted of murdering his wife."

The ominous thunderclap was followed by a bolt of lightning, and Blair closed her eyes against the pain that seared through her.

Chapter Seven

"I don't believe it," Blair stated finally.

"Ask him," Marni advised.

Blair remembered Clint's behavior earlier when she had brought up his wife. Mildred was right; the former Mrs. Hollister was definitely an off-limits subject.

"I can't do that."

"Why not?"

"It's none of my business." Blair's words sounded unconvincing, even to her own ears.

"None of your business! Honey, you're sleeping under the same roof with a convicted felon—a murderer—for God's sake!—and you claim it's none of your business?" Her blue eyes narrowed suspiciously. "Oh, shoot. You like the guy, don't you?"

"I like him," Blair agreed grimly, thinking that the word "like" didn't begin to cover the feelings she'd been experiencing.

"And I thought I was the one with masochistic romantic tendencies. Blair, we're not talking about a jaywalking ticket here. The man killed his wife."

Blair shook her head, rejecting Marni's words. "He couldn't do a thing like that," she protested, remembering the sheen of tears in his eyes as they'd tried to soothe Black Magic. "He can't even stand to see a horse in pain."

"Maybe he isn't jealous of his horses," Marni suggested.

"Exactly what is that supposed to mean?"

"A jury found him guilty of killing his wife in a jealous rage because he caught her with another man."

"Even so," Blair argued, "all he had to do was divorce her."

"Women don't usually pay alimony."

Blair was growing increasingly irritated by the way Marni was dragging out this sordid little story. "Why don't you just tell me what Ramsey Blackwood told you?"

"It wasn't only Ramsey's version. I read it in the paper, Blair. In black and white."

Blair's shoulders sank, and she felt her headache returning with a vengeance. "Marni," she pleaded, "I've been up since three-thirty and I've already had a lousy day. Can't you just spit it out?"

"All right." Marni took a deep breath. "Heather Hollister was a wealthy woman. The prosecuting attorney had witnesses who swore she and Clint argued all the time."

"Lots of husbands and wives argue," Blair pointed out. "But they don't kill each other."

"One of the more frequent arguments was over Heather's refusal to give him the money to buy Risky Pleasure from your grandfather."

"Why would he want to do that? He was already training her."

"It seems he had an obsession about the horse," Marni explained. "He and Jason Langley didn't agree on anything about her, from the day Clint brought her home. He wanted carte blanche in her training, and your grandfather refused.''

Blair tried not to think of the way Clint's gray eyes turned to a polished pewter when he talked about the filly. She didn't want to remember that he himself had told her that Jason hadn't agreed with his plan to race her against Cimarron.

And when she'd asked him why he'd stayed, since her grandfather had fired him after he brought Risky Pleasure home, Clint's explanation had been simply that he had a horse to train. Not that he felt any loyalty to her grandfather. Or to the other horses. No, Blair had a feeling from the moment he'd spotted the rawboned filly, the horse had eclipsed all the others he'd ever trained.

"Blair, there's more." Marni leaned forward, placing her hand on her friend's arm. "Did you ever wonder why there wasn't any funeral for your grandfather?"

"He didn't want one."

"How do you know?"

"Clint told me."

"Just like he told you Jason wanted a quick cremation, right?"

Blair thought she knew where this conversation was going, and she rejected the idea immediately. "If you're accusing him of killing my grandfather, you're way off base. Even if he was the kind of man capable of murder—which he isn't—he had nothing to gain."

"He's already got fifty percent of his precious racehorse," Marni pointed out.

"He's going to have more than that."

Blue eyes widened. "What does that mean?"

Blair's expression warned her friend not to challenge her decision. "I called Ramsey Blackwood first thing this morning and told him I wanted to deed half my interest in Clearwater Hills Farm to Clint.''

Marni stared at Blair as if she'd just grown an extra head. "What on earth for?"

"So he'll stay on here. I need him, Marni."

"As a trainer?"

"Of course. What did you think?"

"I think you're interested in the guy, Blair."

"That's ridiculous," Blair lied swiftly.

"There are other good trainers. If you really tried, with all your money you could probably hire Ben Winters away from Winterhaven Farms."

"Ben's a good trainer," Blair agreed. "But I don't want him; I want Clint Hollister."

Marni expelled a small, defeated sigh. "That's what I'm afraid of. Honey, don't you realize your life could be in danger here?"

"That's ridiculous," Blair retorted, paling as the image of that pitchfork came to mind.

"Is it?"

"Of course!"

"Then why did you look as if you'd just seen a ghost?"

Blair began to pace the floor in long, nervous strides. "I told you, I've had a bad day and not enough sleep."

"Something did happen, didn't it?"

Blair was reminded that she'd never been able to hide anything from her sharp-eyed roommate. "Nothing happened," she insisted. "Nothing at all."

"Except now you've also got yourself one dead race-horse," Marni reminded her. Mildred had filled Marni in on the tragedy.

"Accidents happen," Blair snapped.

"Sure. So do natural deaths. And we'll never know for certain about your grandfather's. But Heather Hollister was definitely killed. By her husband, the same man to whom you want to hand over half your worldly possessions." Marni's expression was atypically sober. "Blair, what if he isn't above killing you in order to get total control of Risky Pleasure? And the farm?"

Blair stared out the window, experiencing that now familiar quickening deep inside her as she watched Clint stride toward a red Blazer that had just pulled up into the driveway.

She turned, pinning a distressed Marni with a stern gaze. "Tell me this," she said tersely. "If Clint Hollister killed his wife, then why isn't he still in prison?"

Marni shrugged. "Ramsey wasn't clear on that point," she admitted. "He said it had something to do with the law. Some complex mumbo jumbo that got Clint out on a technicality." Her eyes handed Blair a warning. "But that doesn't make him less guilty."

"I don't want you to say a word to anyone about this," Blair instructed her firmly. "Not a soul. Do you hear me?"

"Who would I tell? I don't even know anyone other than Ramsey in San Diego."

For someone who professed to be a stranger, Marni had certainly tapped into a gossip line fast enough, Blair considered bleakly. She knew that whatever the explanation, Clint was innocent. He might have frustrated her in the past twenty-four hours and driven her up a wall from time to time, and he might cause her common sense to disappear whenever he looked at her with desire in those wonderful gray eyes. But she knew, without a shadow of a doubt, that the man had never tried to kill her.

Warning Marni once again to silence, she left the room and headed toward the den, drawn there by the sound of male voices.

"Blair, I was just about to send the Saint Bernards out looking for you." Clint smiled as she entered, but his eyes held little seeds of worry.

Blair couldn't quite meet his gaze. "I'm sorry. I was talking with Marni."

"I want you to meet your neighbor, Matt Bradshaw. Matt, this is Blair MacKenzie, Jason's granddaughter."

A tall blond man rose from his chair and extended his hand. "It's a pleasure, Ms. MacKenzie. Your grandfather was always talking about you."

Blair tried to focus on his words as he vigorously pumped her hand. "My grandfather talked about me?"

"All the time. He even kept a scrapbook of every magazine layout you did. In fact..." Brilliant emerald eyes scanned the room, obviously searching for something. "Hey, Clint, what happened to that photo he had framed?"

Clint refused to admit that the glossy color photo was at his house, on his bedside table. "I don't know," he replied with blatant unconcern.

"It was always my favorite thing about coming over here," Matt Bradshaw confessed with a boyishly attractive grin. "That Tigress perfume layout was really something, Ms. MacKenzie."

She managed a tight smile, willing her body to relax. But she could sense Clint's restraint and it made her even more nervous.

"Call me Blair," she suggested. "After all, we are neighbors."

"Blair," he agreed. "And I'm Matt." Then his expression grew serious. "I'm damned sorry about Black Magic, Blair."

She nodded, refusing to let herself cry over the stallion anymore. "Thank you. I'm sorry about Northern Lights, too. I think he's one horse who could have given Cimarron a run for the money at Churchill Downs this year."

Her words obviously piqued Matt's interest. "Your grandfather always said you were beautiful, but he never said anything about your following the horses."

"Blair's been working with Ben Winters," Clint offered, then suddenly remembered that he wasn't supposed to know that little fact. Blair's wide amber eyes revealed both surprise and confusion.

"Ben Winters? I'm suitably impressed." Matt's expression reinforced his words.

Clint was trying to come up with some way to sidetrack the conversation before Blair decided to pin him down on exactly where he'd received his information. He got a reprieve when Marni peeked around the corner of the door.

"Blair, there's someone here to see you."

Ramsey must have come sooner than expected with the papers, Blair thought. "Come in and keep our neighbor company," she invited.

"Marni Roberts," Matt said instantly, as she entered the room.

Marni gave him her bright, professional smile. "How nice that you recognized me," she purred, holding out a perfectly manicured hand.

"It's your eyes."

"My eyes?"

"Ever since you did that shampoo commercial, I've thought you had the most beautiful eyes I'd ever seen." Suddenly he appeared to realize that there were other people in the room. "Oh, damn. I *am* sorry, Blair. I didn't mean that yours weren't lovely. It's just that Ms. Roberts always seemed to be looking directly at me."

Matt Bradshaw groaned with embarrassment as he slumped back down into his chair, rubbing his large palm

over his face. "Don't mind me, folks. I think I'll just sit
here and wait for the ground to swallow me up." To Blair's
amusement, a dark flush rose from the man's open collar.

"Did you really feel that way?" Marni asked.

Matt lifted distressed green eyes up to where Marni now
stood in front of him. "I bet you meet a lot of jerks who
say things like that."

Marni shook her head slowly. "I don't think you're a
jerk at all," she protested softly. "And no, no one has ever
mentioned my eyes." She allowed a little grin. "Usually
they're concentrating on my body."

His gaze accepted the invitation in her tone, moving
from the top of her blond head, down to the polished pink
toenails peeking out of her gold sandals, then back up
again.

"It's very nice, too," he offered politely.

"Thank you. Did Blair say you were her neighbor?"

"Right next door. Although, it's not as close as it would
be if we lived in Manhattan. My place isn't nearly as big as
Clearwater Hills Farm, but I'm getting a good stable, and
I train a few horses for other owners. Do you like horses?"

His face took on an absolutely hopeful expression that
had Blair cringing as she waited for Marni's answer. She'd
never seen her roommate portray any enthusiasm toward
the Thoroughbreds Blair had worked with over the years.

"I don't really know," Marni admitted. "I've never
been around them, except when I visited Blair once in a
while at Aqueduct. I'm afraid I don't know much at all
about racing. But I've heard that it's always lucky to bet
on the gray horse."

Matt laughed, the lines fanning outward from his eyes
crinkling attractively. At the moment, he and Marni could
have been the only two people in the room.

"I'll have to keep that hot tip in mind…. Uh, would you be interested in visiting someday?"

Marni gave his invitation some well-deserved thought. Then she said, "I'd like that."

"Terrific!" Matt rubbed his hands together. "How about tomorrow?"

"Tomorrow?"

"Oh…too soon, huh?"

"Actually, I was thinking about today."

"Hey, today's great," he hastened to assure her. "Why don't you drive back with me after I finish my business here?"

"That sounds nice." She nodded and smiled. "It'll give me time to change into something more suitable."

Blair idly wondered what Marni could have in all those suitcases that would be marginally suitable for exploring training barns. Suddenly she remembered her friend's reason for coming into the den in the first place.

"Excuse me. I'll see who's here and be right back."

"And I'll change," Marni said.

"What on earth do you think you're doing?" Blair asked, once they were out of hearing.

Marni shrugged. "I haven't the faintest idea. Believe me, Blair, I was as surprised as you. I heard the words and realized they were coming out of my mouth, but I sure don't know why or how."

"I thought you'd want to stick around while Ramsey's here."

"Oh, is he coming over?" Marni inquired vaguely.

"Isn't he here now?"

"No."

"Then who was at the door?"

"A delivery man. Were you expecting Ramsey?"

"He's bringing me the papers to sign, remember?"

"Oh, that. I still think you're making an enormous mistake," Marni warned her.

"I don't," Blair returned shortly. "What are you wearing over to Matt's farm? Not that I don't have a pretty good idea."

"Blair, you know I don't have anything for that kind of afternoon!"

"Only because you've never expressed an interest in the great outdoors. I still haven't figured out what you're up to now."

"Nothing. And don't forget who loaned you her Halston for that gallery opening last week. All I'm asking for is a pair of cruddy old jeans and one of those faded shirts you wear all the time. You know, the ones that have all the colors running together."

"They're supposed to bleed. They're madras. Besides, may I point out that you'd look a little silly mucking out a stall in a Halston."

Marni's smooth brow furrowed. "Mucking out a stall? Is that as gross as it sounds?"

"Worse. Take whatever you like," she offered.

Marni's grin was ecstatic. "Thanks, hon. You're a true pal." She headed toward Blair's room, humming an off-key rendition of "Camptown Racetrack" under her breath.

Blair shook her head, bemused over her roommate's uncharacteristic behavior. Then she went to the front door.

"Ms MacKenzie?" The young man standing there had an appreciative gleam in his eyes.

"That's me," she answered briskly. "I believe you have a delivery for me?"

"That's right. I put it in training barn B, like I was told to. I just need your signature."

"What is it?" she asked, taking the plastic pen and clipboard and scribbling her name.

"Flowers," he mumbled, attempting to read upside down. "I thought it was you! Could you sign another one? For me?"

Blair shrugged, doing as requested. "Why on earth would you put flowers in the training barn?"

"I dunno. That's just what was on the delivery slip. Thanks a lot, Ms. MacKenzie."

As the delivery truck drove away, Blair debated returning directly to the den, but curiosity got the better of her. She went out the back door and cut across the paddock to the training barn, where she found the flowers. Throwing a hand over her mouth to stifle the scream that threatened to erupt, she ran back to the house as fast as she could.

"Clint!" Blair burst into the den, interrupting the two men's conversation. "You won't believe what that horrible person's done now!"

Clint felt his stomach turn over as he viewed her anguished face. "What's the matter? Are you all right?" he asked.

She nodded, unable to speak, the words frozen in her throat.

"Is it one of the crew?"

This time she shook her head in the negative.

"One of the horses?" His stomach was doing somersaults now.

"N-n-n-no," she managed to get out.

"Here, Blair." Matt shoved a glass into her hands.

"What's this?"

"Brandy."

"It's too early in the day," she protested weakly.

Clint lifted the glass to her lips. "Matt's right. Drink it, Blair. Then sit down and try to tell us what happened."

She tilted back her head gasping as the liquid heat hit her stomach. But as she drank, the alcohol spread through her system in a comforting warmth.

"It's Black Magic," she said finally.

Both men exchanged puzzled looks. "Maybe it's just sinking in," Matt suggested.

Clint studied Blair intently. "I don't think so."

She was rapidly regaining her senses. "I'll show you," she said, linking her fingers with Clint's as she led him out of the room. He had to fight down the pleasure he received from the simple gesture, reminding himself that something was very, very wrong.

Black Magic had been removed from his stall, but in the stallion's place was a horseshoe of roses, much the same as the ones that had been draped about his neck when he won the Kentucky Derby. But these roses were black and the banner read, "Black Magic—RIP."

"You were right," she said, her voice horribly flat now that her shock had passed. "It was intentional. We have to call the police."

"No!"

Clint's reaction was the same as it had been when she'd suggested that earlier, his tone just as unrelenting, and because Marni had brought home that horrible story, Blair found herself ascribing all sorts of terrible notions to his refusal.

"Why can't you call the police, Clint?" she asked quietly.

Blair hated to see how uncomfortable Clint seemed with the subject. She glanced at Matt, who didn't look too thrilled with the topic, either.

Clint took her unresisting hands in his. Blair told herself she shouldn't be allowing this, but his thumbs were making such soothing circles on the tender skin of her palms.

"Look, we've got horses we're training for other owners," he reminded her.

"And you're afraid that if the word got out that Black Magic was destroyed on purpose, those people would take their horses away from here."

"Exactly."

"That's right," Matt echoed.

"Blair, it wouldn't break you, but you'd be in danger of drowning in red ink within six weeks without the fees these horses are generating. Training fees, brood fees, stud fees..."

"I get the point," she muttered. "Whatever happened to the days of daddy horses and mommy horses making lots of little baby horses who won races and brought in big purses filled with money?"

"I believe that's Sunnybrook Farm you're describing," Clint offered dryly. "This farm is situated in the real world. Things are more complicated."

That's for sure, she considered bleakly.

Matt began to do his own lobbying. "You have enough of your own stock, Blair, so you'd probably survive. But I'd have to close down. If you've been working with Ben Winters, you must know how much even a single horse costs."

"That's the truth," Clint agreed grimly, his face set in harsh lines. "Especially one in training."

Blair felt a prickling of apprehension skim up her spine. Was he talking about Risky Pleasure now? He was willing to risk so much just to hang on to the farm and, by doing that, to the filly. To what lengths would the man go in order to see his dream come true? She shook her head, disallowing the vague little seed of suspicion a chance to sprout.

Marni had misunderstood the newspaper article. She'd obviously been tired last night and undoubtedly drunk some wine. And because she refused to eat any nourishing food, it was quite likely that she'd been even more tipsy than Blair. She simply had not gotten the story straight. That was the only explanation.

"All right," Blair conceded. "But we're going to have to tighten security around here."

"That's exactly what I'd planned to do," Clint said calmly. "So we agree?"

"I suppose so. But I don't particularly like the idea."

"Neither do I, Blair," Clint muttered. "But it's all we can do for now."

Her head was beginning to clear. "Perhaps we can at least check with the florist and see who sent the flowers," she suggested.

"You must have been reading my mind," he replied.

No, Blair mused as the threesome made their way to the house, she hadn't been reading Clint's mind, although she'd dearly love to possess that ability. It was impossible to discern what the man was thinking at any given moment.

"What on earth happened to you?" Marni's clear blue eyes widened as Blair entered her bedroom.

"It's a long, complicated story I'll tell you later. Right now I just want to take a shower and a long nap."

"You certainly look as if you could use both," Marni said, noting Blair's drawn face and the hay on her jeans.

Blair stuck out her tongue. "A fine friend you are." Eyeing Marni suddenly, Blair stopped in her tracks. The jeans Marni had on were looser than the tight designer ones she usually wore, but they weren't so baggy that they were in danger of falling down. She'd unbuttoned just the top buttons of the plaid shirt, the little triangle of creamy skin appearing modestly tantalizing. Her thick blond hair was tied at the nape of her neck with a yellow ribbon.

"You look terrific," Blair stated.

To her amazement, Marni actually blushed. "Thanks. You don't think I look too much like Annie Oakley, do you?"

"Not at all. Turn around."

As Marni complied, she tottered a little on a pair of Blair's wedge-heel boots.

"Those can't possibly fit. You wear a size smaller than I do. With those pointed toes, you must be dying!"

"I can handle it," Marni insisted blithely. "It's just a small matter of positive thinking."

Blair knew how ineffective it was to argue once her friend's mind was made up. Stubbornness was probably the only trait the two women shared. That and loyalty.

"Have it your own way. But don't say I didn't warn you." Blair turned in the doorway of the bathroom. "Oh, by the way, did you have anything to drink last night?"

"Only a couple of glasses of Perrier."

"Are you sure? Not even a glass or two of wine?"

"Do you know how many calories there are in a glass of wine? Eighty. Eighty horrible calories all just waiting to leap onto my hips and put me out of work."

As Marni made the suggestion sound like a Roman banquet, Blair remembered her own dinner last night and glanced down, irrationally expecting to see fat cells popping out in every direction under her snug jeans.

"Then you simply misunderstood," she concluded.

Marni folded her arms and leaned against the door frame while Blair stripped off her clothes for her shower. "We're talking about Clint Hollister now, aren't we?"

Blair reached into the shower stall, turned the water on, then adjusted it to a comfortable temperature. "We are. And I've given it a lot of thought, Marni. If you didn't misunderstand, obviously Ramsey has the story all screwed up."

"Hey, Marni! Ready to go?" Matt's voice bellowed down the hall.

"Coming," she called out gaily. Then her tone became serious. "You know, Blair, I really hate to leave you here alone."

"I'm not alone."

"I know. That's what worries me."

"Clint didn't murder his wife," Blair insisted firmly. "I told you, Ramsey's simply confused."

"I doubt he could be confused about that," Marni argued, raising her voice to be heard above the streaming water.

"If he's so perfect, why are you playing Belle Starr with Matt Bradshaw this afternoon?"

"Ramsey's far from perfect," Marni said as she left the bathroom. "But I still can't believe he'd be mistaken about this, especially since Heather Hollister's maiden name was Blackwood." Marni paused, allowing her words to sink in. "She was Ramsey's daughter, honey."

Blair stood under the shower, wondering if it was the water or her blood that had suddenly turned to ice.

Chapter Eight

Half an hour later Blair entered the sunlit kitchen to find Clint seated at the table, drinking a cup of coffee.

"You look better," he decreed, eyeing her judiciously. "But you're still a little pale."

"I feel as if I've suddenly landed in the middle of a Robert Ludlum novel," she admitted, sinking down into a chair at the table.

"I know the feeling," he said.

"Where's Mildred?"

"I sent her home. I hope you don't mind."

"Of course not," Blair answered automatically. "But why?"

He reached into his shirt pocket and took out a crumpled cigarette pack. He tapped a cigarette on the table, his forehead drawn into thoughtful lines. "I didn't think it was fair to involve her. Who knows what's going to happen next?"

Blair nodded, watching his long fingers as he struck the match. She felt a stab of desire at the memory of those beautiful hands on her body and wondered if Marni could possibly be right. Was she allowing her desire for the man to overrule her common sense?

No, she decided firmly. Even if Clint Hollister hadn't had those gorgeous gray eyes, even if his hair hadn't been the color of sterling silver, even if his body hadn't been hard and well muscled, she would still believe him innocent of Ramsey Blackwood's charges. In fact, the man could look like Quasimodo and she'd know he was incapable of cruelty.

"I've been giving the matter a lot of thought," he said slowly, his expression grim.

"And?"

"I think you should leave, too."

A traitorous little thought tried to make itself heard in the back of her mind, but she squelched it immediately. "Why?"

His attention was drawn to the smoke circles rising slowly to the ceiling, so he missed her fleeting look of distress. "Because it's too dangerous," he replied.

"I'm not afraid," she protested, trying to keep the tremor from her voice.

"Aren't you?" he challenged harshly.

"No," she lied.

His flinty gray gaze speared her. "Then you're an idiot. Because I sure as hell am." His voice softened. "I'm afraid for you, Blair. I think you ought to leave until this is settled."

Blair stood her ground. "I'm not leaving the farm, Clint. I agree with you about Mildred, but I'm not allowing anyone to chase me away. I've worked for this my entire life, and I'll be damned if I'll turn tail and run the first time I encounter some problems."

His dark brows climbed his forehead before crashing back down. "Problems? Is that what you're calling all this?"

Blair sighed. "I don't know what to call it," she admitted. "But I do know you're stuck with me for the duration." She reached out, covering his hand with hers.

Clint looked down at the fair hand and experienced a sudden urge to lift it to his lips and press kisses into the delicate center of the palm. He wondered how he could possibly be feeling desire for her when his life was ripping apart at the seams. He jerked his hand away, reminding himself that he had more important things to consider.

"Are you hungry?" he asked suddenly.

Blair allowed a slight smile. "I'm always hungry. Marni has been warning me for years that I'm going to end up looking like the Pillsbury Doughboy."

"Come on, then," he said, rising from the table. "I'm taking you to lunch."

"Are we going out?" She ran her hands down the front of her clean jeans, wondering if she was appropriately dressed.

"Uh-huh."

"Perhaps I should change my clothes."

"You're perfect," he assured her. "We're going on a picnic. Mildred fixed it before she left."

"A picnic?"

He nodded. "I thought you might like to visit Irish Rover; he's pastured a short drive from here."

Blair's shining look of pleasure gave Clint her answer. After all that had happened that day, it was so nice of him to think of the one thing that could lift her spirits.

"I'd love it," she agreed instantly. "And, Clint..."

"Yeah?"

"Thank you."

He shrugged nonchalantly. "Hey, he's your horse. It's only right I take you out to inspect all your newfound wealth."

There was a gritty tone to his voice that Blair could not decipher, but as they walked out into the bright California sunshine, she decided not to try. For the next few hours, she was going to concentrate on enjoying herself.

They remained silent on the drive to the pasture, both embroiled in their own thoughts. Blair was surprised when Clint stopped the jeep suddenly and pointed out across a grassy field.

"There he is—the horse that built Clearwater Hills Farm."

Blair was out of her seat before Clint could turn off the engine, her eyes lit with a bright, expectant glow. She looked across the pasture toward the twenty-six-year-old horse. His smooth black coat was studded with gray, and his back was a little swayed, but she knew she was looking at a true champion.

Clint came up beside her, put his fingers between his teeth and let out an ear-splitting whistle.

"He's sleeping," Clint explained when the horse didn't flick an ear. "He can still see well enough, but the old guy's pretty deaf. Even whistling doesn't always work. Usually I have to go down and wake him up to call him into his paddock."

"Dear old thing." She approached the horse slowly, allowing him time to discern her presence. As the elderly stallion woke up, he observed her with large, brown eyes. Deciding he liked what he saw, he sashayed toward them.

She rubbed his neck with a long, gentle stroke. "Hello, boy," she murmured. "How's the champ?" Irish Rover snorted happily, nuzzling his nose against the soft curve of her neck. "Oh, Clint, he's so sweet."

"He always has been, to hear Jason tell it. And what a ham! People come by every day to visit him, and he'll actually stand and pose while they take his picture."

Blair's expression sobered momentarily. "I suppose we'll have to stop that for a bit, won't we?"

Clint had already considered the inadvisability of allowing the small but steady stream of Irish Rover fans onto the farm.

"I'm afraid so," he agreed.

"Poor baby," she crooned, patting the white blaze on the horse's face. "You're going to think you've been forgotten. We'll come and visit you every day, though, won't we, Clint?"

"Sure."

"And tomorrow we'll bring a camera."

"A camera? What the hell for?"

"To take his picture. You said he enjoyed that; we don't want him to get depressed because he misses posing for the photographers."

He wondered if she was speaking from personal experience. "Are you going to miss it?" he asked bluntly.

To Clint's amazement, Blair laughed, a light, silvery sound that did something funny to his heart.

"Oh, Clint, I thought you'd agreed to stop typecasting. If I never see another camera lens again, it'll be too soon."

He believed Blair was sincere, but he didn't believe she'd given enough consideration to the life she would be giving up. He'd already decided that her plan to get out of the Tigress contract was an impulsive idea. She'd probably change her mind once she got on the phone with her agent.

"You wouldn't miss the fame?"

"The fame isn't all it's cracked up to be," she said with sudden seriousness.

"At least you don't have to sit home on a Saturday night."

Blair looked up at him, her tawny eyes trying to make him understand that she hadn't found many men who were willing to get to know Blair MacKenzie. Most seemed interested only in her glamorous alter ego.

"I don't date much."

"Why not?" he inquired, even though he knew it was none of his business. But he suddenly had to learn if there was someone special in her life.

She lifted her shoulders in a graceful shrug. "It's too complicated. Besides, you really don't want to hear about my life, Clint. I promise, it would bore you to death."

He no longer could stand being that close to her without touching her. He reached out, his knuckles stroking a light path up her high cheekbones. "You could never bore me, Blair," he said on a deep, vibrant note. "I want to know everything about you. Your likes, your dislikes, where you got that little scar across the bridge of your nose, and how one of the most glamorous women in the country ended up wearing faded jeans and eating bologna sandwiches under a tree."

Blair couldn't miss the desire in Clint's tone. His voice sounded as if it were coming from the inside of a velvet-lined drum, and his fingers were creating sparks on her skin.

"Why?" she whispered.

"For the same reason you want to know everything about me," he answered. "Because you're trying to figure out why your world goes spinning a little crazily out of control every time you're in the same room with a guy who was sent away for killing his wife."

She blanched, all the color draining from her face at his words. "How did you know I had heard about that?"

"Simple. I knew last night that Ramsey wouldn't miss the opportunity to make certain you heard his side. When you came into the den after talking with Marni, you were as pale as driven snow and you wouldn't look me in the eye. Then, back in the barn, when I rejected the idea of calling the police, for an instant there you tried me and found me guilty.''

''That's not true. I never believed a word of that stupid story,'' she protested.

''Some of it's true, Blair.''

She forced herself not to flinch. ''Oh?''

''Heather *was* killed. I was found guilty and spent six months in prison.'' The revelation came out in a low, flat voice that couldn't entirely disguise the pain he'd suffered.

''But you didn't do it.''

He looked down at her, his expression giving nothing away. ''You're that sure? When twelve men and women who spent sixteen long days listening to sworn testimony decided otherwise?''

Blair nodded. ''I'm positive.''

Clint exhaled, and she suddenly realized he'd been holding his breath. ''I want to get it all out into the open, but suddenly I'm starving. How about you?''

''Famished,'' she agreed, letting him take her hand as they walked back up to the car to retrieve the lunch basket Mildred had packed.

Clint laid a blanket out under the spreading branches of a tree. Blair began to unpack their lunch, then started to laugh. ''You said we were having bologna sandwiches.''

''Aren't we?''

''All I can say is perhaps it's better that Mildred isn't around the house right now. If she keeps cooking like this, she and Marni will never get along.'' Blair pulled out the crisp, golden fried chicken, a bowl of marinated pasta salad, a dish of fresh vegetables, deviled eggs and thick slices of home-baked bread.

"Mildred still cooks as if she's feeding that brood of hers," Clint said, eyeing the enormous array of food.

"Oh, my God," Blair gasped, "devil's food cake! I simply cannot resist devil's food cake. I'll be as big as the Goodyear blimp before long."

"I'll make a deal with you," Clint suggested, pouring them each a glass of cold California chablis.

"What's that?"

"You eat whatever you want, sweetheart, and I promise to watch your figure for you." His gray eyes held a pleasant leer that she found unthreatening.

Her own eyes subjected him to an agonizingly slow examination, moving across his wide shoulders, down his chest, over his hips and down the long, muscled expanse of his legs.

"Only if I can watch yours for you," she returned, negotiating the bargain playfully.

"You keep looking at me that way and I'm going to forget all about lunch and start in with dessert."

"You promised," she said softly, her gaze at odds with her words.

"I'm only a man, Blair," he groaned, feeling the tightening in his loins as her eyes turned to molten gold. "I'm made of flesh and blood, not steel." Flesh that was aching for the touch of her satiny body, blood that was rapidly turning to rivers of flame.

Blair could not miss Clint's response to the silken net settling down around them even as she felt her own body warming at the idea of making love to him right now, on the plaid blanket, under the vast expanse of blue sky.

Clint knew that to make love to Blair in this sunlit meadow would be inordinately pleasing; she could thrill his senses in a way no other woman had ever done, and he had no doubt that their lovemaking would be extraordinary. But when it was over, the same problems would be there, only complicated by their sexual intimacy. It was too soon. He sighed, leaning his head back against the tree as he closed his eyes and willed his body to respond to his silent command.

"I promised to tell you about Heather," he said finally.

Blair had been lost in a sensual fantasy of her own, but his gritty tone jolted her back to reality.

"Heather," she echoed flatly. "Did you love her?"

"No."

"Then why did you marry her?"

"I thought she was carrying my baby.

"Oh."

"She miscarried."

"I'm sorry."

"So was I." His gray eyes turned to cold steel, but Blair had the feeling that his anger was directed inward. "I cried when it happened. Can you believe that?"

Yes, she answered silently, remembering his tenderness in the barn. *I can believe that.* She remained silent, though, feeling that the question was rhetorical.

Clint swallowed his wine in long, thirsty gulps, then refilled his glass. Blair shook her head when he held the bottle in her direction. She'd learned her lesson last night.

"I'll admit I never loved Heather, yet I was stunned by how much I wanted that baby. I'd never thought about being a father, but when she showed up at my house with the news, it was suddenly as if she'd given me everything I ever wanted."

"There was always the opportunity for other children," Blair pointed out softly.

Clint made a harsh, scornful sound. "No, there wasn't. Heather had the doctor make certain of that."

"Oh." What on earth could she say to that?

"We got into a hell of an argument over it, and that's when she told me it hadn't even been my child."

Blair was speechless, trying not to think how furious a man would be to hear such news.

"You're wondering if I was angry enough to kill her," he said with unnerving accuracy.

She shook her head, taking a sip of wine, stalling for time until she recovered her voice. "I've already told you, Clint," she finally said, "I don't believe that story."

The harsh lines of his face softened.

"Why did she lie to you in the first place?"

Clint stared out across the flower-dotted green meadow, thinking of the many times he'd asked himself the same question. "She was an incredibly beautiful young woman who'd learned early in life that her looks could get her anything she wanted."

Blair was beginning to understand why Clint had resented her career. He'd been burned once by a woman with more beauty than scruples, so how could he have known that Blair was any different?

"And she wanted you."

"Until she had me. To Heather, seduction was what kept life interesting. I knew the moment she moved into my home that it wasn't going to work, but as long as she was carrying the baby, I was determined to make a go of it. When the accommodations weren't up to what she was used to, Jason let us move into his house. That satisfied her for about two days."

"You could have divorced her," Blair pointed out.

He gave a bitter laugh. "Don't you think I suggested that? Time and time again. No, Heather may not have wanted me, but she'd be damned if she was going to let me find happiness with anyone else, either."

"But—"

"She threatened to kill herself every time I told her I was leaving. The first few times I didn't believe her. After three trips to the hospital to pump out her stomach, I began to realize she was serious."

"Did all this come out in the trial?"

"Of course."

"Then surely the jury could see she was a very unstable woman," Blair protested.

"They could also see several reasons that would make me willing to take drastic measures to get her out of my life. Including that ridiculous charge about Risky Pleasure."

Blair hoped that she could keep her expression from revealing how that particular aspect of the problem had been hard to dispel. Obviously she failed.

"That one bothered you, didn't it?" he asked, tapping a cigarette against the face of his watch before lighting it.

Deciding that the one thing the man deserved was the truth, she nodded reluctantly.

"It obviously bothered the hell out of the jury, too. It wasn't true, Blair."

"I believe that," she said earnestly.

He exhaled the smoke on a harsh breath. "Heather was the jealous one; I knew about the other men in her life and looked the other way. She resented anything or anyone who meant more to me than she did."

"And Risky Pleasure did."

"Yeah. And Heather hated the idea. She grew more and more jealous of Risky Pleasure and started telling everyone that I was obsessed with the filly. That I wanted the horse all to myself. She'd get drunk at parties and tell anyone who'd listen that I'd threatened her in order to force her to give me the money to buy the filly from Jason."

"Oh, Clint, how horrible for you.... Let's not talk about it anymore," Blair said, hating the anguish she saw carved into his rugged face.

"I've gotten this far," he stated dully, "I may as well finish the story."

"You don't have to tell me this; I know how it must hurt."

He viewed the gentle concern in her tawny eyes and wondered how two women who'd come into the world graced with such uncommon beauty could be so different.

"It's important that I do," he insisted. "Because I don't want it hovering unanswered between us. I've learned the hard way that if you ignore a problem, it can only get worse."

He inhaled on the cigarette, closing his eyes as he breathed in the strangely calming smoke. "When Heather didn't show up for a few days, it never occurred to me to call the police. It wasn't the first time she'd taken off. To tell you the truth, I always secretly hoped she wouldn't come back."

"I can understand that," Blair murmured.

"I'm glad you can, because the police and the DA couldn't. Neither could the jury. When Heather's body was found in that motel out of town, I was the logical suspect."

"Are you telling me you were convicted on circumstantial evidence?"

He gave her a mirthless smile. "The real world isn't like Perry Mason, Blair. The culprit doesn't crack on the stand and admit his guilt. But Jason never once doubted my innocence. He had investigators out combing the country, trying to find the last man Heather had been with."

"I'm glad you weren't entirely alone," Blair said quietly, wondering if she had misjudged her grandfather. Hadn't she convicted him of being a cruel, unloving man after only listening to her mother's side of the story? David MacKenzie, oddly enough, had always defended Jason Langley whenever the subject had come up. In later years, Kate had learned to discuss the matter out of her husband's hearing.

"I'd been in prison six months when one of the investigators Jason had hired ran across an assault charge in Fresno. A woman was accusing a man she'd met in a singles bar of beating her up. When the detective went out and interviewed her, she said the man had bragged that he'd already killed one woman, so it wouldn't be that difficult to do it a second time."

This was Ramsey Blackwood's legal mumbo jumbo that got Clint out of jail? Blair thought incredulously. "I take it he turned out to be the one."

Clint nodded. "It took a while to prove the case, but finally, when faced with all the evidence, the guy confessed."

"Clint," Blair said thoughtfully, "would Ramsey have any reason to hold a grudge against you, even knowing you didn't kill his daughter?"

He ground the cigarette out on a rock before answering. "You're thinking he might be behind all this."

Blair nodded. "It's a possibility."

Clint shook his head. "I've thought the same thing over and over again. I've even confronted him with it."

"And?"

He raked his fingers through his hair. "He denies it, of course. But he wouldn't have any reason to be pulling the same stunts over at Matt's. It doesn't make sense."

They fell silent, and Blair's mind tossed the problem around like a leaf caught in a whirlpool. It circled and circled, never quite getting free.

"He could be doing it to throw you off the track," she suggested.

Clint looked at her with renewed respect. "That's not an impossible scenario," he admitted. "But why now? Why didn't all these things happen three years ago, when Heather was first killed? Or when I was released from prison?"

Blair's face fell as she attempted to think of a logical explanation and came up empty. "I don't know," she admitted. "So I suppose we're back to square one."

"It seems so," he muttered. Then he eyed the still-untouched food. "I thought you were famished."

While Blair couldn't completely put away her worries, Clint had relieved her mind a great deal by telling her about Heather. She vowed first thing to let Marni know as much of the truth as possible, without revealing the secrets of Clint's ill-fated marriage.

As if by unspoken agreement, they kept their conversation on the positive aspects of the farm, discussing the upcoming racing season.

"Ready to go back?" he asked finally, without a great deal of enthusiasm. He rose, brushing crumbs from his faded indigo jeans.

"I suppose so," she murmured, accepting his outstretched hand. Blair was no more eager than he to return to the problems they'd managed to put away as they were sharing Mildred's expertly prepared lunch. She fell silent while they packed up the basket and drove back to the house.

"We still haven't gone over this season's racing schedule," Clint reminded her as they pulled up to the house.

"Why don't we go over the list tonight after dinner?" she suggested.

His eyes flicked over her slender frame, and he grinned. Where on earth did she put it all, he wondered, remembering the Herculean lunch she'd eaten. "Sure. That is, if you're going to be ready for food again before next weekend."

Blair wrinkled her nose at him in a gesture he found ill suited for the Tigress Woman, but perfectly suited to the jeans-clad lady jumping down from the Jeep.

"I told you, I've got a fantastic metabolism," she said.

This time his gaze took a more leisurely tour of her body, and Blair felt as if his silvery eyes were probing right through to her lacy underwear. "I can see that," he murmured, his husky tone affecting her like a physical caress.

She forced a ragged laugh. "And I exercise," she reminded him.

"Ah, yes, that mysterious exercise." His eyes settled onto the soft swell of her breasts, and Blair's nipples tightened as they pressed against the cotton fabric, reaching for his touch. "Tell me, do you prefer doing it indoors or out in the exhilarating fresh air?"

From the warm look in his eyes, Blair had a funny feeling he wasn't talking about physical fitness any longer. Her heart was beating at a rate that could not possibly be normal for anyone. She was amazed he couldn't see its wild thudding under her shirt.

"Fresh air in Manhattan?" She tried to laugh as her gaze was enmeshed in molten silver pools of masculine desire.

"Inside, then," he guessed, dragging his eyes to her lips. The strawberries Mildred had included in the picnic had dyed the soft skin a deep pink. He yearned for a taste of them.

"Inside," she agreed, feeling as if she were sinking into quicksand.

Clint nodded his head, shoving his hands deep into his pockets to keep from touching her. "There's nothing wrong with indoor sports," he allowed. "But now that you live in sunny California, you should probably consider moving some of your activities outdoors. Have you ever done it at night? Bathed in the glow of a full moon?"

Although they were still ostensibly discussing exercise, his low tone painted sensual pictures in her mind. Blair envisioned Clint making love to her on that plaid blanket, lying under a black velvet canopy of diamond-bright stars, the air perfumed with the scent of California poppies and sweet lupine. She trembled slightly at the provocative image.

"How long has it been since you've seen stars?" he asked suddenly, once again giving Blair the unnerving feeling that he could read her mind.

"Why did you ask that?" she asked defensively.

He shrugged. "I thought when things settle down around here, you might like to go moonlight riding along the beach."

It sounded marvelous. It also sounded far more romantic than she was up to handling right now.

"But I thought you weren't going to let this well-photographed fanny onto one of your precious horses."

He grinned. "That was before I learned that well-shaped rear end was quite accustomed to sitting in a saddle."

Suddenly Blair remembered his words to Matt. "That's right! How did you find out about Ben Winters, anyway?"

A slight shadow came over his eyes. He busied himself by lifting the basket out of the backseat of the Jeep. "Here."

"Thanks," she murmured absently, taking the wicker picnic hamper. "Ben Winters?" she prodded him softly.

"Marni told Blackwood, who told me," he admitted, looking decidedly uncomfortable.

"But that means you've talked to him today."

She wondered if Ramsey Blackwood had called and told Clint he was receiving half the farm. Was that what had caused his change in attitude toward her?

Clint groaned inwardly, reminding himself about tangled webs of prevarication. He tapped a cigarette on the hood of the Jeep before sticking it between his lips.

Recognizing the stalling tactic, Blair merely waited.

"Last night," he admitted, deciding there had been enough half-truths between them already.

"Last night? But you were with me last night." Her smooth brow furrowed, and suddenly she remembered. "He was the one who called after I'd gone to bed, wasn't he? I asked you who it was, and you told me a friend offering condolences." Blair didn't like the way Clint's eyes shifted from her curious gaze as he inhaled on that ever-present cigarette. "Why didn't you tell me it was Ramsey?"

"He's not my favorite topic of conversation, Blair. Surely you can understand that."

She leaned against the Jeep, looking at him thoughtfully. Clint forced the muscles of his face into a casual expression.

"Of course I can. Which makes it all the more curious why in the world he'd be calling you up to tell you what he'd learned about me from Marni." Suddenly she remembered her friend's complaint that morning. "That's what last night's dinner invitation was about, wasn't it? Ramsey was pumping Marni for information."

"Blackwood doesn't keep me informed about his social calendar, Blair. I assume he invited the woman to his house because she's young, beautiful and famous." Clint suddenly spun around on a booted heel, turning in the direction of the paddock.

"So why did he spend the entire evening asking about me?" Blair challenged after him. "And how did you know they had dinner at his house?"

Then she recalled Clint's willingness to wait up for her friend. "That's how you knew when she was coming home, isn't it? He called you the minute he stuck her in that damn taxi.... Why, Clint?"

His tanned face could have been carved from granite as he looked at her over his shoulder. "I thought you trusted me."

"I do," she insisted, wishing she'd been able to put more emphasis on her declaration.

"Then why don't you start acting as if you do?" he growled before marching off again.

Furious, Blair reached down, picked up a small rock from the gravel driveway and threw it at the back of his head. It missed only by inches, and Clint skidded to a halt.

Blair held her breath, waiting for the inevitable explosion, but when he pivoted slowly around, his expression was less formidable.

"Baseball?" he inquired dryly.

She didn't know whether to laugh or cry as he turned their argument back to that ridiculous guessing game.

"If it was baseball, Mr. Hotshot Trainer, I wouldn't have missed!"

"You're angry," he diagnosed correctly.

"Furious," she admitted.

"Want to try for two out of three?" he asked, taking off his hat, baring his silvery head for a target.

"Don't tempt me," she warned.

"I could ask the same thing of you," he said huskily as he watched her breasts rise and fall under her cotton shirt.

Blair shook her head, trying not to respond to the sensual teasing in his voice. "Why don't you just get to work while I try to figure out that Chinese puzzle Jason Langley called his accounting system. The man hadn't balanced his personal checkbook for the last ten years!"

"Jason could get a little absentminded," Clint acknowledged. "He usually left the important things to his lawyer or his accountant."

"I'm not thrilled with the entries made by his accountant, either," Blair confessed. "I still haven't figured out what half of them mean.... Like 'high tower.' My grandfather never owned a horse with that name, did he?"

"Never. But it does ring a bell."

"Well, whatever it was, it didn't come cheap. He spent more than a million dollars on it last year."

Clint expelled a low whistle. "That's not chicken feed. Let me think about it, and I'll try to remember where I heard the name, okay?"

She nodded. "Okay."

"I've got to supervise the final feeding now, but I'll see you later for dinner."

Blair tried to remind herself that she was angry at Clint for not being totally open with her. Yet she was finding it so difficult to refuse the invitation in those lustrous gray eyes. She nodded her acquiescence.

"Would you like to go out? If you feel like seafood, we could always drive into the city."

"Shouldn't we stay here? To watch after things?"

"Yeah, we probably should," Clint agreed. "Since we're on our own, want to grill a couple of steaks?"

"Sounds great. I'll take two out of the freezer."

"What about your friend?"

Blair laughed, her irritation dissolving. "Marni would die before allowing all those calories to pass through her lips."

"It doesn't seem to have done you any harm." His gaze paid masculine compliments. "Gymnastics," he guessed suddenly.

"Nope."

"Too bad," he murmured, putting his hat back on and turning away again. "That one offered an intriguing realm of possibilities."

Chapter Nine

Clint couldn't get Blair out of his mind as he attended to the afternoon feeding. She was definitely not what he'd been expecting, and he was admittedly fascinated by the woman; she had far more depth than what was displayed by her advertising campaigns.

"There you are!"

When the all-too-familiar voice of Ramsey Blackwood jerked him from his thoughts, Clint muttered a low oath. The one thing he didn't need today was a visit from his former father-in-law. Especially after the way the man had made certain that Blair heard about his shoddy little story. Blackwood's side of it, at any rate.

He slowly put down the grain bucket. "Even a rattlesnake gives a warning before it attacks, Blackwood."

"Ms MacKenzie didn't waste any time in going to you for confirmation of your past indiscretions, did she?" Ramsey said thoughtfully. "That young woman is reminding me more and more of her obstreperous old grandfather."

"May I point out that obstreperous old man kept you in Mercedes cars over the years?"

Ramsey Blackwood gave him a mirthless smile. "I earned every penny I made from that coldhearted old skinflint. And you're a fine one to talk, Hollister, since you've made out like a bandit."

Clint pulled out a cigarette, breaking his own commandment about no smoking in the barn. "I never expected Jason to will me fifty percent of Risky Pleasure."

"Oh, that was probably overly generous, but this new twist is quite a coup." The man's eyes narrowed wickedly. "As far as gigolos go, you're probably the best paid in history. When I suggested a little romance might go a long way toward convincing a woman to change her mind, I certainly didn't expect you to make it an Olympian sport."

"What the hell are you talking about?" Clint grated out between clenched teeth, his patience at a very low ebb.

"Your receiving fifty percent of Clearwater Hills Farm, of course. Tell me, Hollister, did you come right out and ask for it, or did you let the lady believe it was all her idea?"

Clint almost choked on the smoke filling his lungs as Ramsey's words sank in. "What?"

The attorney's lips pursed into a charade of a smile. "Now you're going to play it coy and tell me you didn't know."

"Not only did I not know, I don't believe it."

"Interesting," Ramsey murmured to himself. "Well, it's true. She called me before dawn this morning and instructed me to make out the papers."

"Do you have them with you?"

"Of course."

"Let me see them."

"They're not yours." At Clint's glower, Ramsey curved his fingers a bit tighter about the handle of his alligator-skin attaché case.

"Let me see them, Blackwood, or I'll break your fingers taking that case away from you."

"I'd press charges," the lawyer warned.

Clint tipped his hat back with his thumb, rocking back and forth on his heels. He dropped the cigarette to the floor of the barn, making certain he ground it out before returning his attention to Ramsey.

"You do that, counselor. It sure as hell wouldn't be the first time." He moved forward, his hand outstretched.

"I made a mistake, Hollister. I honestly thought you were guilty." The man backed away a few steps, clutching the briefcase to his chest.

"Don't give me that. You just wanted me out of here because I wouldn't encourage Jason to buy into your crazy investment schemes."

"You owed it to Heather to try. I offered you a generous commission on every one of those deals; you could have been set for life. How happy do you think she was, living here as the wife of a hired hand?" The attorney's tone was blatantly scornful. "And after the life she'd been used to."

"I'd say about as happy as she was living in that La Jolla mansion of yours. I saw the scars on her wrists. She was in trouble long before I stepped into the picture."

Ramsey waved his hand, airily dismissing his daughter. "Look, I was only trying to help. Jason Langley was a wealthy man, but except for the money he spent on these stupid nags, he might as well have kept his money in the mattress."

"These stupid nags made him all that money in the first place, because he understood them. He was smart enough to stay out of investments he didn't know anything about.... Now that we've cleared the air on that little subject, I'd like to see those papers."

Ramsey put the case down on a bale of hay, opened it and extracted a manila envelope, which he handed over to

Clint. He eyed the younger man thoughtfully as Clint skimmed the pages of legalese.

"You know, Hollister, this could still work out for the best. If you've got her eating out of your hand enough to deed half this place to you in two days, you could probably talk her into selling by the end of the week. I call my buyer, you and the young lady make a tidy profit, and everyone ends up the winner."

"Including you," Clint added, "since you're holding out for a ten percent commission."

"It's a fair deal. Besides, you'd still end up with forty-five percent, which is damn good pay for a night of bedroom acrobatics."

Clint felt his fury rising and fought against the urge to rid the world of the supercilious attorney once and for all. "You're forgetting something," he said.

"And that is?"

"If Blair doesn't sell, I own fifty percent."

"She'll never make it," Ramsey blustered.

"I'm betting she will."

"Hollister, look at this reasonably. The woman can't possibly run a farm this size."

"We're going to run it together. Besides, you're not giving the lady credit. She's more than just a pretty face." Clint gave the older man a false smile. "Now why don't you go back to your office, and I'll see that Ms. Mac-Kenzie gets these papers."

Ramsey held his hand out, shaking his head at the same time. "I don't think that's a good idea."

"You've got five minutes to get off this farm," Clint warned him in a low voice. "And if you know what's good for you, you won't show that two-sided face on the property again. Is that understood?"

"You can't fire me!"

"I wasn't talking about firing you, counselor."

There was a silky threat in Clint's voice that Ramsey appeared unwilling to challenge. He backed slowly out of the barn, climbed into his gray Mercedes and roared down the road.

Blair was on the phone when Clint entered the kitchen.

"That's okay, Marni," she was saying. "Stay as long as you like. I'm glad you're having a good time."

She hung up, a fond smile curving her lips. "Now that's a pair I'd never have in my wildest dreams imagined together. I'm amazed they're finding anything to talk about. She's not coming home for dinner, by the way."

Blair expected Clint to make some suggestive comment about the two of them having the house all to themselves, but he surprised her by shrugging carelessly and saying nothing.

"Clint, is something wrong?"

"What could be wrong?"

She didn't like the cold glitter in his eyes. "Around this place, just about anything. Has something else happened?"

He removed the papers from his back pocket. "Your attorney brought these by for you. I told him I'd see that you got them."

"Oh, damn. I wanted to surprise you!" Then her amber eyes widened. "Clint, what are you doing?"

He ripped the papers in half, then in half again, repeating the process until the confettilike pieces had drifted over the floor, resembling unmelted snow.

"I'm not for sale, Blair. At any price." He turned and walked out of the house.

She stared mutely at the scattered shreds of what had been her special surprise. Then she ran outside and grabbed him by the arm. "What did that grandstand play in there mean?"

He shrugged off her hand as easily as if she'd been a troublesome gnat. "All you rich girls seem to find it amusing sport to play with people's lives. I thought you were different, Blair, but obviously I was wrong. You're just like Heather, Kate—"

"Just one minute, mister," she interrupted, stiffening her back. "How dare you compare my mother with a woman you've already admitted had no more morals than a common alley cat!"

"Kate Langley may not have fooled around on David MacKenzie, but she sure as hell ruined his life."

"She loved him!" Blair shouted.

"Then she should have loved him enough to let him go. But no, she had to trap him into marriage and force him to give up what he probably did better than anyone before or after him."

"A lot you know." Blair tossed her head angrily. "My father was a good and sweet man, but Irish Rover was obviously a fluke, because he never trained another champion."

Clint's laugh was bitter. "Of course he didn't, you little fool. Jason wouldn't let him."

"What did my grandfather have to do with it? My father left Clearwater Hills Farm."

"Right. And Jason made certain each farm knew that if it wanted any Irish Rover or Moonglow blood in its stables, it had better not hire David MacKenzie!"

His words came at her like deadly bullets, and Blair sucked in a deep breath as they struck at the very core of her heart. She remembered her mother bitterly complaining about their small homes, their constant traveling. It had never made sense to her that Kate had placed the

blame for all their misfortunes on Jason Langley, but
suddenly the pieces fitted into place. She felt as if she were
going to be ill.

"My father was that good?" she whispered.

Clint was not immune to the pain that his own display
of exacerbation had just caused her. "He was the best."

"I'm selling the farm," she announced suddenly.
"What do you want to pay for it?"

"Me?" He stared at her.

"Name a price, Clint. Any number from one to ten will
do."

"Blair, be serious."

Her eyes were as hard as agates. "Oh, I'm deadly serious, Clint. And if you're not going to make an offer, I'll
just have to come up with something. How does one dol-
lar sound?"

He didn't like the way she looked. Two scarlet flags were
the only color in her face, her lips were pressed into a grim
line and her gaze had frozen to ice.

"Blair—"

"Sold, to the man in the gray Stetson," she announced
with a smile that chilled his soul. "Stop by the house later
this afternoon, cowboy, and I'll sign the place over to you
and give you the key. Right now I'm going to pack."

She spun around, making her way to the house on legs
that threatened to fold at any minute. Clint caught up with
her easily, one hand gripping her shoulder. "Blair, I'm
sorry. I thought you knew."

She stared up at him. "My God, Clint, if I'd known that
Jason Langley ruined my father's chances to train champions, do you think I'd have stepped one foot on this
farm? I can't accept anything from such a cruel and
heartless man."

Blair squared her shoulders. "The only reason I got into modeling in the first place was because it paid so well. I've been saving for years to start my own stable. Oh, nothing on the grand scale of this, of course," she admitted, her gaze raking over the rolling fields of grassland. "But at least I'll know I bought it with my own money—and not Jason Langley's thirty pieces of silver!"

"Jason always intended for you to have the farm, Blair," Clint argued. "That's why he wouldn't sell out, even when he knew he didn't have long to live. He wanted all this to be yours."

"What makes you think I give a damn about what Jason Langley wanted?" she spat out.

"What about what David MacKenzie wanted?"

Blair avoided his steady gray gaze, her eyes moving rapidly over the distant fields. "What does that mean?"

"Do you think he spent all those years training you just to have you work in second-class stables? He trained you for here, Blair. And according to Ben Winters, you're ready."

That got her attention. "You've talked with Ben?"

"Before lunch. He had nothing but praise for you—even if you are a woman."

She groaned. "I've heard that before."

"Then you'll stay? It's what your father would have wanted."

Blair thought back to how diligently her father had worked with her, teaching her everything he knew about Thoroughbreds. Clint was right. Her father had obviously been preparing her to train champions; to return to Clearwater Hills Farm to reclaim her birthright. If she let him down now, she'd be guilty of the same bullheaded, unbending attitude that had characterized Jason Langley. Mildred had already warned her not to allow her deep-seated trait of stubbornness to ruin any more lives. Including her own. As furious as she was about her situation, Blair couldn't let her father down.

"I'll stay," she agreed reluctantly. "How about you?"

"I don't want fifty percent of your farm, Blair."

"I need you," she protested. "I don't care what Ben says. I'm not ready to train all these horses by myself."

"Then I'll stay on for a while."

"How long?"

"As long as you need me." He turned away then, continuing toward the training barn.

That was something, Blair considered, wondering what Clint would have said if she'd told him she needed him for a lot more than to help train her horses. That confession was better kept to herself, she decided, heading back to the house.

Clint had just reached the training barn when it hit him where he'd heard the words "high tower." Jason had yelled them into the phone about two weeks before he died. It hadn't been like Jason to spend a million dollars without discussing it with Clint. And yet for a year, according to Blair, he'd done exactly that. Why?

"IT DIDN'T WORK," the man admitted, keeping his voice low as he spoke into the telephone. "She's unbelievably stubborn."

"You're an attractive enough man; surely you can convince her it would be in her best interests to sell," the woman suggested.

"From the way she was looking at Hollister this morning, I wouldn't stand a chance."

"Clint Hollister," the woman muttered acidly. "That man has been a thorn in my side from the beginning. It'll be a pleasure taking care of him."

"I thought you said there wasn't going to be any violence."

"Unnecessary violence," she corrected. "And that's up to you."

The man heard the water in the shower being turned off. "Look, I'm not alone here. I've got to hang up," he said. "I'll see you Friday night."

"It won't be soon enough. I've missed you, darling."

The invitation in her throaty voice was unmistakable, and he felt his blood warming in response, as it always did. "Me, too."

She laughed. "I can tell. Don't let your houseguest wear you out, sweetheart. I'm expecting marvelous things from you on Friday."

He hung up just as the door to the den opened. "What kept you?" he asked with a boyishly attractive grin. "I was getting lonely."

IT WAS AS IF BOTH Clint and Blair had decided to work overtime to keep their relationship on a strictly professional level. Although their shared dinner was not without the odd moment of sensual yearning, they steadfastly ignored each one, keeping the conversation on horses, the farm and the season's racing schedule. Clearwater Hills Farm's early waking hour allowed Blair to escape to her own room soon after dinner was over, but sleep was an illusive target. Her dreams were filled with Clint Hollister, who appeared to her in a myriad of moods, like the facets of a child's kaleidoscope.

They spoke only a few words as they worked together in the predawn hours of the next day, feeding the horses in training and then watching the workouts, but each was vividly aware of the other's presence. Last night's self-restraint seemed to be eroding, like tides undermining the foundations of a sand castle, and Blair was never so glad to see anyone as she was when she walked into the kitchen and found Marni sitting at the kitchen table.

"Hi! Where's Matt?" she asked.

"He's coming. He just wanted to talk to Clint for a minute about Dancing Lady. She's run on three soft racetracks in a row back East and came home with a fungus on the heels of her foot."

Blair had been pouring herself a cup of coffee, but at Marni's matter-of-fact tone she turned to stare at her longtime friend. "Sounds as if you two found something to talk about," she finally stated noncommittally.

"All night, in fact," Marni said. "Matt was as surprised as I was to look up at the clock and see it was time for the morning feeding."

"You stayed up all night? Talking?" Blair hadn't been overly surprised when she awoke this morning to find that Marni hadn't come home. But she'd pictured quite a different scenario going on next door.

"Well, not just talking."

"I thought not," Blair murmured.

"We spend some of the time watching videotapes of races. Oh, Blair, it's such an exciting business...you've no idea!"

"I think I can imagine."

Marni realized what she'd said and began to laugh. "Of course you can. But I never realized there was so much more to horse racing than the betting window. Why didn't you ever tell me?"

"Perhaps my feelings don't carry as much weight as Matt Bradshaw's."

Marni's blue eyes held a faraway look, and a little smile curved her full lips. "He's a wonderful man, Blair, like no one I've ever met."

Blair sat down at the table. "This sounds serious."

Marni made a face. "I think it is. I wouldn't get blisters and saddle sores for any other man I know."

"Saddle sores? You actually rode a horse?"

"Bounced is probably a better description," she admitted, grimacing slightly in remembrance. "My rear is probably black and blue by now."

"How were the boots?"

"I've blisters over blisters. I'm going to buy a pair of my own this afternoon. Right now it's a toss-up which of us is limping worse—Dancing Lady or me."

Blair tried to picture Marni on a horse and came up blank.

"Blair, do you think it's possible to fall in love at first sight?"

"I didn't used to," she answered slowly, staring down into her coffee, as if seeking an answer in the black depths. "But I'm beginning to wonder."

Both women fell silent, content to linger in their own thoughts.

"Good morning, Blair. Boy does that coffee smell great!"

As Matt came into the kitchen, he gave Blair a wide, friendly smile. It didn't escape her notice that the smile he shared with Marni was warmer, more intimate, and sparked with a definite promise.

"Good morning. Would you like some breakfast? Clint and I ate before the workouts, but you're probably starved."

He shook his blond head. "Thanks, anyway, but Marni and I already ate. She makes a dynamite Spanish omelet."

Marni a cook? Blair wouldn't remember the last time she'd seen her eat anything that resembled a full meal. When Blair's questioning gaze caught her friend's eye,

Marni only shrugged, allowing a slight, inwardly directed smile.

"How's Tidal Wave?" Clint asked Matt as he pulled up a chair and straddled it, leaning his arms along the top. "Are you going to run him in the Santa Anita Derby?"

"I think he has a good chance," Matt replied. "With Dancing Lady's problems, he's about all I've got to run these days."

"Things will pick up," Clint said reassuringly.

Matt managed a grin. "Sure they will," he agreed with false heartiness. "That thought is what's keeping me going these days."

They fell silent for a few minutes; then Matt rose from the table. "Well, we'd better be going. I promised Marni another riding lesson. She's catching on faster than anyone I've ever known."

As Marni rose to follow him, she stopped suddenly, looking back over her shoulder. "Oh, dear, we almost forgot to invite you two."

"Invite us to what?" Blair asked.

"The party Matt is throwing Friday night. He spent an hour calling people, but we almost forgot to tell the two most important guests."

"What's the party for?" Clint asked, though he was not in any mood to celebrate.

"I thought Marni might like to meet a few of the local folk," Matt said offhandedly.

"It's going to be a lot of fun," Marni coaxed prettily.

Blair knew it would hurt her friend's feelings if she failed to show up. "I'll drop in. But I can't stay long," she warned.

Marni's smile was beatific, and even Matt looked pleased. "Clint," he said. "Can we count on you?"

"Just for one quick drink. I don't want to leave the farm for long."

"Great. See you later," Matt said with hearty enthusiasm.

"Later," Blair and Clint murmured in unison as the pair left, arm in arm.

"He certainly is good-natured," Blair observed, "considering that it sounds as if he's in worse shape than we are."

"Matt's had a run of bad luck the past few years," Clint told her. "But your friend seems to have made quite a difference in his attitude."

"Marni has that effect on men," Blair allowed.

"Really?"

"Really," she said dryly. "Don't tell me you haven't noticed."

"Not really. I suppose I've been too busy watching you."

Clint's gaze bathed her face in a warm glow that went all the way to her toes. Once again a sensual net drifted over them, and without realizing that either one had moved, Blair was in his arms.

"Oh, sweetheart," he whispered, his lips against hers, so that Blair felt the words as well as heard them. "What you do to me with those huge, gold eyes."

She closed her eyes, delighting in the sound of his voice, the way his words breathed a caress on her skin, the warmth of his wide hands as his fingers splayed against her back, urging her closer still. She could feel him against her, from her breasts to her thighs, and it seemed that the heat from both their bodies was melding them into a single delicious entity.

"Is this one of those passes you didn't want to keep dodging?" he asked, his thumbs creating both ecstasy and havoc to her senses as they played lightly, tantalizingly up and down her sides, barely skimming her breasts.

"Yes." She managed to whisper her answer into his mouth, their breath mingling in a soft, scented cloud.

"Should I stop?" His lips plucked at hers, punctuating the words with little kisses.

Her fingers were toying with the hair at the back of his neck, delighting in the feel of the silky silver that curled so enticingly against his collar.

"Don't you dare," she said, tugging at a silver curl playfully. "I told you, Clint, this is one of those passes I *don't* want to dodge."

As his lips suddenly pressed against hers with an urgent, searching hunger, Blair tugged his shirt loose, her nails sinking into the muscled flesh of his back.

"That's right," he groaned, "let me feel your claws, Tigress lady. Let me know that you want me as badly as I want you."

A vague warning rippled through her as Clint's huskily muttered words sank in. He was just like the others, obviously more interested in bedding the famous Tigress Woman than making love to Blair MacKenzie.

Clint had not known he'd said the words out loud, but when her body went stiff in his arms, he realized that he'd made the primitive fantasy an obvious one.

"Blair," he muttered achingly, "you're taking it all wrong."

Her fingers left off kneading the muscles of his back and pressed against his chest as she attempted to put some space between them.

"I don't think I am," she said firmly, even now hoping that she might be wrong, that she'd overreacted to what was simply an honest slip in the heat of passion. "Admit it, Clint. You're like every other man in the country. You want to make it with the Tigress Woman!''

If she'd known that damn ad campaign was going to turn her world upside down, she would never have agreed to do it. But at the time she'd been desperate for the money offered, and there was certainly nothing obscene in the photos. The obscenities were in the minds of men like Clint Hollister.

She tried to squirm away, but Clint's superior strength held her in his arms, not hurting her, but not permitting her freedom, either.

"I'm not like every other man in the country," he rasped. "I'm not like any man you've ever been with."

"Your modesty overwhelms me," she said recklessly. "But you're right, Clint. All the men I've made love to over the years have been gentlemen."

She neglected to say that there'd been only three in all her nearly thirty years and that one had been her husband, who couldn't honestly claim that description, either. Her love life was not Clint Hollister's business—not that experimental time at twenty, when she'd been positive she was the only virgin left in New York City; not her ill-fated marriage to a young photographer who'd never forgiven her for achieving fame without him; nor the comfortable, but unexciting affair she'd shared with her accountant from Brooklyn. Tom had been sweet, and Blair had loved him dearly, but their dreams and aspirations had been too different to make a long-lasting relationship possible.

Clint's hands locked firmly around her shoulders. "You've got the quickest tongue in the West, sweetheart. If you don't watch it, one of these days it's going to get you in a lot of trouble."

Blair trembled slightly at the cold warning in his tone, reminding herself that Clint Hollister was a man who rode his passions hard.

"In the first place, I've never claimed to be a gentleman. And in the second, of course I want to make love to the Tigress Woman."

"I knew it," Blair muttered, attempting to twist out of his arms once again.

"You're a damn fool, Blair MacKenzie," he growled, his fingers tightening even more. "I ought to beat you, but then I'd have to convince you all over again that I'm not the kind of guy who'd ever strike a woman. No matter how much she deserves it."

His tone was definitely accusatory, and Blair's eyes shot golden sparks as she glared up at him. "You're the one who admitted you only want a roll in the hay with some distorted image of me you've cooked up—some sick fantasy you've derived from what was supposed to be a simple perfume ad!"

Clint wanted to shake Blair until her lovely teeth rattled. How could she not see it? Not feel it? Before he gave into his instinct, he released her and groped for a cigarette, lighting it quickly.

Blair watched his chest rise as he inhaled, remembering how wonderful the warm skin of his back had felt to her fingertips. The sensual memory returned with devastating exactness when her gaze couldn't resist following the dark whorl of chest hair to where it disappeared beneath his belt. Her fingers almost itched with the desire to explore the intriguing path.

"What are you thinking right this minute?"

His bland voice cut through her intimate reverie, and Blair jerked her eyes back up to his face. "Nothing," she lied poorly.

He drew in on the cigarette, a vaguely amused expression on his face. "Liar. We both know exactly what you were thinking. Face it, Blair—that advertising agency picked you out of thousands of other equally beautiful women because you *are* the Tigress Woman."

"So now the man's an expert on Madison Avenue," she shot back.

"I'm an expert on *you*," he corrected smoothly. "I know that despite your attempts to remain cool and collected, you're the most passionate woman I've ever held in my arms. It doesn't do any good to deny it, Blair, because your body gives you away whenever it flames for me. I know you're feeling what I am when those beautiful eyes light up like shooting stars and those luscious lips cry out against mine."

"Your ego is honestly not to be believed," she murmured, hating the way her whole being was responding to his huskily issued accusation, warming at the words in exactly the same way it never failed to respond to his touch.

"Don't fight it, Blair," he suggested, stabbing out the cigarette in a copper ashtray. "All you're doing is postponing the inevitable.... Ready to go supervise the morning runs?"

"Of course I am," she agreed waspishly, marching out the door.

Muttering a low oath, Clint followed, thinking that Blair MacKenzie redefined "stubborn." In that respect, along with her love for the horses, she was reminding him more and more of Jason Langley.

Chapter Ten

The next three days passed without any renewed seduction attempts from Clint. Not that it would honestly be seduction, Blair told herself reluctantly. She had to admit she was becoming more and more drawn to the rugged Thoroughbred trainer.

He possessed a gentleness that she was certain very few people witnessed. It was obvious in the way he treated the horses, especially Risky Pleasure. His soft words and tender touches had her wishing fleetingly that he'd behave with such warmth toward her. Then she'd have to shake herself, remembering that she'd been the one to set the rule about their relationship remaining strictly business.

They worked well together, she acknowledged. Fortunately, they shared the same ideas about training Thoroughbreds, except for the hay storage, and she'd been waiting for the right moment to bring up the subject. Things had been going so smoothly, she wasn't looking forward to rocking the boat.

Blair reminded herself of that one morning while watching the workouts. Clint was standing next to her, one booted foot on the bottom rail of the fence surrounding the oval track. Although the morning air was brisk and cool, Blair could feel the warmth radiating from his body.

"Oh, I meant to tell you something," he said offhandedly as Matador came charging past.

"What?" she murmured, her gaze shifting down to the stopwatch she held in her hand. Blair didn't think she could ever tire of watching the glorious Thoroughbreds run.

"I'm building a single-level hay shed between the training barns."

Her eyes widened as she turned to look up at him. "Really? What made you change your mind?"

"Nothing. I always felt the same way you did," he admitted a bit sheepishly. "It was Jason who refused to consider it. He wasn't usually against new ideas, but every once in a while he'd dig his heels in, and it would take a stick of dynamite to get him to budge."

She studied Clint appraisingly, believing his statement about her grandfather. "Why didn't you tell me that when I first brought it up?"

He grinned, reaching out to tug on her thick braid. "I didn't want you to get the idea I'd let a woman walk all over me."

"Well, I certainly never thought that. You gave me some rough moments, Clint Hollister. I didn't think we'd ever be able to work together."

"Neither did I. But it looks as if we were both wrong, doesn't it? I think we make a pretty good team, Blair."

His deep voice caressed her name, and she knew her eyes were giving her away as they locked with his. "Me, too," she said softly.

"Blair..." Clint hesitated, trying to choose his words carefully. He didn't want her to run off, but he was also going crazy from wanting her. He'd thought that if he kept things casual, Blair would eventually give in to the shared desire that continued to spark between them at odd, unexpected moments. Marni had been spending almost all her time at Matt's; she'd breeze in occasionally to pick up a new change of clothes. That left the two of them alone in the house, their bedrooms just a few feet apart.

He'd been waiting for her to come to him, but so far, Blair MacKenzie was demonstrating a streak of Langley determination that made him want to wring her lissome neck.

Blair found herself trapped in a gleaming silver lair and wondered how long she could continue to fight her rebellious body. In fact, she considered with brutal self-honesty, if it were only her body that mattered, she might give in to the pleasure she knew could be found in Clint's arms. But something was happening to her heart, and that was an entirely different story.

She couldn't risk a brief, passionate affair, knowing that she'd feel miserable when it came to an end. And how could she continue to work with him then, if he shared his bed with some other warm and willing woman? The answer was that she couldn't. And since she needed his Thoroughbred expertise every bit as much as she needed him as a lover, she'd have to resist temptation.

She was trying to find the words to explain this when Matador's high whinny made her jerk her eyes back to the track. The gelding had taken off at a full gallop, as if the devil himself were after him, and Blair gasped as she saw the young girl, Annie, hanging on for her life.

"Clint!" Blair grasped his arm. "He's not slowing down at the fence!"

Matador suddenly swerved, throwing the rider against the rail. She fell to the ground, and Blair and Clint held their collective breaths, praying the wild eyed Thoroughbred wouldn't crush her.

"I'll get him," Jerry cried out suddenly, jumping onto a training horse and taking off after Matador.

"Jerry can handle Matador," Clint assured Blair as they ran toward the fallen rider. "He used to groom him. Right now Annie needs our attention."

The young girl was sitting up, holding her arm gingerly. Her face was abnormally pale, and her eyes were wide dark circles.

"I'm sorry, Ms. MacKenzie, Clint," she said immediately. "But he didn't give me any warning. One minute we were going along fine, then he took off as if he'd been stung by a hornet, or something."

"Don't worry about that," Blair said, her words seconded by Clint. "How are you?"

"I think I broke my arm," Annie said, flinching as Clint's strong fingers circled the bone.

"I think you did," he agreed. "Can you walk to the garage? We'll take you to the hospital and get your arm set."

"I can walk, but what about Matador?"

Clint's gaze cut to the far end of the track. "Jerry's got him," he assured her. "Everything's fine."

Annie's dark brown eyes suddenly filled with tears. "Not everything," she wailed. "Now I won't be able to ride Risky Pleasure against Cimarron!"

Blair shot Clint a challenging look. "Does everyone around this place know about your crazy idea?"

He shrugged. "I suppose it's been discussed."

"And I suppose they're all behind you one hundred percent," she replied archly. Glancing down into Annie's face, Blair sighed. "Stupid question. Forget I even bothered to ask."

"She's a wonderful horse, Ms. MacKenzie," Annie said fervently, momentarily seeming to forget her pain in her enthusiasm. "I know she can win." Her young face fell. "Even if I won't be riding her."

Blair knew when she was licked. "The name is Blair," she said absently. "And I've already promised Clint that I'd consider the idea.... Now, let's get you to the car."

"You won't be sorry," Annie insisted as Clint and Blair supported her on the way to the house. "She'll win. Really she will."

"That seems to be the concensus of opinion," Blair muttered, steadfastly ignoring the knowing glint in Clint's gray eyes.

CLINT AND BLAIR were directed to the waiting room by an officious admitting nurse who assured them that Annie's fracture was a simple one. Unable to sit still, Blair paced the floor, feeling inexplicably guilty.

"You didn't throw her into that fence, you know," Clint said suddenly, observing Blair's stricken expression.

She stopped in her tracks, eyeing him appraisingly across the intervening space. "How did you know what I was thinking?"

"I'm beginning to understand you."

"Oh, are you?"

He appeared unperturbed by her challenging tone. "I know that you're pacing a path in that tile trying to figure out what you could have done to prevent Annie's accident."

"Is that what you think it was? Another *accident*?"

"I don't know," he admitted. "I only know you don't have any reason to feel guilty."

Blair sank into a chair, her fingers rubbing circles on her throbbing temples. "I always thought I was so independent," she said softly. "I've spent the last eleven years with advertising people, makeup people, photographers and

wardrobe personnel. Whenever I go out on a job, I'm sur-
rounded by individuals whose job is to make me look as
glamorous as possible.''

He took the chair beside her, putting his arm around her
slumped shoulders. ''And although they always seemed to
be working for you, you're beginning to think perhaps it
was the other way around and that you were nothing but
a pretty set decoration for them.''

''Damn it, Clint, it's very disconcerting when you read
my mind,'' she complained. ''I'm supposed to be running
Clearwater Hills Farm, but suddenly I'm wondering if I
can do it.''

''That's what they want you to be thinking,'' he returned grittily.

She closed her eyes momentarily, gathering strength to
continue the conversation. When she opened them, she
was shaken by the concern she was viewing in his dark gray
eyes.

''You really don't think Matador's spooking like that
was an accident, do you?''

''Do you?'' he countered.

When Blair answered, she was trying to convince herself as well as Clint. ''It's not impossible. I saw him race
at Aqueduct and he practically bit the man's arm off at the
starting gate. Let's face it, the horse doesn't exactly have
the personality of Irish Rover.''

''He doesn't like anyone to hold his head,'' Clint explained. ''Once we refused to allow any help in the starting gate, we didn't have any more trouble with him.
Besides, Annie's been riding him every morning for a year.
He's never given her any problem.''

''Oh.'' She fell silent for a moment. ''Do you think it
might have been a hornet? Or a wasp?''

''Not in that early morning air. It was too cold.''

"Oh." Her flat tone echoed the depression she saw in his eyes. Before she could ask what he suggested they do next, Jerry appeared in the doorway.

"Is she all right?" His freckled young face was a mask of concern.

"She's going to be fine," Clint assured him.

Jerry looked unrelieved. "I should have done something. If only I had been riding Matador..."

"The two of you are really something," Clint said in disgust. "Will you both get it through your heads that you're not to blame?"

Blair turned her guilty gaze out the window, and Jerry appeared suitably chastised.

"The doctor should be finishing up," Clint told him. "Why don't you go retrieve Annie and we'll get out of here."

The young man's eyes lit up as he left the waiting room.

"It appears we have a case of young love on our hands," Blair murmured, a soft smile transforming the hard line of her lips.

"It used to be a problem when Annie worked for Matt," Clint allowed. "Jerry was over there as much as he was at our place."

"Annie used to work for Matt?"

"She exercised Northern Dancer."

"Oh."

"Yeah...Anyway, when Matt had to lay her off, Jerry convinced me she'd be an asset to have at Clearwater Hills Farm."

"You must agree, if you promised her the chance to ride Risky Pleasure against Cimarron."

"She's raced some at Santa Anita and Del Mar, so she's not without experience. Add to that fact that Risky Pleasure responds better to Annie than to any rider she's had, and I'd say going with Annie instead of a more established pro isn't such a bad idea."

"It's unorthodox."

Clint grinned. "So is the entire idea."

"You've got a point," Blair agreed with an answering smile.

At that moment Annie appeared, her forearm encased in a white plaster cast. Jerry hovered protectively beside her.

"I suppose you'll be sending me home," Annie said.

"Of course not," Blair assured her. "Clearwater Hills Farm needs you. We wouldn't let you go just because of a little thing like a broken arm."

"I can't ride," Annie pointed out.

Blair put her arm around the girl's thin shoulders. "Don't worry about that. You'll be back on the track before we know it. In the meantime, there are absolutely scads and scads of things for you to do, aren't there, Clint?"

"Scads," he repeated blankly, having no idea what Blair had in mind.

"See?" Blair's smile could have lit up San Diego County. "How about a soda before we go back to the farm?" she suggested cheerily. "I have a sudden urge for a double malted."

"THAT WAS NICE OF YOU," Clint said that evening as they sat watching television in the den, neither paying a great deal of attention to the movie.

"Nice?" she repeated.

"Keeping Annie on. You know as well as I do she's useless right now."

"That's not true at all," Blair countered. "She happens to be a whiz at figures. I've got her helping me with the books."

"You didn't know that when you assured her we had scads and scads of things for her to do." His tone was laced with affection, his smile warm.

Blair arched a challenging dark brow. "I suppose you would have sent her home?"

His grin reached his eyes, turning them to a lustrous pewter. "No. I would have lied. Just the way you did."

Blair returned his smile. "I knew it," she murmured, focusing her attention on the television screen again. She'd seen *Chinatown* so many times she could probably recite all the actors' lines verbatim, she considered, entranced as always by Jack Nicholson's performance. Then a faint idea began to flicker on the edges of her mind.

"Clint?"

"Yeah?" he asked absently.

"Have any of the farms around here sold in the last few months?"

"A few. It's getting harder and harder to make a profit these days."

"That's true," she said, remembering what Matt had told her about his economic woes. "Did they all sell to the same person?"

"I don't think so." Clint turned toward her, eyeing her interestedly. "Why?"

"I don't know," she replied cautiously, aware that she'd hate it if he laughed at her. "Perhaps it's just this movie, with Jack Nicholson tracking down all the bad guys who are buying up Los Angeles, but it suddenly occurred to me that perhaps that's what's going on here."

"Jason was approached last month, but he turned the offer down," Clint said, the wheels beginning to spin in his head. *Blackwood. It had to be.* "Want to go into town tomorrow morning?" he asked suddenly.

"Let me guess—we're visiting the county recorder's office."

He grinned. "It's amazing that you can have so many brains in that gorgeous head."

"I think I'll take that as a compliment, as backhanded as it was." Blair pointed the remote control at the television, darkening the screen. "I don't know about you, but I'm exhausted. I'm going to bed."

"Want some company?" he asked, his eyes gleaming.

Blair shook her head. "Just when I was starting to think you might be one of the good guys."

He rose from the couch, cupping her chin in his fingers as he held her smiling gaze to his. "I am," he assured her in a deep, husky voice. "Why don't you quit playing hard to get, sweetheart, and I'll show you exactly how good I can be."

Her soft smile didn't waver. "You're incorrigible."

His thumb lightly stroked her throat, causing her pulse to leap beneath his touch. "Would you have it any other way? I'd hate to think I was boring you, Blair...after all those high-powered New York men you're used to."

Blair had never known a man who could compare with Clint Hollister for raw power, but she saw no reason to let him in on that little secret.

"The one thing you never do, Clint," she professed, laughing lightly, "is bore me." She reached up and patted his cheek. "Good night."

"Aren't you going to kiss me good night?" he asked, touching her hair.

"I don't know if that's such a good idea."

"I'm only asking for a kiss, Blair, not a lifetime commitment."

Their eyes met—hers darkly gold, his brightly silvered—in a jeweled moment that was like nothing Blair had ever experienced. Her pupils widened, obscuring the brilliant irises, as she watched Clint's head come slowly, inexorably nearer.

His lips were warm, so marvelously, wonderfully warm; his touch was gentle, without being at all hesitant. Clint Hollister was kissing her as if it was his perfect right, and as Blair's arms reached up to encircle his neck, she could not think of one logical reason why she shouldn't be doing this.

"Blair."

Her name was a sultry summer breeze against her lips, and she closed her eyes, concentrating on the sensation of pleasure that radiated outward from his touch. She had no idea how long the kiss lasted, she was floating happily on gentle tides of desire, succumbing to the sweetness of his lips. Finally, after what could have been a few moments, an hour or an eternity, they came up for air, each appearing abnormally shaken.

"Wow," he murmured, reaching out to trace her full upper lip.

"Wow," she agreed softly, trembling under his touch.

"I think we're playing with fire, Ms. MacKenzie," he stated soberly, realizing that, as much as he'd been hungering for Blair's luscious body, something else was happening. He wasn't sure he cared for it, but like everything else these days, it appeared to be out of his control.

Her confused gaze mirrored his own troubled thoughts. "I think so, too, Mr. Hollister." It was a whisper, but Clint had no trouble hearing it in the stillness of the room.

"So what do you suggest we do?"

It took every bit of willpower Blair possessed to resist the dark hunger in his eyes. "I suggest we both get a good night's sleep. Things always appear clearer in the morning.''

"Are you saying I won't still want you in the morning?" His tone was incredulous.

Blair shook her head, and Clint had the feeling that her crooked smile was directed inward. "No, I'm saying that in the morning perhaps we'll both have enough sense not to do anything about it." She rose up on her toes, pressing a quick, hard kiss against his lips. "Good night, Clint," she murmured and left the room before she could change her mind.

Clint watched her go. Then, heaving a resigned sigh, he went to his own room, where he tossed and turned the rest of the night as he thought about Blair MacKenzie sleeping just down the hall.

BLAIR AND CLINT were given little time to ponder their changing relationship. They spent the next day in the basement of the county recorder's office, pouring over stacks of dusty files.

"I found another one." Blair's tone was flat, instead of exultant, as it had been at the beginning of the search through the numerous pages of real estate transactions.

"Recognize the name?"

She shook her head. "No. It's a different company from the others. Guardian Development Corporation. Does that ring any bells?"

"Not a one," he admitted. "So far we've come up with seven separate sales to seven different developers, all in the same general location. Damn, I was hoping we'd find the answer in here."

Blair wiped a dark smudge on her yellow linen dress. "All we're finding is dust. This last book even had a page missing," she complained. "Whatever happened to the computer age?"

"The clerk said they were a little behind," he reminded her, taking down another leather-bound volume. "We should actually be grateful. It might be cleaner, but can you imagine looking at this many listings on microfiche? You'd have one helluva headache before you'd gotten through the first six months."

"Speaking of that..." Blair said wearily, propping her elbows on the table as she rubbed her temples with her thumbs. "All this has happened so suddenly," she complained. "Just a few weeks ago I was sitting at my kitchen table in Manhattan with my accountant, trying to come up with the money to buy a small farm somewhere and a couple of yearlings at this year's sales. Now..." Her voice drifted off.

"Accountant," he said thoughtfully. "Let me see your list."

She handed over the piece of paper on which she written the names of the development companies in a smooth, slanting hand.

"I think we've just found a loose thread," he said, a tremor of excitement in his voice.

"What is it?"

His index finger moved down the sheet of paper, stopping in the middle of the list. "This one."

"Hanson Properties?"

"That's it."

"That's what?"

"You've been sorting through Jason's books. What's his accountant's name?"

Blair's smooth forehead wrinkled in thought. "Brian Hanson."

"Bingo!" he exclaimed with the enthusiasm one might give the winner of the sixty-four-thousand-dollar question.

Blair shook her head. "Clint, Hanson is not an uncommon name. I'll bet we could find a dozen of them in the phone book."

"I've got a better idea. We'll check the incorporation records to see who the officers of Hanson Properties are. If one of them is Brian Hanson, then at least we'll know we're on the right track."

"And if it isn't?" Blair was suddenly very tired, discouraged and hungry. At that moment the task looked about as easy as locating the proverbial needle in a haystack.

"Then it's back to the drawing board. Got any better ideas?"

She sighed. "No, not a one."

An hour later, Blair found the answer. "Well, there goes that idea," she muttered.

"Dead end?" Clint looked up from his own stack of record books.

"The Hanson of Hanson Properties isn't Brian at all," she said on an exasperated sigh. "It's Robin."

Before Clint could answer, the door to the records room opened, and an officious-looking woman filled the space. When they'd arrived hours earlier, Blair had secretly imagined the records clerk as one of those dragons in the video games, faithfully guarding the treasures of the realm. The woman had not been extremely helpful, but neither had she been impervious to Clint Hollister's personality. He'd obviously found the magic word that charmed this particular female dragon into submission, and she'd ultimately opened her precious records to them.

"I'm sorry, but you'll have to leave," she said. "We close at five o'clock."

"It can't be that late," Clint protested.

Blair could believe it. Hobgoblins of hunger had been trying to make themselves heard in her stomach for the past hour.

"I'm sorry, but it is," the woman replied. "Our clocks are very accurate; we always open at nine o'clock and close at five. On the dot."

Clint groaned. "We'll have to come back tomorrow."

Blair nodded, trying to look enthusiastic. She failed. As they walked out of the dark basement room into the bright afternoon sunshine, the thudding of her headache only increased.

"You must be starving," he said on a note of apology while he opened the car door for her. "We'll stop for something on the way home."

She nodded, still receiving a thrill whenever she thought of the farm as home.

Fifteen minutes later, although Blair realized Clint had chosen the restaurant with care, she was too tired to be aware of what she was eating. Seeming to sense her mood, he didn't try to keep a conversation going, and for that she was grateful.

Afterward, back in his car, she leaned her head against the seat and closed her eyes in exhaustion. It seemed to Blair that only a moment had passed before she felt a light, feathery touch on her cheek.

"Hey, Sleeping Beauty, it's time to wake up. Your prince has just brought you back to the castle."

Blair opened her eyes slowly and saw Clint's head incredibly close to hers.

"Want me to carry you into bed?" he asked huskily.

She was sleepy, not crazy. "No, thank you. I can manage."

He smiled. "Coward."

"You'd only be disappointed anyway," she whispered shakily. "I'm too exhausted to be much of a Tigress Woman tonight."

"Don't worry about it. Tonight you remind me of a warm, cuddly tabby cat." He ran his hand down her back. "Purr for me, pretty tabby."

"Clint, please," she murmured, her tone one of both demurral and request. She wondered when she'd become such a vacillating individual. *Kiss me, don't kiss me. Touch me, keep away. Come here, go.* She'd been giving Clint an extraordinary series of contradictory messages, and she wouldn't have blamed him if he packed up and walked out on the crazy lady who seemed incapable of making up her own mind about anything.

Clint heard the confusion in her voice and forced himself to remember that Blair needed him for far more right now than a night of lovemaking. While it would take only a few more kisses, a touch here…and there…and yes, there as well, he mused, his eyes drifting over her slender body, tomorrow morning she'd wake up and regret her momentary weakness. He'd have to bide his time until she was ready to come to him willingly, until she was as desperate for him as he was for her.

"Come on, sweetheart," he said, releasing her suddenly. "We've got an early morning tomorrow." He opened his door, climbed out of the bucket seat, then helped her out from the car, his arm around her waist to steady her as they entered the house.

"I'm going to go check on things," he said. "Why don't you go to bed?"

"This early?"

His gray eyes swept over her appraisingly. "You look beat," he observed, noting the shadows under her eyes.

"You wouldn't want to disappoint everyone at Matt's party tomorrow night, would you?"

The party. It had completely slipped her mind. "I suppose we have to go," she said without a great deal of enthusiasm.

"I think we'd better. You know as well as I do that everyone will be expecting the Tigress Woman to show up," he pointed out accurately.

"I'm getting really tired of her," Blair said.

Clint's gaze was inordinately fond. "You know," he murmured, "I'm beginning to believe you about that."

"I'm glad." Her wide amber eyes held an infinite number of messages, each more enticing than the last. Clint had to shove his hands into his pockets to keep from touching her.

"I'll see you in the morning," he said gruffly, turning away from temptation. "Johnny Doyle's going to be taking Annie's place until she's able to ride again. I want to give him some instructions on how to ride Matador."

"Morning," she agreed softly, watching him leave.

As tired as she was, Blair found sleep an impossibility and decided instead to catch up on the local news. The papers had been stacking up all week, and after first allowing herself the luxury of enjoying seven straight days of comic strips, she began reading the remainder of the news.

Although not a fan of society-page gossip, Blair had spent too many years modeling not to have her eye caught by a photograph of women in expensive evening gowns, hosting a fund-raising ball for this year's "in" disease. Not knowing anyone in San Diego, she skimmed the caption, paying scant attention to the names. Then she went back to one name, captured by its familiarity. Holding her breath, she quickly scanned the accompanying article.

Blair then ran out to Johnny Doyle's room in search of Clint, only to discover he'd already left. Muttering a soft oath, she returned to the house, but it was deserted. After a cursory check in training barn B, she finally located Clint in the smaller of the two training barns, currying Risky Pleasure.

"I've been looking all over for you," she panted.

He dropped the currycomb, staring at her as he took in her flushed face and very wide, amber eyes. He had her in his arms in seconds, his worried gaze roving her face.

"What's wrong? Are you all right?"

Her frantic search had left her breathless, and Clint was forced to wait until she could talk. "Look!" She shoved the newspaper page into his hands.

His gray eyes scanned the print in a cursory glance. "Dear Abby? You look as if you've just gone ten rounds with Joe Frazier, and all because you want me to read an advice column?"

She shook her head. "No. Here." She poked at the page, showing him the picture.

"'Society Ball to Benefit Less Fortunate,'" he read. "So? Don't tell me we have to go. Heather used to drag me to those things, and I really hate them, Blair."

"Damn it!" she cried. "Read the names!"

He shook his head with barely concealed impatience, but Blair watched as the idea struck home. "Robin Hanson?"

"That's not all," she said proudly. "Read the second paragraph."

"'The hostesses of the successful fund-raiser were Buffy Meredith, wife of financier Kent Meredith; Joan Palmer Thompson, wife of newly elected city councilman Steve Thompson; Robin Hanson, wife of Brian Hanson...' Brian Hanson," Clint repeated. "Damn. I should have remembered her name! Congratulations, sweetheart, you may have just found the key!''

The paper fell to the floor, and Blair found herself lifted off her feet as Clint swung her around, giving her a deep, congratulatory kiss. Blair's mouth fused to his willingly, hungrily; the entire world centered on his marvelous lips. As he lowered her slowly back to the floor, the giddy mood suddenly changed, his kiss growing more demanding even while it gave more heated pleasure.

Through the fog clouding her mind, Blair could focus only on this glorious kiss that swept the world away from under her feet and left her floating on a cloud of sheer desire. It went on and on, and even when she found herself unable to breathe, Blair hoped it would continue endlessly. Finally, Clint dragged his mouth away, pressing it into her dark chestnut hair as he held her head against his shoulder.

''Blair,'' he murmured, his breath a warm, welcome breeze.

''What?'' she responded dazedly, her eyes still closed to the dizzy, dancing way his kiss had made her feel.

His palm stroked the back of her head. ''Nothing. Just Blair.''

''Oh.'' She looped her arms about his waist, looking up at him, her tawny eyes gleaming with unsatiated desire. ''What do we do now?''

He grinned suggestively. ''About what?''

''About Robin Hanson,'' she reminded him firmly. ''That *is* why I came out here, remember?''

''Robin Hanson,'' he agreed without a great deal of enthusiasm. ''Let's wait until tomorrow night and play the thing by ear.''

''Tomorrow night?''

"Brian Hanson is also Matt's accountant," Clint told her. "They're bound to be at the party."

"I'm going to go crazy until then," she complained.

His hands tightened about her waist. "I've got a few suggestions on how to while away those hours," he said in a deep, husky voice.

Blair fought against her own desire. "I thought we'd agreed to keep this strictly business."

"We did. But I'd better warn you, cold showers are beginning to lose their effectiveness." His eyes darkened. "I want you, Blair."

"Do you always get everything you want?" she asked quietly.

His answer was succinct. "Yes."

She turned away, rubbing her temples with her fingers. "You make it sound so simple, but it isn't."

As Clint observed her standing with her head bent, he had to restrain himself from taking her into his arms again. Where she belonged.

Of course Blair was confused, he admitted reluctantly to himself. She'd come to the farm with no intention of inheriting anything. Then, just when she thought she was taking over a thriving business, she'd been flung headfirst into turmoil. Perhaps he should wait until all this was settled, and she could come to him without anything standing in their way. But God, how he wanted her!

He bent to pick up the currycomb. "I'd better get back to work."

"It's late," she reminded him needlessly.

He shrugged. "I've fallen behind by spending all day at the courthouse."

He began working with Risky Pleasure.

"Jerry could do that," she pointed out softly.

"I'd prefer to do it myself."

Blair stifled a sigh at his suddenly withdrawn attitude. "Fine. I'll see you in the morning, then."

He merely grunted a reply. The filly neighed her objection as Clint stopped to watch Blair leave. Muttering a low curse, he finished the currying with a few careless strokes. Then he left the barn and sat down on a bale of hay to smoke a cigarette and watch the deep indigo clouds play tag across the black velvet sky.

Chapter Eleven

To add to Blair's distress, Marni returned to the house the next morning, declaring her decision to move in with Matt.

"Are you sure this is what you want do do?" Blair asked as she sat down on the end of Marni's bed. Her friend was throwing things haphazardly into suitcases.

"I've never been so certain of anything in my life."

"But it's only been a week."

"That's about five days longer than I needed," Marni stated blithely. "Here." She held out her jewelry box. "You may as well keep this stuff. I can't see myself wearing rhinestones to muck out a stall, can you?"

"You actually do that, too?"

"Of course. I've discovered that I'm quite handy to have around, despite what my mother always told me."

Blair knew that Marni's mother had been partially responsible for her lack of self-esteem. According to Marni, the woman's pet phrase had always been, "I don't approve of a thing the girl does, but she *is* pretty." Marni had taken that thoughtless comment, wrapped it about her, absorbed it, and in the end, had finally come to believe that her beauty was her only value.

Blair had always known differently, but apparently it had taken Matt Bradshaw to make Marni believe otherwise. For that, Blair was glad, yet she still felt that events were happening too soon.

"I don't think you should rush into anything," she cautioned again, watching Marni pack a vast array of designer dresses, several of which she had designed herself. While Marni steadfastly insisted that she didn't have a domestic bone in her body, she did possess a unique sense of style and a flair for knowing instinctively what was flattering to her. Every so often she professed a desire to design a line of her own, but a new assignment or a new man made her forget the idea.

Blair's warning fell on deaf ears as Marni proceeded to change the subject. "So, what's happening with you and the hunk?"

Blair decided not to relate the latest bit of information concerning Robin Hanson. Even though Marni was a loyal enough friend, she never had been the soul of discretion.

"I'm still trying to break my contract," Blair said.

"Tough, huh?"

"Ironclad."

Marni eyed her thoughtfully. "I suppose you're still dead set against selling."

"Of course I am."

Marni nodded. "That's what I told Matt."

"You two were discussing me?"

Marni shrugged. "It wasn't anything personal, Blair. We were just talking about how hard it was to run a farm, and he asked if I thought you were really up to it." She grinned. "I told him it was always a mistake to underestimate you when you set your mind to something." She closed the suitcase. "Well, good luck...I guess I'll see you tonight."

"Tonight," Blair echoed, rising to walk Marni out to Matt's Blazer.

As Marni climbed into the driver's seat, Blair asked, "Where's Matt?"

"He had to go into the city to see about buying a stallion to replace Northern Lights," Marni said. A small frown furrowed her flawless forehead. "I hope it works out; he seemed a little edgy when he left."

"I hope *everything* works out," Blair said honestly. "For both of you."

Marni grinned. "It will," she vowed, twisting the key in the ignition. "This time I've hit the jackpot."

As Blair watched the Blazer disappear in a cloud of dust, she could only hope that this time Marni knew what she was doing.

THE MAN LAY on his back, smoking a cigarette and staring up at the ceiling. "I still don't like it," he announced.

The woman's fingers were playing in the mat of hair covering his chest. "I'm finding that a bit difficult to believe. Do you realize how many men would sell their souls to be in your position?"

He turned his head on the pillow, his eyes spearing her. "Is that what I've done?"

She laughed, sitting up in bed to light her own cigarette. "Don't go getting a conscience at this late date, darling. Besides, it's not as if you're debauching some innocent virgin. She's a grown woman. She knows what she's getting into."

He shook his head. "She thinks I love her."

Slender shoulders lifted in a careless shrug. "So? You won't have been the first man to tell a little white lie in bed."

"Or you the first woman?"

Her eyes narrowed. "What does that mean?"

He took a long drag on the cigarette, while he chose his words carefully. "Sometimes I get the feeling you're just using me—that when all this is over, you'll be on your merry way and leave me with nothing."

She arched an auburn brow. "You're calling all those millions of pretty dollars nothing?"

"Damn it, I didn't get into this for the money. I agreed to the entire deal because I love you!" he argued heatedly.

Her silvery laugh was laced with scorn. "What a selective memory you have, my sweet. What about the fact that you were on the brink of bankruptcy before we offered you a chance to bail yourself out and make a tidy profit as well?"

"You promised it'd be a piece of cake," he reminded her. "So far, it's been anything but."

"We're making progress," she assured him. "I guarantee that after tomorrow night, Clearwater Hills Farm will fall into our laps."

"And then what?" he challenged.

She looked at him curiously. "We'll all be filthy rich, of course. Just as I promised."

"And what about you and me?"

She leaned over and pressed a kiss against his firmly set mouth. "We'll continue as usual. Nothing's going to change with us."

"What about your husband? Where does he fit into this little scenario?"

"After a decent interval, I'll divorce Brian," she assured him silkily. "We don't want to rush into things; it'll look too suspicious."

The man glared up at the ceiling. "I hate this."

She plucked the cigarette from his fingers and put it out in a crystal ashtray. Her own followed. "Don't pout, darling," Robin Hanson murmured, her fingers blazing a tantalizing trail down his chest. "I can think of much better things to do than fight."

Smothering a frustrated oath, he drew her into his arms, succumbing as he always did to her expert touch.

LATER THAT EVENING Blair stood in front of her mirror, eyeing her reflection judiciously. She'd managed to cover up the purple shadows under her eyes that gave away her recent lack of sleep, but a pair of lines bracketed her lips, displaying her tension. While she was convinced that Robin Hanson somehow held the key to what was going on, she didn't have the slightest idea how she was going to go about getting the woman to admit it.

"Blair?" Clint called in to her. "Are you ready?"

"Just about," she murmured. "Come on in."

He opened the door, stopping to stare at the vision standing only a few feet away. Her hair, which she usually wore pulled back, lay loose around her shoulders in a soft, dark cloud. It was thick and wavy, gleaming in the low lamplight. She was wearing makeup, he realized, something she seldom did since her arrival. Her full lips were painted a lush red; her eyes were rimmed with slashes of dark kohl. As he approached, he inhaled the heady, evocative scent of Tigress perfume.

"Would I be hanged for a chauvinist if I admitted to a few lustful feelings right now?" he asked in a husky voice.

Holding out her arms, Blair twirled, the red chiffon swirling above her knees. The halter dress plunged to the waist in back, while the front slit allowed a tantalizing glimpse of creamy skin.

"You said they were probably expecting the Tigress Woman tonight," she reminded him. "I thought the least I could do for Matt, since Marni thinks he's the greatest thing since multi-vitamins, is oblige."

"I think I should have kept my big mouth shut," Clint muttered. "Every man in the place will be walking into walls when you show up wearing that dress."

Blair couldn't miss the irritation in his tone. She grinned. "Why, Clint Hollister, are you jealous?"

"Of course," he answered instantly. "I suppose now you're going to accuse me of being overly possessive and chauvinistic."

She shook her head. "No," she replied, thoughtfully, "I think I like it." Her brown eyes took a leisurely tour of Clint, drinking in the sight of so much man. She'd always considered him breathtakingly masculine in his working clothes, but there was something about him in evening dress that accentuated his manliness even more.

"In fact," she decided aloud, "I'm probably going to experience a little of that green-eyed monster myself. You're going to have women throwing themselves at your feet tonight, Clint Hollister."

Her softly spoken words and gleaming eyes caused his blood to surge more hotly through his veins. "I've got an idea."

Her eyes didn't move from his. "Oh?"

"Let's stay home."

Oh, how she'd like that! Blair felt her knees weaken at the look Clint was giving her. "What about Robin Hanson?"

If anyone had told Clint that he'd ever be so uninterested in Clearwater Hills Farm, he would have called that person crazy. But at this moment, he didn't give a damn about the farm, or Robin Hanson, or any of the problems he'd been having. Every nerve in his body was on red alert, wanting, needing Blair MacKenzie. Then he remembered that without the farm there'd be no reason for Blair to re-

main in California. She'd be back in New York, resuming
her jet-set existence—and out of his life.

He raked his fingers through his hair in obvious frustration. "You're right," he agreed. "Let's go before one
of us changes his mind."

The aura of sensuality that had swirled about them was
not dissipated by the crisp evening air. It took all Clint's
inner restraint not to turn the car around and forgo Matt's
party for more pleasurable pursuits. He forced his mind on
the problem at hand.

"I'll tell you what," he suggested. "When we get there,
we'll split up. You see what you can get out of Brian Hanson, and I'll tackle his wife."

"That will be quite a sacrifice," she said dryly.

He gave her a questioning look. "What's that supposed
to mean?"

"I saw the woman's picture in the paper, Clint," Blair
reminded him. "She's beautiful."

"And about as cold as a glacier."

"I'm not even going to ask how you discovered that."

"You don't have to take a woman to bed to know that
she's frigid. Or, on the flip side, to realize that some
women are much warmer than they'd like to appear." He
slanted her a knowing glance.

Blair steadfastly ignored the message in his silver gaze.
"So, what's Brian Hanson like? Is he cold, too?"

Clint considered her words carefully. "He's good-
looking enough, I suppose—in an Ivy League sort of way."

"Sounds interesting," Blair said teasingly. "Perhaps this
party won't be so dull after all."

"Don't take your job too seriously, Blair. I've always
thought Brian Hanson's charm was the kind that washed
off in the shower. Besides, I'd hate to ruin Matt's party by

having to punch out his accountant for getting too friendly with my woman."

Blair stared at him. "You can't be serious!"

"I was only speaking figuratively," Clint muttered unconvincingly, damning himself for allowing that thought to escape.

Blair looked at him for a long, silent time before turning her attention to the well of darkness outside the car window. A few minutes later they had arrived at Matt Bradshaw's farm.

As she entered Matt's house, Blair wondered if the man actually possessed so many friends, or if half of San Diego County had shown up out of simple curiosity. Before she could even make her way across the crowded living room, she had autographed seven covers of *Sports Illustrated*'s annual swimsuit issue, fielded two not-so-subtle passes, and survived the blistering glares from several women who obviously perceived Blair to be a threat.

"I'd say you're an unqualified hit," Clint murmured in her ear, grabbing two glasses of champagne from a tray held by a passing waiter.

Blair thanked him with a smile, then took a sip of the sparkling California wine. "The Tigress Woman is a hit," she corrected blandly.

"You really think of her as a separate entity, don't you?"

"Of course," Blair answered without hesitation. "You were right about one thing, Clint."

He arched an inquiring brow, inviting elaboration.

"I can't see her mucking out a stall, either," Blair admitted with a grin Clint suspected was directed at herself.

"You may have a point," he agreed, his hand cupping her elbow as they cut a swath through the throng of fashionably attired men and women. "However, I still contend that her spirit dwells inside the body of a woman who's every bit as enticing in jeans.''

Blair was saved by Matt from answering this huskily stated declaration. Their host suddenly appeared in front of her, looking exceedingly handsome in his formal evening wear.

"Blair!" he welcomed her with a warm smile. "You look absolutely ravishing tonight."

"Thank you, Matt. This is quite some party. I didn't expect to see so many people."

"You and Marni proved quite a draw," he said, confirming Blair's earlier suspicion. "Speaking of which, there's someone who's been dying to meet you." His attention slid to Clint. "You won't mind if I borrow Blair for a few minutes, will you, Clint?"

"As long as you remember to bring her back," Clint drawled with a laconic air of possessiveness that should have irritated Blair but for some strange reason didn't.

"I promise not to let Brian abscond with her," Matt told him with a laugh.

At the mention of Jason Langley's accountant, Blair and Clint exchanged a quick, meaningful glance.

"Have fun," Clint advised her. Blair nodded, allowing Matt to take her hand and lead her across the room. As they approached the waiting man, Blair's heart began to pound, and she hoped that her nervousness wouldn't give her away.

"Brian," Matt exclaimed heartily, "I'm sure you recognize Blair MacKenzie. Blair, this is Brian Hanson."

The tall, urbane man's blue eyes were bright with masculine appreciation and with something else Blair couldn't quite recognize.

"Ms. MacKenzie," he said, taking the hand Matt had just abandoned, "you've no idea what a pleasure it is to meet you in person. Jason spoke very highly of you."

"It's a pleasure to meet you, Mr. Hanson," she said, restraining herself from jerking her hand away as his thumb brushed provocatively against her palm.

"Call me Brian," he suggested. "I hope we'll become very close friends." The message in his deep voice was unmistakable.

Matt cleared his throat. "Well, I'd better go check on the ice."

Brian Hanson's eyes didn't leave Blair's face. "Why don't you do that?" he agreed. "I'd like to become better acquainted with your new neighbor."

Matt looked decidedly uneasy as he nodded, then disappeared into the crowd of party guests.

"So," Blair began casually, extracting her hand from the man's increasingly familiar touch, "you were my grandfather's accountant."

"As well as his friend," Brian replied. "I still can't believe he's gone."

Blair didn't know what to say to that, so she probed a little further. "I've been having some difficulty with the farm's books. Perhaps you can explain a few of the entries to me." She gave him a coaxing, feminine smile.

"I'd be happy to discuss his accounts with you," Brian said amiably. "During business hours. After all, this *is* a party and we should be enjoying ourselves. Would you care to dance?"

"I'm a little tired," she demurred. "Why don't we go somewhere a little quieter, and you can fill me in on high tower."

There was a moment of silence, during which Blair couldn't miss the sudden narrowing of Brian Hanson's eyes as he observed her with renewed interest.

"High tower? It doesn't ring a bell."

"My grandfather spent quite a bit of money on it over the past year."

"High tower," he repeated softly, more to himself than to her. "Sorry, I can't recall any such name." He treated her to a reassuring smile. "But that doesn't really mean anything. I never was able to keep those horses' names straight."

"High tower isn't a horse."

He arched a blond brow. "Oh? Are you certain of that?"

Blair nodded, sipping on her champagne and studying him over the rim of her glass. Brian Hanson's blue eyes suddenly held a core of ice.

"Positive," she said. "Mr. Hollister assured me that there had never been a horse by that name on the farm."

"Hollister." He spat the name out as if it had a bad aftertaste. Then he put his hand on Blair's back and began to lead her abruptly from the room toward a pair of French doors.

Decidedly uneasy about the idea of being alone on the deserted terrace with Brian Hanson, she looked around for Clint but was unable to find him in the throng of people.

"What do you know about your grandfather's trainer?" Brian asked the moment they were alone.

Blair managed a casual shrug. "I know he's the best in the business."

"Do you know the man's been in prison?"

Hanson certainly didn't pull any punches, Blair considered. "Yes. I also know he was innocent." She tried not to flinch as the accountant's fingers brushed up her arm.

"I do hope you're not getting involved with the man," he said, his voice holding a definite warning. "Clint Hollister is nothing but bad news. In fact, I wouldn't be at all surprised if he had something to do with Jason Langley's death."

"If you truly believe that," she challenged softly, "why didn't you go to the authorities?"

"With Jason's history of heart trouble, it would be impossible to prove."

"Then why—"

"Jason Langley wanted to sell Clearwater Hills Farm, but Hollister fought the sale tooth and nail. He didn't want to end up out on the street."

Blair took a calming sip of champagne. "He'd hardly end up out on the street," she murmured. "I know of a number of farms that would jump at the chance to hire him."

"As a trainer," Brian agreed. "But he was far more than that to Jason. He'd infiltrated himself into the man's confidence. In fact, for the past year he had carte blanche as to the running of the place. Jason was too ill to watch over things as he should have, which gave Hollister the chance to take control. He wouldn't have been able to grasp such power anywhere else, and he knew it."

"If my grandfather wanted to sell the farm," Blair argued, "why did he leave it to me?"

"That was an old will," Brian explained. "Jason was still planning to leave everything to you. And with the profit he would have made from the sale, you would have ended up an extremely wealthy woman."

Blair ran a crimson-tinted fingernail around the rim of her glass. "My grandfather really wanted to sell the farm?"

Hanson nodded. "He did. As a matter of fact, he had an appointment with a group of prospective buyers the afternoon of his death. Unfortunately, he didn't survive to make that meeting."

His eyes glittered in the reflected glow of the landscape lights. "Now do you see why I have my own suspicions concerning Clint Hollister?"

Blair managed a slight nod, reminding herself that nothing would be accomplished by telling this man she knew he was lying. Clint might drive her up a wall sometimes; he might have a proprietary attitude toward Clearwater Hills Farm, and he admitted that he and Jason had fought continuously over management policies. But just as she'd known he had not killed his wife, she knew with an ironclad certainty that he had had nothing to do with her grandfather's death.

"I think I need another drink," she murmured, wanting to escape the steely-eyed gaze of the man beside her.

"I'll get it for you," Brian suggested immediately, reaching for her empty glass.

Blair shook her head and gave him a crooked smile. "Thank you anyway, Mr. Hanson, but I'd like a couple of minutes alone to freshen up." She attempted a more convincing smile. "The problem with being the Tigress Woman is that everyone expects perfection."

His eyes warmed as they took a slow tour of her body. "I'd say you're managing to come very close to that ideal right now, Ms. MacKenzie," he murmured.

She forced a light, musical laugh. "Thank you, Mr. Hanson. You're very good for a woman's ego. What a shame you're married."

"Who said I'm married?" he countered.

"I saw your wife's picture in the society pages. She's a very lovely woman."

"She is," he agreed blithely. Blair had to fight from cringing as his hand once again trailed up her arm. "And we have a very good marriage. We understand each other."

His tone was unmistakable, and Blair backed away. "How nice for you both," she said, feigning ignorance of the sensual invitation in his deep voice. "Well, I've enjoyed our little chat. I suppose I'll see you later."

He nodded. "You can count on it, Ms. MacKenzie."

As she wove her way back through the crowd, Blair scanned the room for Clint. Where was he? She couldn't wait to tell him about Brian Hanson's accusations. She finally spotted him in a far corner of the room, talking with a tall, willowy redhead she recognized immediately as Robin Hanson.

Clint's silver head was inclined toward the woman, whose hands were fluttering like graceful birds as she spoke. When she laughed and placed one of those hands on his arm, Blair was stunned by the jolt of jealousy that forked through her. She was considering going over there and establishing her territorial rights when a tuxedo-clad roadblock suddenly popped up in front of her.

"Ms. MacKenzie, may I have a word with you?"

While Blair had not taken to Ramsey Blackwood from the start, knowing what he'd done to Clint certainly didn't help establish the man into her good graces.

"I'm sorry," she said, "but I promised Mr. Hollister this next dance."

Ramsey's eyes followed hers. "Your partner seems otherwise occupied," he observed blandly. "I'm sure he won't miss you."

That was what Blair was afraid of. "Can't it wait?"

"No, it can't," he said firmly.

She stifled a sigh, but followed the lawyer into Matt's deserted den. "What is it, Mr. Blackwood?" she inquired, not bothering to restrain her irritation.

He took the chair behind the wide oak desk, braced his elbows on the arms of the chair and observed her over linked fingers as he swiveled back and forth. His expression was sympathetic.

"Your grandfather and I were close friends," he began. "Therefore I feel a fatherly responsibility toward you."

She sat down opposite him, crossing her legs with a graceful, fluid gesture. The look in Ramsey Blackwood's eyes as they locked onto the fleeting flash of thigh was far from paternal.

"Now you're going to warn me against getting involved with Clint Hollister," Blair guessed.

"He's already proved fatal for one woman," Ramsey grated out with ill-concealed bitterness. "I'd hate to see you suffer the same fate."

Blair leaned forward in order to stress her point. "I'm honestly sorry about your daughter," she said. "But Clint didn't kill her."

"If you mean he didn't wield the knife, you're probably correct," Ramsey allowed. "But he drove Heather to it with his obsession about Clearwater Hills Farm. *And* that damnable horse."

"Risky Pleasure," Blair murmured.

"That's the one. He'd do anything to keep from giving up that filly, Ms. MacKenzie. Just as he'd do anything to keep from leaving Clearwater Hills Farm."

Aware of the acrimony between the two men, Blair considered the source, discounting Ramsey's harsh accusation. She was, however, curious about one thing.

"Mr. Blackwood, do you know anything about something called high tower?"

For a moment there was a flicker in the depths of his eyes, but Ramsey's expression remained inscrutably bland. "Not a thing. Why?"

"It doesn't matter," she said, instinctively understanding that for some reason Ramsey Blackwood was prepared to lie. "May I ask you one more question?"

"Of course."

"Did my grandfather intend to sell Clearwater Hills Farm?"

"That was the plan. Unfortunately, he suffered that fatal heart attack before he could finalize the deal." Ramsey's gaze narrowed. "Are you considering selling, Ms. MacKenzie?"

Blair rose. "Not at all, Mr. Blackwood," she stated firmly. "I'm here to stay." Her back was straight as she made her way to the closed door.

"Ms. MacKenzie?" Ramsey called after her.

She eyed him over her shoulder. "Yes?"

"Watch your step very carefully. Despite his charms, Clint Hollister can be a very formidable enemy."

"I wasn't aware we were enemies."

"You have something the man wants," Blackwood pointed out smoothly. "Something he's always wanted. I'd say that puts you in a decidedly perilous position.... I want you to know that you can always count on me if you need help."

"I'll keep that in mind," Blair murmured, wanting nothing more than to escape this party and go home before she had to listen to one more accusation concerning Clint.

Chapter Twelve

Blair's search for Clint was interrupted briefly by a scene she inadvertently came across as she passed one of the bedrooms. Robin Hanson and Matt were engaged in a casual conversation, although Blair wondered what they could possibly be discussing that demanded privacy. But lingering exacerbation created by her earlier confrontations kept her from dwelling on the matter.

"There you are," Clint said as she reentered the living room. "I've been looking all over for you."

"I've been looking for you, too."

"Well, you've found me," he said with a smile.

"Let's get out of here," Blair suggested suddenly.

Clint's smile faded. "Sure," he agreed, eyeing her curiously. "I'd have thought this party would be right up your alley."

Blair stopped, her eyes flashing as she looked up at him. "Don't tell me we're back to my so-called jet-set existence."

It was impossible to miss the pain in her eyes, yet Clint had the vague impression that his words were not the cause. No, something else had her inordinately disturbed, he decided, and she was simply taking out her unhappiness on him.

"Not at all," he said amiably. "I just thought every woman liked the opportunity to get dressed up and dazzle us poor, unsuspecting males."

"Well, you thought wrong," she snapped, marching toward the front door.

Stifling a weary sigh, Clint followed. Blair remained silent during the short drive back to the farm, and Clint resolved not to pressure her. He was, however, uneasy about what Ramsey Blackwood might have told her to make her that miserable. He hadn't missed seeing the two of them disappear into the den, and he had forced himself to take a long walk out to Matt's barns in order to avoid confronting her directly about her conversation with his former father-in-law.

The phone was ringing as they entered the house. "Hello," Blair snapped into the mouthpiece.

"Blair?" Marni's voice held curiosity and concern. "Is everything all right? You left before we had a chance to talk."

"Everything's fine," she lied. "I just got a blinding headache and Clint agreed to take me home."

"Oh...Well, I hope you feel better soon."

"I'm sure I will."

"You're still not upset about my moving in with Matt, are you?"

"Not at all. It's your life. I hope everything works out this time."

"It will," Marni professed fervently. "He says he loves me, Blair."

Blair sought an excuse to end the conversation. "Look, honey, my head is honestly killing me. Why don't we get together for lunch tomorrow?"

"That'll be fun," Marni said. "Let's go into San Diego and visit Old Town. I'd love an opportunity to do something touristy. Go to bed, now, and I'll see you tomorrow.''

"Tomorrow." Blair hung up, staring for a long, silent moment at the telephone.

"Want to talk about it?" Clint asked.

She turned around, unnerved by both the gentle concern she heard in his voice and the slight hesitation that made him appear uncharacteristically vulnerable.

"Not really."

"Want a couple of aspirins?"

"No, thanks."

"I thought you had a headache."

"I just wanted to get out of there, okay?" she retorted.

He held up his hands. "Sure."

Blair settled down into a chair and picked up a novel she'd left on the table, pretending to immerse herself in the story. Following her lead, Clint took a chair across the room, waiting for Blair to give some clue as to what had gone wrong.

When she sighed for the third time, Clint looked up from the racing magazine he'd been pretending to read. "Problem?"

"The house just seems empty without Marni."

"She's probably been here only two hours since she arrived," he pointed out.

"I know. It's just that..."

"Jealous?" he asked casually, putting the magazine down on a table beside the chair and lighting a cigarette.

"Jealous? Why on earth would I be jealous of my best friend?"

He shrugged. "I don't know, but isn't love the ultimate female fantasy?" Blair thought she saw something flicker for a moment in his eyes, but then it was gone before she could decipher its meaning.

"Not mine."

"Ah, yes," he said, drawing on the cigarette thoughtfully, "you're one of those women who never managed to exchange your adolescent love of horses for that of a man."

"What a ridiculous thing to say," she snapped. "Although it's about as sexist a statement as I'd expect you to come up with. Using that line of reasoning, you're so in love with Risky Pleasure you wouldn't fall in love with the perfect woman if she fell stark naked into your lap."

Clint was silent as he considered that prospect. "It's an intriguing scenario," he murmured, his gray gaze moving with agonizing slowness over her taut body. "Had you been considering throwing yourself into my lap, Blair?"

"I was speaking hypothetically," she said icily, refusing to let him see how the desire gleaming in his beautiful eyes was threatening to melt her bones.

He rose wearily, grinding out the cigarette. "Of course you were," he agreed flatly. "Doing that would take more guts than you'd ever have."

He marched from the room, leaving her to stare after him. The ashtray hit the door frame after his head had already cleared the space, sending ashes scattering down onto the Mexican tile flooring.

Blair paced the room furiously, her arms wrapped around herself as if to hold in her temper. She was feeling about as explosive as Vesuvius right now, and if Clint Hollister dared to show himself again, she'd certainly tell him a thing or two. She muttered every curse word she could think of under her breath, receiving a glimmer of satisfaction as her language began to resemble that of a longshoreman.

She'd just come up with a particularly graphic expression she'd seen scrawled on a bathroom wall in a Greenwich Village bar and was repeating it over and over, preparing to fling it into Clint's dark face, when she finally realized he wasn't returning. The house had grown silent as a tomb, and she could only surmise that he'd gone to bed.

She slumped down into a chair, staring off into space, her mind churning over his accusations. Did she appear as cold and heartless as he'd so brutally stated? If so, she had definitely handled things all wrong.

CLINT LAY IN BED, his head braced by his arms. He stared up at the ceiling, wishing that he hadn't had the misfortune to fall head over heels in love with a woman as shortsighted and stubborn as Blair MacKenzie. He had just about exhausted his supply of derogatory terms when the tentative knock at the door caught his attention.

"Come in," he muttered, knowing there was only one other person in the house. He wasn't in any mood to continue that argument.

She opened the door hesitantly, her eyes blinking as she attempted to adjust to the darkness. Clint sighed and reached out to turn on the bedside lamp.

Blair was wearing a flannel robe, tied kimono-style, and suddenly he remembered the Garfield nightshirt. She sure as hell didn't dress like a high-priced fashion model at night. For one wild, fleeting moment, he had entertained the idea that she might be coming to him in a filmy, seductive nightgown, her surrender achieved. But no such luck.

"What can I do for you, Blair?" he asked, sitting up in bed and reaching for his cigarettes.

He wasn't wearing a pajama top, she noted instantly, wondering if he had anything at all on under that rumpled navy sheet. Her mind began to paint erotic pictures, and a soft shade of rose colored her cheeks.

Clint stopped in the act of tapping the cigarette against the table and watched Blair's complexion change color and the pupils of her eyes widen even further, moving like molten obsidian over the gleaming topaz. As she approached the bed, he inhaled the come-hither scent of Tigress perfume.

"Blair," he said, knowing that this time there would be no turning back if she took one step nearer, "what in the hell do you want?"

She gave him a smile like the one Eve must have given to Adam when she handed him the apple. Blair's lustrous gaze held his as she slowly untied the belt of the robe. She slid it off her shoulders, moving toward him with the sensuous glide of a jungle animal, her seductive intent gleaming in her catlike eyes. She stood inches away from the bed, clad in a sea-green nightgown with lacy inserts so sheer they could have been spun from spiderwebs.

"I want to make love with you, Clint," she answered his grittily issued question calmly.

His eyes had been devouring the soft curves of her body, but now they came back to hers.

"I want you, Blair. I think I've wanted you since that first moment I saw you standing by Blackwood's car, so prim and proper in that tailored suit and silly little hat."

He swallowed, and Blair caught the movement in his throat, wondering how even that simple act could heighten the needs battering inside her.

Clint wished she wouldn't look at him that way. He had to get this said, had to explain, to allow her to understand fully. But he was rapidly losing his concentration, and when he continued speaking, his voice was only an incomprehensible buzz in his ear.

"I wanted to undress you, to peel away that false image you wore until you were in my arms, warm and willing, as if you'd waited all your life to come to me in just this way."

His voice grew more husky and it seemed as if his tenuous grasp on sanity were rapidly slipping away. "But 'willing' is the definitive word here, Blair. I don't want you to do anything you don't honestly want."

She forced herself to listen to Clint's words. He'd yet to touch her, but she was already trembling like a leaf in gale-force winds. The absolute power this man had over her was both frightening and exciting, and Blair knew they'd been moving toward this moment from the beginning.

She held out her hands. Beyond words, her gesture and the desire sparking her tawny eyes were all the answer Clint needed.

Throwing back the sheet, he left the bed, gathered her into his arms and gave her a long, lingering kiss that only had her wanting more. As her hands moved slowly across his back, exploring the muscles that went taut under her palms, Blair experienced a warm, fluttering ache to know this man totally. Her hands moved lower, and Clint groaned, pressing her against him, his flesh warming her, his desire making hers flame all the higher.

"You're wearing too many clothes," he complained, his hands caressing her body and causing it to hum under his expert touch like a live wire.

"Yes," she whispered.

His fingers slid the ribbon straps from her shoulders, and the nightgown fell to the floor in a silky puddle, allowing him a weakening gaze at her firm, uplifted breasts. "Beautiful," he murmured, stroking her satiny skin.

Blair's pulse leaped at the featherlight caress; he could feel it under his hands, and it beat against his lips as they explored her flesh. Clint imagined he could taste it as his tongue flicked across her nipple.

She moaned, arching her back, inviting him to take her more fully into his mouth, which he did, moving from breast to breast, treating each in turn to the tender torment that was driving Blair beyond reason.

"Better," he said happily, moving his lips steadily downward. His deep voice vibrated against her stomach, echoing the pulsating desire spiraling out from her innermost core.

"Better," she agreed on a gasp as his tongue made a warm, wet foray into her navel.

When he lowered her to the bed, Blair had the sensation of floating, and she wondered idly if Clint possessed the power of levitation among his vast talents. Then, as she sank into the mattress, she felt herself growing heavy, her limbs weighted, her mind languid with a thick, heavy pleasure.

"Beautiful," he murmured again, "so beautiful." He kissed her, a deep, drugging kiss that engulfed her in tides of aching warmth. He lifted his head and gazed down at her, his eyes gleaming a molten silver, his hands moving over her body in devastating trails that made her arch instinctively, seeking release.

"I've waited too long for this to rush it now," he said softly, his lips brushing lightly at her gleaming skin, tasting of her warm flesh.

Through the thick cloud fogging her mind, Blair suddenly realized that the situation had somehow reversed itself. She'd come into Clint's room to seduce him. Instead, he was the one doing all the giving.

"I wanted to make love to you," she objected on a tattered moan as his lips discovered a flash point of pleasure on her ankle.

"We've all night," he argued, his tongue tracing a damp path up her leg.

"But your pleasure—Oh!" His teeth had nipped at the delicate cord at the back of her knee.

"My pleasure comes from pleasuring you," he murmured, his mouth loitering at the silk of her inner thighs, delighting in the way she trembled when his tongue drew ever-widening circles on her skin.

Blair moaned his name, twisting to find relief; his teasing caresses were driving her to the point of despair. The deepening ache had turned into a steady, pulsating throb, moving through her body like heated honey; and when his tongue finally stabbed into the core of her, she felt something shatter within, like the finest crystal under a high note.

She cried out for him to hold her, to make her safe, and Clint obliged, taking her into his arms and murmuring soft, inarticulate words of comfort into her ear. Slowly, gradually, she stopped trembling, and lying in the circle of Clint's strong arms, Blair was shaken by a sudden renewal of desire that shot through her like a white-hot flame. Her body was acutely, fiercely, alive.

Clint was stunned by Blair's sudden change in mood as her hands, which had been gently stroking his body, turned greedy, drawing muffled groans from him as they sought to discover intimate secrets.

Blair marveled at his strength as he wondered at her softness, her fingers exploring every taut muscle, every straining sinew. She moved her fingers over him, and when that wasn't enough, her lips followed the heated path her hands had forged, tasting the intoxicating tang of his warm male flesh. Her teeth nipped at his moist skin, and when her tongue stroked away the little marks, Clint's body was wracked with a series of harsh shudders.

"Blair, I can't take much more," he warned, reaching for her in an attempt to end this tantalizing torture before he plunged over the brink of madness.

She easily avoided him, rising to her knees, her hair a dark curtain that brushed over the skin of his chest with a mind-blinding touch. Blair had never known such power, and as her avid mouth followed the dark arrow of hair downward, bliss just a moment away, she became the Tigress Woman—primitive, uninhibited, alive with savage passion.

When her lips embraced him, Blair was suddenly aware of a new sensation, that of possession. She wanted him. Not just for these few wild moments of unrestrained passion, but forever. He was hers, only hers, and the idea was so stimulating, so thrilling, that she threw her body onto his, pressing against his burning flesh, moving against him until Clint could stand no more.

He turned her over on her back, his blood transformed to flames that seared through his veins as he took her, driving her into the softness of the mattress with a hunger that transcended all bounds of time and space. Her long legs wrapped themselves about his hips and she matched his strength with hers, his soaring passion with her own, until together they crested, their exultant cries smothered by each other's lips.

Afterward, the shudders continued to course through her body. Lying passively in his arms, Blair could feel the still-wild pounding of his heart against her breasts.

Clint lifted his head and looked down at her, amusement blending with the leftover passion in his eyes. "I knew there was a tigress lurking in that beautiful body."

Smiling, Blair reached up to stroke his cheek with slightly trembling fingers. "It just took the right man to bring it out."

He pressed his lips against hers. "It's us," he murmured. "We make the magic together."

She sighed happily. "That's true. I've never known anything like it." She rained a series of light kisses across his collarbone. "Think how those photographs could have come out if you'd been in the studio with me."

Clint's body warmed anew with the memory of the brilliant passion he'd witnessed in her eyes as he'd entered her, claiming her heart and soul, as well as her body, for all time. "They'd have been X-rated." His teeth nipped lightly at her earlobe, then lured her lips back to his.

"Mmm. But it would have made all the long hours under those hot lights a lot more fun."

"I think we can create enough of our own heat, don't you?"

She laughed, her fingers playing in his dark chest hair. "Definitely."

They fell silent, smiling at each other, lost in their own memories of what they'd just shared and in their own idyllic thoughts of the future.

"I love you."

They both said it together, as attuned in their need to state their feelings aloud as they had been in everything else. Clint looked down into her soft, loving gaze, and suddenly his mind churned up the sight of that pitchfork that had come so near to costing him everything he'd ever wanted in a woman.

"What's the matter?" she asked softly, seeing a frightening look of desperation flash into his gray eyes.

"I can't lose you, Blair."

Her expression was slightly puzzled as she framed his face with her hands. "I'm not going anywhere," she said.

Clint refused to allow himself any more thoughts of the problem that had begun with the farm and now encompassed his entire life. Nothing would happen to her, he swore. He'd see to it. They belonged together, he and Blair, and he wasn't going to allow anything to interfere.

As he stared down at her, the icy feeling of trepidation was replaced by a wild surge of need, and he took her again, desperately, urgently.

BLAIR WAS DREAMING of a stable of winning Thoroughbreds that were racing down the track, the jockeys all clad in the green-and-white silks of Clearwater Hills Farms. She and Clint were on the sidelines, cheering wildly, their arms wrapped about each other. When the entire field crossed the finish line together, they were ecstatic.

Clint kissed her thoroughly before they made their way to the winner's circle, where they were greeted with chaos. All the horses were rearing back, tossing their riders to the ground while they fought for their rightful position as victor. Their angry neighs filled the air, and their front hooves struck out at one another. As the dream grew more and more violent, the horses' screams more strident, Blair's eyes flew open.

An icy fear skimmed down her spine when she realized that the terrified screams were no dream. She pulled out of Clint's arms and ran to the bedroom window. He muttered an objection, reaching out in his sleep to the warm spot where she'd been only moments earlier.

"Oh, my God! Clint, the training barn's on fire!"

He was instantly awake and at her side. The cries of the horses filled the perfumed night air. "Damn! This has got to stop!" He tacked on a virulent series of oaths as he groped about in the dark for his clothes.

Blair turned on the lamp and found her robe under the comforter, which had slid to the floor during their lovemaking. She slipped the robe on, tying the belt while Clint struggled into a pair of jeans and his boots, forgoing socks in his haste.

Together, they ran outside, calling for water to anyone capable of hearing. Clint flung open the barn door, releasing clouds of billowing black smoke. The horses were rearing up as they had done in Blair's dreams, their hooves striking out at the smoke as if they could force it away with their efforts. Their eyes were wide and wild, their necks bathed in sweat, their mouths foaming with their instinctive fear of fire.

"Here." She shoved the sheet she'd pulled from the bed before leaving the room, into Clint's hands. "I thought this might help."

His admiring gaze normally would have given her inordinate pleasure, but there was no time for that at the moment.

"Thanks," he said, tearing the navy cloth into long strips. "You take one side and I'll take the other. Where in the hell is everyone, anyway?"

Knowing it was a rhetorical question, Blair didn't bother to answer. She grabbed a handful of the makeshift blindfolds and tied one of them around Star Dancer's wild black eyes. She stroked the stallion's soaking neck, murmuring encouraging words as she threw on his bridle and tugged hard, urging him out of the stall. The effort seemed to take hours, but finally he was outdoors, breathing in the fresh air, his chest heaving with exertion. By now the crew had arrived, and Blair handed him over to a young girl who'd recently been hired as a hot walker, the lowest rung of the ladder. It was her job to cool the horses down after exercise.

"Here," Blair said, "take him somewhere and hose him off. Then come right back."

"Yes, ma'am," the teenager answered, her own eyes wide with fright.

Blair allowed herself a backward glance, pleased to see that the girl was talking soothingly to the hysterical stallion as she led him away. Blair ran back to the barn, where three more horses were being evacuated by grooms. She did some quick calculations. They should be able to save most of the horses. She experienced an immense sense of gratitude when she spotted Annie assisting Jerry, managing incredibly well for a person with one arm in a sling.

Someone ran by, dragging a large hose into the barn and turning the stream of water in the direction of the bales of stacked hay from which was pouring forth the dense, acrid smoke.

Everyone continued to work at a frantic pace, and finally Clint led Storm Warning from the barn. Blair couldn't help crying out when she saw the stallion, whose skin was charred to a hateful black crisp. She grabbed a hose and began running cold water onto the horse's face, neck and eyes while Clint ran for ice and blankets.

As they worked feverishly, draping the horse in the wet blankets and ice-filled towels, Blair was unaware of the tears pouring down her cheeks. She couldn't remember when she'd been so glad to see anyone as she was when Bill Collins suddenly came into view.

"Jerry called me," the vet explained. He began to examine the stallion. Let's see what we have here."

"I'm not putting him away," Blair stated firmly, expecting an argument from Clint or Bill Collins.

Both men surprised her. "I'm with Blair," Clint seconded instantly.

"You might not have to," Bill said. "His heart rate isn't nearly as bad as it could be. Also, the mucous membranes are pink and normal. We might be able to save him. But it won't be easy," he added.

"We don't care," Blair and Clint said in unison. As Clint squeezed her hand reassuringly, Blair considered that just perhaps her world hadn't come to an end, after all.

They helped the vet replace the blankets and wrap the horse's legs. "We should move him to a clinic," Bill advised, "so he can get constant care."

"Blair and I will take turns," Clint said, "won't we?"

She nodded. "Around the clock."

"I can't guarantee he'll make it," Bill warned. "More than sixty percent of his body is burned, and a large part of the burns are third-degree. You know as well as I do that when an animal suffers burns over fifty percent of its body, the prognosis isn't good."

"He'll make it," Blair insisted. "I know he will."

"Then let's get started. I'll want him somewhere quiet, away from the other horses."

Clint suggested a small building that had once been used as a breeding barn. Far away from the bustle of the paddock, it should serve their purpose. Blair crooned comfortingly to Storm Warning as they led him away; she was encouraged by the way he perked up his ears in response. The attempt to save him wasn't futile. She knew it!

Blair and Clint stood by as Bill gave the stallion an injection of painkiller, as well as penicillin. With a centrifuge, the vet measured the horse's cell volume, finding him to be dehydrated. But Bill had come well prepared. Within minutes two IV's were set up, and Storm Warning was given more vitamin B to help against shock. The horse was catheterized and a tube inserted in his stomach so that additional fluids could be administered orally. When he began to swell in the early hours of the morning, he was given steroids to stabilize the swelling.

It was a long and tiring night, since more than once it looked as if they'd lose the stallion, but Blair and Clint never stopped talking to him or stroking his head or encouraging him not to give up. Storm Warning proved himself to be one plucky horse; he remained calm, responding to the three humans trying so desperately to save him. By the time the sun had risen on the eastern horizon, the swelling had gone down perceptibly and his skin was moist.

"I'm slowing the IV," Bill informed them. "For now, all we can do is keep an eye on him. He's going to need a lot of attention over the next several weeks, though."

Blair and Clint nodded wearily, Clint suddenly breaking into a deep coughing fit that had Blair worried. They'd soaked their own strips of cloth in water and covered their noses and mouths, but Clint had worked the longest without such assistance.

"Are you all right?" she asked.

He took a few deep breaths, which only brought about another bout of coughing. "Fine," he said finally as he came up for air.

"Are you sure?"

He shook his head, raking his hands through his darkened hair. "I'll be okay. I just inhaled some smoke when I first went in."

"Thank God the others are safe," she murmured.

"Thank *you*. If you hadn't wakened when you did, it could have been a real disaster."

"It was meant to be a disaster, wasn't it?" she asked softly, shivering as she considered their unseen enemy out there, lurking somewhere in the darkness.

Clint didn't answer; no answer was necessary. Seeing Blair's tremors, he asked, "Cold?"

"Frightened," she admitted, no longer hesitant to let him know her feelings after what they'd shared that evening. Had it only been that evening? It seemed like a hundred years ago.

He put his arm around her. "I know."

Before she could answer, a wide-eyed groom named Dennis Marston arrived at the door to tell them that the firemen had gone and things were under control.

"I'll stay with Storm Warning," he volunteered, "while you two get some rest."

"I don't know." Blair hesitated.

"Hey, it'll be all right," he assured her. "Storm Warning and I are old friends. Aren't we, guy?" he asked, going over to stroke what was left of the stallion's thick mane.

Storm Warning made the decision for Blair by nuzzling his head against the young man's chest. Dennis was the stallion's groom, and his love for the burned horse was evident.

"All right," she agreed. "Thank you, Dennis."

As he turned his gaze from the stallion, the young man's eyes were suspiciously moist. "Don't thank me, Ms. MacKenzie," he said huskily. "I'd never let anything happen to any of my horses."

"You've managed to hire a very loyal crew," she murmured to Clint as they walked across the yard.

"They're good kids. They love the horses like their own."

"Like you and Risky Pleasure."

He nodded. "Would you mind if I checked her before we went in?"

Blair shook her head, taking his hand in hers. "Not at all," she said. They went over to the smaller barn that had escaped the fire.

Blair and Clint were brought up short as they reached Risky Pleasure's stall. It was empty.

Chapter Thirteen

The commotion had not gone unnoticed, and several individuals from neighboring farms had arrived on the heels
of the pumper truck, ready to help. Hours later, only Matt
and Marni remained. At this point, it appeared all they
could offer was moral support. "Who would do such a
thing?" Marni asked, handing both Blair and Clint a drink
as they entered the kitchen, their faces identical masks of
despair.

"I don't know," Clint muttered, before tossing off the
drink. "But when I find out, I'm going to make certain the
bastard pays."

Blair stared blankly at the glass her friend had pushed
into her hands.

"It's brandy," Marni said. "It'll help."

Blair thought that nothing would help the way she felt
right now, but at Matt's added coaxing she gave in, feeling an explosion of warmth when the alcohol hit her
stomach.

"I think I'm going to be sick," she said suddenly.

Clint reached out for her, but Marni quickly stopped
him. "I'll take care of her, Clint. You sit down before you
drop."

Marni put her arm around Blair's shoulder and led her to the bathroom, then stood back as the combination of smoke, fear and despair made Blair ill.

"I'm sorry," she muttered, sinking down on the floor with her knees drawn up against her chest. Feeling inordinately dizzy, she lowered her forehead to her knees and drank in deep breaths of air. She could still smell the acrid smoke in her nostrils and thought she was going to be sick all over again.

"Don't be silly," Marni scolded. "You've been through a terrible ordeal. You're allowed to fall apart a little bit. You can't always be in control, Blair. The sooner you learn that, the happier you'll be."

Blair thought back to those glorious hours before her world had come apart at the seams. "You're right," she surprised her friend by saying. "Clint said almost the same thing to me."

"And?"

"And now I've got to help him find Risky Pleasure." Blair struggled to her feet.

"What you need to do is rest," Marni countered ineffectually, heaving a frustrated sigh as she followed Blair back down the hallway to the kitchen.

Clint was slumped at the table, his head in his hands.

"Feeling better?" Matt asked Blair, his green eyes solicitous.

"A little." Her voice was still not strong.

Clint lifted his head, managing a weak smile. "Shouldn't you be lying down?"

"Probably." She moved beside him, running her fingers through his smoky hair. "But so should you, and you're still up."

"I've got to wait for the police."

"It's my farm," she reminded him. "So it's my responsibility."

His arm went around her waist. "I thought we'd come to an understanding about that."

Blair viewed the weariness in his eyes and could have wept. "We did," she agreed. "We're in this together, all the way, Clint."

This time his smile was a little stronger. "That's better." He pulled her down onto his lap, and she rested her head on his shoulder.

"I can stay and give the police the report," Matt offered. "You two look beat."

"We'll be okay. Which is a helluva lot more than I can say for Risky Pleasure," Clint muttered.

"You've no idea who's doing all this?" Marni asked, her eyes shadowed with a faint fear.

"We had a couple of ideas," Clint said slowly, "but they're not panning out too well."

A gloomy silence settled over the room. Then Clint sat up suddenly, almost dumping Blair from his lap. "Jerry!"

"What?" the other three asked in unison.

Clint turned to Blair. "When we were all working to get the horses out of the training barn, did you see Jerry anywhere around?"

Blair thought back. "Yes," she said. "I saw him working with Annie when we first discovered the fire."

"Did you see him later?"

She shook her head. "Now that you mention it, I didn't.... Oh, Clint, you don't think he set that fire, do you? Jerry would never hurt any of the horses. And he'd never do anything to Risky Pleasure—you know how he adores that filly."

"I thought he did. Let's go check."

Blair struggled to keep up with Clint as they made their way across the yard to the building that housed the groom's quarters.

"Well?" Clint said, his gray eyes raking over Jerry's empty room.

Blair's bleak gaze followed his. "He's gone," she stated flatly.

"With our horse." Clint's voice trembled with pent-up rage.

Blair put a hand on his arm. "There must be a reason."

"Yeah. And when we find the kid, I'm going to beat it out of him."

She didn't answer that, knowing that Clint was speaking out of frustration. "Does he have any family around here?"

"No. They all live back East."

"Perhaps he just took her out for a while to calm her down," Blair suggested hopefully. "Maybe he doesn't have anything to do with this at all."

"Sure," Clint shot back, "why don't you tell me another fairy tale while you're at it?" A moment later he groaned, rubbing his hand over his face. When he took the hand away, his eyes revealed contrition. "I'm sorry, babe. I've no right to take this out on you."

She went up on her toes and kissed his cheek. "Don't worry about that." Then she saw the police cruiser pull into the driveway. "We'd better go talk to them," she said without a great deal of enthusiasm.

After the police had taken their report, Marni pointed out a fact that all of them, in their distress, had overlooked.

"Doesn't it seem odd to you that they'd steal Risky Pleasure?"

Clint shrugged his shoulders. "These days nothing would surprise me," he grunted.

Marni was undeterred. "But if they really were responsible for Black Magic's broken leg, then why didn't they just destroy Risky Pleasure in her stall? Why go to all the trouble of spiriting her out of here in the first place?"

"There's always the possibility of ransom," Clint mused.

"If it's simply a need for money, then why all the other incidents?" Marni argued.

The four were silent, mulling the problem over. "I'll be damned if I know," Clint muttered finally.

Blair's heart turned over at the defeat in his tone, the exhaustion etched on every hard line of his face. His silvery hair was tousled from his raking his fingers through it, and his skin was still darkened with smudges from the heavy smoke.

"Bed," Marni stated firmly. "You two need some sleep. Matt and I will try to find out if anyone else around here knows what Jerry was up to."

This time Clint didn't argue. "Just a few short hours. We still have Storm Warning to worry about."

There was never any question about Blair's going to her room and Clint to his. After that evening it seemed natural that they'd both share the bed in which only a few hours before, they'd pledged a new beginning.

It felt so right, Blair thought as she lay in Clint's strong arms. So good. Feeling safe with him beside her, she closed her eyes and allowed her exhaustion to overtake her. Soon they were both asleep.

WITH BLAIR AND CLINT safely asleep and Marni taking a nap in her old room, Matt sat alone in the den, staring into space. For the past two weeks he'd been feeling as if he were slowly, inexorably, sinking into quicksand. That morning he realized he was in danger of going in over his head.

Heaving a weary sigh, he dialed the number of Robin Hanson. "That was a lousy thing to do," he said the moment she answered the phone.

"It was a necessary thing to do," she amended. "Remember, darling, nice guys finish last. I've always thought of myself as a winner."

"What the hell did you do with the filly?" he grated out.

"Filly?"

"Risky Pleasure."

"I assume she's still in residence at the farm."

"Don't play coy with me, sweetheart. You know as well as I do she's disappeared."

There was a long, thoughtful silence on the other end of the telephone. "That's an interesting twist," Robin murmured. "But we didn't have anything to do with horse-napping the filly."

Matt suddenly felt like wringing the woman's neck. "If you're lying to me, Robin, so help me God..."

"Believe me, darling, I have no idea what happened to Hollister's precious horse. Although I wish I had thought of absconding with her," she added. "It's a delicious idea. He must be frantic."

"You can be a real black widow when you want to be," he muttered, unable to miss the enthusiasm in her voice.

"Flattery will get you nowhere, darling," she said silkily. "Keep me informed about the filly; I don't like the idea of someone else suddenly entering this little game we've got going for ourselves."

"Do you think Blackwood's behind it?"

"That's a possibility. Quite honestly, I wouldn't have thought the man had the guts to do anything like this, but you never know what an individual will do when several million dollars are at stake."

That's for sure, Matt considered bleakly as he hung up, wishing he'd never gotten involved in this mess to begin with. When he'd first been approached by Hightower to sell his land for the site of a new electronics factory, he'd believed it was the answer to all his prayers. A series of losing seasons had been capped off by Northern Light's accident, and he'd been on the brink of bankruptcy.

But one condition of the deal had been that he promise not to mention the sale while Hightower Development began quietly to buy up all the surrounding land. VideoTec was going to employ several thousand people, and all those new workers would need housing. While the idea of the rolling grasslands covered with rows and rows of tract housing was definitely unappealing, Matt had managed to convince himself that progress was inevitable. If he didn't cooperate, they'd simply find someone else. So he'd remained silent, watching as the bogus real estate companies began buying up the land.

He'd never expected things to get out of hand this way. Just as he'd never expected Jason Langley to have that fatal heart attack while confronting him with his suspicions. Jason had surprised everyone by his sudden insistence on reviewing all his financial records. For years he'd allowed his attorney and accountant to tend to the business end of Clearwater Hills Farm, directing his attention to the only thing that interested him: the horses.

But once Jason had accepted the fact that he didn't have long to live, he'd wanted to know exactly what he was leaving to his granddaughter. It hadn't taken him long to discover the discrepancy in the books or unearth his neighbor's part in the unusual amount of real estate transactions going on. He'd lost his temper, a not unusual occurrence, but that time it had been fatal.

Afraid that others would follow the trail, Matt had paid his own visit to the hall of records, removed the damning page that listed his sale to VideoTec, through Hightower enterprises, and burned it in his fireplace. He'd thought that would be the end of everything. But then Blair had shown up, refusing to sell, and things had turned decidedly nasty when Hanson's hired thugs had shattered Black Magic's leg.

In an effort to forestall any further tragedies, Matt had entered into the affair with Marni, hoping she could convince her friend to cut her losses and go back to New York. He felt guilty about using Marni that way. She was a nice woman and deserved better, but he'd been desperate, and at the time it seemed a viable solution.

Unfortunately, the entire idea proved a dismal failure, for Marni steadfastly insisted that Blair had a mind of her own and would listen to no one when it came to surrendering her lifelong dream.

Matt shook his head, afraid to consider what might happen next.

BILL COLLINS HAD STAYED ON catching a few hours of needed sleep. He was back tending Storm Warning when Blair and Clint showed up after their naps.

"He's holding his own," the vet assured them. "In fact, as bad as he looks, he just might be in better shape than Sun Devil."

"Sun Devil?" Blair said. "He wasn't burned."

Bill shook his head. "I know, Blair. But he inhaled a lot of smoke."

"Pneumonia," Clint muttered.

The vet shook his head. "It doesn't look good."

Clint raked his fingers through his hair. "I've seen horses through pneumonia before, and we can do it again with Sun Devil," he vowed.

"Of course we will," Blair seconded fervently. "What's your plan for Storm Warning?" she asked, stroking the stallion's head tenderly. The horse's eyes were burned so badly they were swollen shut, but that didn't stop him from responding to Blair's voice and gentle touch.

"It'll be a long process," Bill warned. "And expensive. And there are no guarantees."

"I don't care about expense," Blair said firmly.

"Our first concern is to make certain he survives his shock. We seem to be doing pretty well there," he assured Blair and Clint. "Next, we have to worry about pneumonia, so I'll be giving him penicillin for his lungs. I'm also treating him with chloramphenicol for his eyes and butazolidin for pain; we'll continue that treatment, as well as vitamin injections.

"If we manage to get through those dangers, then we still have to worry about infection. I've put a call in for some synthetic skin for grafts. We'll have to make sheet blankets to cover him during the healing process, to keep him from rubbing off the skin grafts. Silver sulfadiazine should help prevent him from wanting to scratch; it's been successful in treating burns on humans."

Bill's expression was professionally cautious. "Even if everything goes well," he concluded, "you're looking at a year at least before you'll have a healthy horse."

Blair and Clint exchanged a long look. Then Clint spoke for both of them, taking Blair's hand and giving it a tight, reassuring squeeze. "We're not going anywhere."

The following days blended together into an exhausting combination of vigil and work. Clint and Blair rotated shifts, taking turns tending to Storm Warning while the crews cleaned up the mess left behind by the fire. Neither Clint nor Blair was surprised when the fire department ruled the blaze arson; neither were they surprised when the police failed to locate Risky Pleasure. The filly seemed to have vanished into thin air.

"She has to be somewhere," Blair muttered as she exited the shower after a tiring six-hour shift of trying to keep the stallion from sloughing off his burned skin.

Clint was seated on the edge of the bed, pulling on his boots. "Now that's a brilliant observation if I've ever heard one."

Blair didn't take his gritty tone personally. He'd gotten little sleep since the fire and was obviously walking an emotional tightrope right now. The work entailed with nursing Sun Devil and Storm Warning had not allowed him the privilege of worrying about the filly during his waking hours, but Blair could see that sleep had been as difficult for him as it was for her.

"What about Annie's family?" she asked.

"I told you, they all live here in San Diego. Besides, the police checked that out already." He raked his fingers through his hair in obvious frustration. "Damn!"

"What is it?"

"There's a grandmother I forgot about. Annie's so damned Americanized, I tend to forget her family came from across the border."

"And the grandmother still lives there?"

"Tijuana, I think. But I'd better call Matt and find out exactly where."

As he rose to make his way to the phone, Blair reached out, putting her hand on his arm. "Don't do that," she advised softly.

"Why not?"

"There's something I meant to tell you about, something that happened at the party."

She told Clint about Brian Hanson's assertion that Jason had intended to sell the farm, a fact that had been seconded by Ramsey.

Clint muttered a harsh expletive, then asked, "What does that have to do with Matt?"

Blair went on to explain the scene she'd inadvertantly witnessed. "I can't prove anything is going on between them, but it just didn't look right," she stated quietly.

"That's why you were in such a bad mood that night, wasn't it?" Clint sank down onto the edge of the bed.

"I was upset about the accusations against you. But yes, I was also worried about Marni," she admitted.

"Why didn't you tell me?"

"I was going to. But then we made love and I forgot. After that, there was the fire, and we've both been so busy, it slipped my mind.... What if Matt's behind all this?" she suggested softly.

"That's a harsh accusation, Blair."

"I know," she whispered. They stared at each other, their expressions bleak.

"I suppose I can find out where Annie's grandmother lives just as easily from her parents."

"I think that would be best."

Clint stood up, his eyes displaying his discomfort with this latest twist. "Matt's always been a friend," he said. "I hate what I'm thinking."

Blair's eyes were mirror images of Clint's. "Me, too." She felt like crying when he left the room, his wide shoulders slumped with the weight of suspicions.

As THEY DROVE toward the border that afternoon, pulling an empty horse trailer in case they were lucky enough to find the pilfered filly, Blair attempted logic. Writing down all the pieces they'd found of this puzzle, she hoped to force them into a workable whole.

"That's it!" she said suddenly.

Clint glanced over at the notepad. "What's it?"

"Hightower! We've been looking at it all along and never even knew it!"

"Would you care to explain that a little further?"

She read off the list of new property owners in the area. "Hanson Properties, Ingram Property Management, Guardian Development Company, Henderson Land Company, Thompson Development, Owens Land Management, Western Corporation, Evergreen Real Estate and Randall Investments."

"So?"

"Look at the first initials," she said, tapping each letter with the point of her pencil. They're an acronym."

"I'll be damned. They spell out 'high tower.'"

"Hightower," she confirmed.

"So it *is* all one company."

"One company that seems determined to buy up every last piece of property out here. I'm surprised the zoning board has been rubber-stamping the applications for land-use change, though."

"That was undoubtedly the easy part," Clint informed her. "This is a rapidly expanding area, and the zoning board is up to its eyebrows in applications. All you need is one crooked board member to push the paper through, and unless they get a big hue and cry from the general population, the applications pass without much of a fight."

"And San Diego residents are too busy fighting beach-front development to care what happens up here," she surmised.

Clint nodded. "Got it. Jason and I went to some of the meetings. A few of the other landowners did, too, but we were like that small voice crying out in the wilderness. No one heard us."

Blair considered that idea, considered losing her beautiful farm and grew more furious by the moment. "They're not going to run me off my property," she declared fervently.

Clint chuckled in spite of his depressed mood. "Now you sound like some heroine out of a Saturday afternoon matinee."

Her eyes softened. "Then we're in great shape. Because you remind me of all those heroes I used to swoon over."

"Aren't you laying it on a little thick?"

"Not at all. I do love you, Clint." She reached out, putting her hand on his leg and stroking it lightly.

"I love you, too, sweetheart," he replied in a husky voice. "But if you don't put that cute little hand back where it belongs, I'm going to have to pull over to the side of the road."

At the way the obvious desire in Clint's voice warmed her blood, Blair regarded his suggestion as ideal. But she knew they had far more important things to do, so she did as he asked.

"Do you think Risky Pleasure will be in Tijuana, Clint?"

"I don't know," he admitted. But I can't think of anywhere else to try. It's possible Jerry is hiding her at Annie's grandmother's place."

"Is it that easy to smuggle a horse across the border?"

"If thousands of illegals can enter the country every night, it shouldn't be that difficult to move a single horse in the opposite direction."

"But why would he take her in the first place?"

Clint shook his head. "I'll be damned if I know."

As he fell silent, Blair watched the scenery flash by the truck window. They'd left the eastern grasslands and were now driving along the coast.

"Cold?" Clint observed Blair's slight tremor.

"No, but I just had a thought."

"Must not have been very pleasant."

"It wasn't. I was wondering if this could all be a trap to lure us out of the country so that we can't get any help."

Clint rubbed his jaw. "I thought of that," he told her. "In fact, I'd considered not allowing you to come along."

"Not come along?" Blair's eyes widened and her tone was incredulous. "Do you honestly think you could have kept me away?"

Clint managed a low laugh. "I said I'd *considered* it. I also dismissed the idea immediately. Keeping you out of action would probably require several lengths of strong rope, and I'm not prepared to take the inevitable consequences when I'd finally have to untie you."

Blair, too, laughed for a moment; then her expression sobered. "I know we're going to find her, Clint. I just know it."

"Ah, I forgot—Madame Tigress has a crystal ball. Did you perchance, happen to see a big-boned filly in there?"

"Of course," Blair answered promptly. "And she's beating the socks off Cimarron."

"You're agreeing to the match race?"

"Of course I'm agreeing," she said softly, leaning over to brush a light kiss against his cheek.

Clint was suddenly overcome with waves of fear like nothing he'd every known. What if he were to lose her? The thought continued to torment him as they crossed the border into Tijuana, drove past the shopping stalls, and slowed to make way for the hordes of tourists filling the narrow streets. Making a quick decision, Clint braked to a stop.

"Why are we stopping?" Blair asked, eyeing him curiously. They were outside a small café, but she knew Clint had not developed a sudden urge for a taco.

"I'm not taking you with me."

"That's ridiculous!"

"No, it's not. I've no intention of taking you into a dangerous situation like this."

"Clint…"

"Look, Blair, it might be different if I believed you'd stick to playing the maiden-in-distress part, but I've got the uneasy feeling you watched all those Saturday afternoon matinees and picked up the wrong role model. I'm only thinking of you, sweetheart."

"If you were really thinking of me," she argued, "you'd let me come with you. I can't stand the idea of your going to Annie's grandmother's all alone. I'd never forgive myself if you got hurt."

"How the hell do you think I'd feel if *you* got hurt?" he shot back.

"I promise not to do anything foolish. Besides, we don't even know if Risky Pleasure is down here. Please let me stay," she wheedled, her tawny eyes entreating him to her line of reasoning.

Clint felt as if he were drowning in deep pools of molten gold. "Damn it, Blair, this is crazy."

"Clint…"

The impatient blare of a taxi horn interrupted them, reminding Clint that he was effectively blocking the flow of traffic. He shifted into gear, cursing softly under his breath. "You are not coming with me, and that's the end of it. It's too dangerous for a woman."

Blair felt like hitting him over the top of his hard, chauvinist head. "Fine," she snapped, moving to open the truck door. "I'll just get out right here. I'm sure I'll be completely safe wandering around this place until whenever you get back. I've heard that border-town reputations are exaggerated anyway."

He grabbed her arm, yanking her back into the truck. "Damn it, you win. You're coming along."

Clint's blistering expression echoed his angry tone, but since she'd gotten her way Blair decided the prudent thing to do now would be to ignore his irritation and not flaunt her victory.

She folded her hands in her lap with all the complaisance of an obedient schoolgirl. "Thank you, Clint," she said softly. "I promise not to get in your way."

His only response was a muffled oath, but as she dared a surreptitious glance out of the corner of her eye, Blair thought she saw a ghost of a smile playing on his lips.

Chapter Fourteen

"This certainly explains all the illegal aliens," Blair murmured as they drove past the rows and rows of shanties made of tar paper and flattened oil drums. The dark gray storm clouds hovering overhead only added to the bleak scene.

"There are almost eight hundred thousand people living in Tijuana these days. They pour in from the interior, seeking higher wages and a better way of life. Unfortunately, all too many of them only end up worse off than they were in the first place. It takes more than a dream to make it, I'm afraid."

Blair remained silent, uncomfortable with the inevitable comparison in life-styles. The view became more rural, and she watched the little pastures strung with wires that housed chickens, donkeys, once in a while a cow or a swaybacked horse. Then one animal in particular caught her eye.

"Clint!" She grabbed his arm, almost causing him to steer off the dirt roadway.

"Hey!" He brought the truck to an abrupt halt. "If you don't mind, Blair, I'd like to get there all in one piece."

She ignored his gritty tone, pointing instead out the window. "Look at that horse."

At Clint's first cursory glance, he was inclined to disregard the large, rawboned filly. But as he studied her further, he felt a faint stirring of hope. "It sure as hell looks like her," he agreed. "But the star is missing. And she doesn't have the stockings."

"And the tail is the wrong color," Blair added. "But she could've been dyed, Clint. I tell you, that's Risky Pleasure."

The more he looked, the more Clint felt Blair was right. "Let's go take a closer look."

As if on cue, the storm hit the moment they exited the truck, the sky opening up as dime-sized raindrops began to fall around them.

"Terrific timing," he growled, making his way through the downpour to the horse, who was standing in the middle of the field, ears up, eyeing them with curiosity.

"Wonderful timing," Blair corrected, clapping her hands. "Look at her, Clint!"

As they watched, the water running off the horse turned into dark brown rivulets, and signs of the familiar white star and stockings came into view. Clint broke into a jog with Blair on his heels, both of them calling out to the filly, who neighed happily in response.

"Shoe polish," he laughed, throwing an arm around Risky Pleasure's neck. "The kid used shoe polish for camouflage!"

"Surely he didn't expect to get away with that."

"It was just a temporary measure. In fact, I think I've finally got everything figured out."

"Well, I'm sure glad someone does," Blair muttered, "because I'm still lost."

"I'll tell you later," he promised. "First let's get Risky Pleasure out of this rain before she ends up looking like a zebra."

While they walked back to the truck, Blair talked a hundred miles an hour to the filly, who appeared to be nodding and neighing in agreement to her owner's enthusiasm. Within minutes Risky Pleasure was loaded into the horse trailer. Blair and Clint were congratulating themselves on a job well done when a dark car suddenly appeared around the curve and screeched to a stop in front of them. As two men jumped out, Blair realized she was finally face to face with the individuals responsible for all the troubles at the farm. These were the people who'd caused Black Magic's death.

At the memory of that sweet stallion, fury whipped through her. She squared her shoulders and moved toward the men, her topaz eyes shooting sparks.

"Blair!" Clint pushed her name through gritted teeth as his fingers curled around her elbow, stopping her in her tracks. One of the men had pulled out a revolver; the other man was pointing a twelve-gauge shotgun at them.

The taller of the two strangers nodded approvingly. "Very good, Hollister. If you know what's good for Miss MacKenzie, you'll advise her to do as we say. Now, both of you, against the trailer."

Blair and Clint exchanged a look, then slowly did as instructed, turning their backs on the men and placing their palms against the side of the fiberglass horse trailer. If the anger directed her way from Clint's gray eyes was any indication, Blair considered for a fleeting instant that she'd be safer in the hands of these thugs.

The click of a cylinder from behind caused her blood suddenly to run cold, and she shut her eyes, seeing swirling bright spots on a background of black velvet. When the explosion sounded seconds later, she tried to scream, but only a ragged croak escaped her white lips.

As Blair slowly realized that she had not been shot, that awareness brought even a worse thought. Clint. *Dear God, these men had shot Clint!* But when she opened her eyes, he was still standing beside her, a grim expression carved onto his face.

"Dangerous country," the man with the shotgun said casually. Blair cast a wary glance over her shoulder, looking at the scattered remains of what she could only surmise had been a desert snake.

"Rattler," he informed her, seeing the direction of her gaze. "Wouldn't do to let you get bit, Miss MacKenzie. That's a damn painful way to go. I had something a little quicker in mind myself."

"Terrific," Clint muttered. "Now do you see why I didn't want you along?"

"We're in this together," she reminded him under her breath. "All the way. Besides, there's something I haven't told you...."

"All right, you two, knock off the chatter," the smaller man instructed, his voice sounding like a bald tire on a gravel road.

"Who are you?" Blair asked angrily. "And what do you want with us?"

"Lady, if you don't shut up, I'm going to do it for you." he advised calmly.

"And how do you suggest doing that?" she demanded, trying to judge the shorter man's weight and height. It just might work. But she'd never before used her hard-practiced skills in an actual attack. What if she failed?

"Blair, just do what they ask," Clint insisted, "before you end up getting yourself killed."

Killed? Her wide eyes returned to the barrel of the weapon pointed in her direction, and her vivid awareness of the actual danger of her situation caused her to sway slightly.

Both men shouted as Clint reached out, wrapping his arm around her waist to steady her. "She tripped, dammit! What did you think, that she was going to try to escape with those guns aimed at her back?"

"Just shut up, Hollister, and put your hands back against the trailer," the smaller man ordered. "Vince, check 'em out."

Clint complied, his eyes ordering Blair to do likewise. Vince patted them down, searching for weapons. Clint had to bite down the useless rage that surged through him as the man's hands moved along Blair's body. It wasn't the time. Not yet. He had to keep them talking.

"They're both clean, Phil." Vince returned to stand beside his partner.

"Did Blackwood set you up to this?" Clint asked conversationally.

Both men laughed harshly. "Blackwood's the next on the list. We're going to take care of him after we finish with you."

"You've got a busy day planned."

"You made it easier. It was obvious the kid had swiped the horse, but nobody at Hightower knew where he hid it. All we had to do was follow you two, and here we are."

Blair risked a glance back over her shoulder. The men were too far away. She couldn't risk it. Not yet.

"What do you want with Risky Pleasure?" she asked, stalling for time.

"Hell," Vince said, "we don't give a damn about the stupid nag. But Hanson's worried that the kid knows something. We figured if we tagged along after you and the cowboy here, we could find the kid and make sure he didn't show up later with some fool blackmail scheme."

Blair's blood ran cold as she realized they intended to kill Jerry. As well as her and Clint.

"I'm surprised Matt didn't think of Annie's grand-mother," Clint remarked casually. "He is involved in all this, isn't he?"

Phil nodded. "He got a little squeamish when the job got serious. He wanted to back out after Vince here did in that stallion, but there was always that little matter of Langley's death."

"Matt killed my grandfather?" Blair gasped.

The man shrugged. "He says it was an accident. Who knows what really happened? The old bastard was dead, one way or the other."

"So Matt was stuck," Clint stated flatly, thinking how he'd always considered Matt Bradshaw his friend.

It didn't escape Clint's notice that they were telling him far too many things about the nature of the incidents at Clearwater Hills Farm. The only way they'd be so open was if they planned to kill him and Blair. He wished he could assure her that he had no intention of allowing that to happen. He could only hope she wasn't too frightened.

Meanwhile, Blair was trying to remain calm. There had to be a way out of this. She knew that whatever these Hightower people wanted with her property, they were not above killing to achieve it.

"You really are the Tigress Woman, aren't you?" Phil asked suddenly, his gaze narrowing. "I didn't see it at first. But your eyes give you away."

"Is that good or bad?" she managed to say.

"Depends on how you look at it, I suppose. Come here," he instructed, his pale blue eyes suddenly gleaming with a bright light.

Blair didn't move. The man slowly lifted his arm, aiming the revolver at Clint. "I asked you nicely to come over here, Miss MacKenzie. I don't want to have to repeat it."

"Blair..." Clint reached out, not wanting her anywhere near those thugs.

The deadly sound of the shotgun being cocked sounded like a rifle shot in the steady *plunk plunk* of the falling rain.

"You stay where you are, Hollister, or Vince will pull that trigger. This is between the little lady and me."

"Let her go," Clint said, slowly withdrawing his hand. "She doesn't have anything to do with this."

"I'm afraid she does," Phil argued. "That's right, come over here, Tigress Woman," he said, nodding his approval as Blair approached. "I think it's time we got to know each other a little better, don't you?"

Clint fought against the murderous rage that surged through him, threatening to eat away any semblance of sanity. She didn't need blind heroics now. When he made his move, he would have to be certain that he could pull it off.

"She doesn't own the farm anymore," he said. "She deeded it over to me."

"Tell me another one," Vince laughed. "You may be a helluva horse trainer, Hollister, but you're a lousy liar."

"It's true," Clint said calmly. "It's amazing what a woman will do if you tell her you love her."

At Blair's sudden intake of breath, Phil's eyes moved back and forth between the couple. The pained expression on her face made him seem more willing to accept Clint's story.

"Well, well. While this sure as hell makes everything more interesting, I'm afraid it doesn't change things. You know, all this would've been a lot easier if Vince here hadn't missed with that damn pitchfork.''

"I knew it wasn't an accident,'' Clint muttered.

"With you out of the way, Hollister, the little lady here would have had to give up and take that cute little tail back to New York on the first plane.''

"The pitchfork was meant for Clint?'' Blair asked weakly, thinking how much she would have missed if these horrible men had succeeded in killing him.

"What did you think? That it was for you?'' Phil asked incredulously.

Blair could only nod.

"Hell, there wasn't any reason to do away with you then,'' he said. "Of course, you know too much now, I'm afraid. We're going to have to do away with both of you.''

His eyes gleamed as they moved down her slender frame, taking in the rain-soaked clothes that clung to her body like a second skin. The cold had hardened her nipples, and they pressed against the wet sweater, arresting Phil's heated gaze.

"Although in your case, Tigress Woman, I think we can make certain your last few hours are enjoyable.''

His leer caused terror to spiral up her spine, and goose bumps rose on her skin when he reached out and dragged her back against him, his arm crushing against her breasts as his other hand still pointed the gun at Clint.

Clint was on the verge of losing control at the way Phil was looking down at Blair. Now Vince, too, seemed to be more interested in what the Tigress Woman could provide in the way of recreation. Both men were gazing at her as if she were their own personal smorgasbord and they'd been starving for months.

Knowing full well the fantasies those Tigress Woman layouts could instill, Clint forced himself to allow them their tawdry mental images for the time being. At least that activity took their attention away from him.

He slowly walked his fingers along the edge of the trailer. Out of the corner of her eye, Blair saw what he was doing. She had to keep their captors from noticing Clint's surreptitious movements.

"Can't we make some kind of deal?" she asked in a breathless little voice, her eyes wide and guileless.

"Lady, be reasonable," Vince complained, a red flush rising from his collar as he watched the rise and fall of her breasts. "You know too much."

"I won't tell," she promised, her voice half honey, half smoke as she took a chance and reached out to place a supplicating hand on his arm. By his glazed look, Blair knew that Vince was not immune to her stroking fingers. "Besides, I can pay you a lot more than Mr. Hanson is paying."

"I don't know...."

"Don't be an idiot," Phil argued. "We've got a job to do, pure and simple. Since when do you start getting all wishy-washy over a broad?"

"I just thought—"

"You're not paid to think," the smaller man, who was still holding Blair, snapped back. "You'll do whatever I tell you. And I'm telling you to take care of Hollister while I spend a little time with Miss MacKenzie."

"I take my orders from Hanson, not you," Vince said.

"Is that a fact?" Phil loosened his hold on Blair as he glared up at his partner. "May I remind you who went to college with Hanson in the first place?"

"I'm getting sick of hearing about that fancy-pants college you two went to," Vince growled.

While they'd been arguing, Clint had loosened Risky Pleasure's reins. Suddenly he slapped the horse on the rump, causing her to escape the trailer and take off at a full gallop. The commotion caught the men off guard, and with a mighty roar, Clint threw himself against them, knocking Vince to the ground. The shotgun sank ineffectually into the deep mud.

"Hold it right there," Phil ordered, flinging Blair away from him, attempting to aim the revolver at Clint, who was rolling on the ground with the larger, but less agile, Vince.

Her captor let out a loud shout as Blair suddenly grabbed his outstretched arm and flipped him onto his back. He landed on a flat rock, gasping for breath like a grounded carp. Blair picked up the gun he'd dropped, her hands trembling as she aimed it at his head.

"Blair, give it to me!"

Her attention returned to Clint, who was straddling Vince and pounding his fists into the man's doughy face. She quickly handed the revolver over, more than willing to allow Clint to take charge of the situation.

"Get some rope out of the trailer, will you, honey?" he asked calmly, covering the two men. "I think we'd better tie our friends up before they get themselves into more mischief."

Blair retrieved the length of rope quickly, relaxing only when Clint had tightly bound their hands and ankles.

"At least I've discovered the mysterious exercise program," he said with a chuckle. "My God, I could have guessed for a million years and never come up with jujitsu. Why didn't you tell me?"

Blair smiled. "I was saving it in case you ever got out of line. Then, by the time you did, I sure wasn't going to beat you up for doing what I'd wanted all along."

He pulled her into his arms, his lips bestowing hard little kisses all over her face. He'd come so close to losing her!

"There are a lot easier ways to get me on my back, sweetheart," he drawled.

Really?" Her arms looped around his waist as she smiled up at him.

"Really. All you have to do is ask."

They exchanged a long, delicious kiss, oblivious to the slanting rain pelting them.

"Hey, we're getting soaked out here!"

Clint's gaze slid to the two men lying in a pool of brackish mud. "So you are," he stated calmly. "They're getting cold," he said to Blair.

"What a pity."

"I suppose the least we can do is take them into town and have them thrown in jail."

"I suppose so."

"Hey! You can't leave us in some foreign jail. We might never get out!" Phil complained.

"He's got a point," Clint said.

"He certainly does," Blair agreed.

"Would you miss him if he never got back to the States?"

Blair shook her head. "Not me. How about you?"

"Hey, you two, quit joking around!" Phil shouted. "Mexico always waives extradition!"

Clint appeared thoughtful. "I wonder how much it would take to bribe a few government officials in order to keep good old Vince and Phil as guests here for a few years."

Blair's topaz eyes grew incredulous. "Why, Clint Hollister, are you suggesting that these two men could become lost in the system?"

"Hey, wait a minute, we've got rights, too, you know!" Vince bellowed.

"Do you hear anything?" Clint asked Blair.

"Just the rain."

"Speaking of rain, we've got a horse who's dripping shoe polish out there somewhere. I suppose we should go find her."

Blair, peering past Clint's shoulder, suddenly smiled. "That won't be necessary."

Clint turned to see Risky Pleasure walking across the field, Jerry and Annie seated on her bare back. Both their faces displayed their nervousness.

"I'm sorry," Jerry said as he slid to the ground. "I know it was a lousy thing to do. But all I could think of was getting Risky Pleasure away from the farm to where she'd be safe."

"You had us worried to death," Blair felt the need to point out, despite the young man's good intentions. "Do you have any idea what Clint's been going through? What I've been going through?"

Jerry hung his head. "I guess I didn't think it through very well," he admitted. Annie remained silent, looking as if she expected both of them to be fired at any moment.

"You certainly didn't," Blair agreed.

Clint pressed a finger against her lips. "It's all over. And despite everything, Risky Pleasure is safe and sound."

"Thank God," Blair said fervently. "We may have you two to thank for that," she told them with a slight smile.

"Come on," Clint suggested. "Let's take these thugs into town and go home."

Annie finally managed to speak. "We're not fired?"

Clint grinned. "Are you kidding? Who's going to take care of the filly if we get rid of Jerry?"

"And if we fired you, Annie," Blair added, "we'd have to start looking for someone else to ride Risky Pleasure against Cimarron."

Jerry and Annie's answering smiles threatened to banish the slate-gray rain clouds as they hurried to load the filly into the trailer.

It took the remainder of the day to get the necessary papers that would permit them to bring Risky Pleasure back across the border. But the next morning Clint and Blair were sharing breakfast in the farm's sunlit kitchen.

"All the time I thought it was Blackwood," Clint mused aloud. "I never suspected Matt."

"Well, Ramsey wasn't exactly innocent," Blair pointed out. "After all, he had gone in with Brian Hanson to skim funds from the farm and divert them to Hightower properties."

"Yeah, but he honestly thought he was doing Jason a favor," Clint said reluctantly. "The old man wouldn't agree to invest in the company, so Blackwood figured that once he could show the profit, Jason would admit he'd been wrong....Which was a pipe dream if I ever heard one," Clint muttered. He knew that if Jason Langley could ever have admitted to being wrong, he would have invited Blair and her parents back to Clearwater Hills Farm years ago.

"It's interesting that Ramsey had no idea that Hightower was behind the drive to buy up all the land," Blair observed.

"It only proves there's no honor among thieves. He swears that when he was approached by Ingram Property Management and offered that commission to get Jason to sell, he planned to use his funds to pay back the money he'd embezzled. That way he could get the records in order before the old man found out what had been going on behind his back. But Jason did find out." Clint remembered that heated telephone call.

"You don't really think they killed him, do you?"

"Uh-uh." Clint patted her hand comfortingly. "I believe Matt on that one. Jason knew he only had a short time left to live. That's why he was going through his papers, in order to have everything in shape when you took over."

Clint suddenly grinned. "Oh, by the way, while Ramsey was turning everything over to the DA, an interesting little letter popped up."

"Oh?" Blair asked casually, rising from the table to get the coffee pot. She was refilling their cups when his next words almost caused her to drop the pot in surprise.

"Jason kept track of you over the years. He'd even had weekly conversations with Ben Winters."

"You've got to be kidding!"

"Seems he knew just about everything there was to know about you, sweetheart. Including the fact that you've got a stubborn streak a mile wide."

"I do not," Blair said, having the grace to flush as Clint laughed. "Well, perhaps a few feet wide," she admitted.

"That's why he left Risky Pleasure to both of us."

"I don't understand."

"He knew we were both so much alike we'd fall in love, but at the same time he figured you'd be like the irresistible force running headlong into the immovable object. So he chose the one thing neither of us could resist."

"Risky Pleasure."

"That's it," Clint agreed. "He may have been an irascible old bastard, but he seemed to know people as well as he did horseflesh. He figured the filly would force us to work together until we realized we were perfect for each other."

Blair and Clint exchanged a long look, both knowing that they'd been manipulated every step of the way. But neither had a single regret.

Then she returned her mind to the subject at hand. "What's going to happen to Ramsey now? And Matt? And the men behind Hightower?"

"The Hightower people have so many counts of racketeering charges against them, they'll be lucky to get out of prison in this century. And since Matt has turned state's evidence, he's been guaranteed immunity from prosecution, although he'll have to live with what he did for the rest of his life."

"Poor Marni," Blair murmured.

"It must have been hard on her."

Blair sighed, remembering the tearful conversation she'd had with her best friend after returning home last night. "It was. But I think it did her some good. She's determined to get her life in order and stop depending on men for self-esteem."

"I hope she makes it."

"Me, too," Blair agreed fervently. "I hope you don't mind, Clint, but I offered to let her stay here as long as she wants."

"It's your home, Blair.

She nodded thoughtfully, determined to change that situation as soon as possible. "What about Ramsey? What's going to happen to him?"

Clint shrugged. "He'll be disbarred, but since he wasn't in on any of the other crimes, he'll probably get off with probation or a light sentence for embezzlement. The guy is like a cat with nine lives—he'll always manage to land on his feet."

She sighed, thinking how much pain the man had caused Clint.

"Tired?"

Blair nodded, rubbing a hand against the back of her neck. "Very."

"It's been a rough few days. You should probably be in bed."

Her eyes met his, encountering an unmistakable sensual invitation. "That's not such a bad idea."

"I'm just full of great ideas."

Blair merely raised a dark brow in response.

Clint grinned and lifted her into his arms. "I've always believed actions speak louder than words," he claimed, carrying her down the long hallway.

Chapter Fifteen

As much as Blair wanted to make love to Clint, there were still some problems that had to be resolved. Lying on the bed, she did her best to ignore the gleam in his gray eyes and discuss their future.

"Clint," she murmured as he slowly undid the buttons of her blouse, "we need to talk."

"Umm. You're beautiful." He parted the material, bending his head to kiss her breasts with a lazy tenderness.

As anticipation began to build, Blair had difficulty in keeping her mind on her planned speech. "Clint," she protested softly, her voice drifting off while his lips traveled a teasing journey along her jaw. "The farm. We need to talk about the farm."

"Later." His lips moved over her face, feathering tantalizing kisses everywhere but on her lips, which hungered for his touch.

Blair raked her fingers through the lush silver waves of his hair, turning her own head in an attempt to capture those elusive lips. Finally she placed both her palms against his cheeks and held him still while she brushed her mouth over his.

"Later," she agreed, nibbling at his lips.

The kiss was cataclysmic, rocking Blair to her very core. Her eyes flew open, colliding with Clint's like a clash of cymbals. The hunger she witnessed there equaled her own, and as she clung to him, there were no more words.

CLINT WOKE to find Blair still in his arms, curled tightly at his side. Her hair was spread over the pillowcase like strands of spun silk, and he breathed in the wildflower scent of her shampoo as he pressed his lips against her head.

She sighed happily, rolling over onto her back, stretching her arms above her head.

"Gato del Sol," he murmured with a smile.

"Mmm?"

"Remember the Derby winner a few years back? He was named after a barn cat who liked to lie around, fat and sassy, in the warm afternoon sunbeams. That's what you reminded me of just now."

"Are you accusing me of being fat and sassy?"

Clint propped himself up on one elbow, tracing her slender curves with his fingertips. "Perhaps fat doesn't fit," he agreed huskily, "but if they give awards for sassy, sweetheart, you're a shoo-in for first place."

Blair laughed lightly. "I think I'll take that as a compliment."

"Good, because that's how it's meant. Most of the time," he tacked on.

"Now we're back to my stubborn streak, I suppose." She sighed dramatically.

"You are a little headstrong, darlin'."

"You're not exactly Mr. Agreeable all the time, either, Clint Hollister."

Blair's scowl only caused Clint to grin wider. "At least it'll never get boring around here."

She fought to compose her face. "Not as long as you remember who's boss."

Clint released her slowly, then sat up, resting his head against the pillow as he reached over and pulled a cigarette from the pack on the table beside the bed. Blair watched nervously as he tapped the cigarette against the wood, the sound unnaturally loud in the stifling silence that swirled between them.

"I see," he said finally, striking a match with barely controlled violence.

"I don't think you do," Blair began to argue, sitting up as well.

He lifted his hands to cut her off, then let them fall to the sheets. "Go on. I didn't mean to interrupt the boss when she was about to lay down the law." His gray eyes followed a spiral of smoke to the ceiling with apparent interest.

Blair flinched as he imbued the words with an acid scorn. She had to fight to keep her composure. "I want us to have equal say in the training of the horses," she stated firmly.

"Impossible. What happens when we disagree? You can only have one trainer, Blair. It gets too confusing for the horse otherwise."

She had already considered that aspect of the situation and was prepared for his objection. "There will be no problems with continuity in training because in cases of disagreements, your word carries the day."

"Really?" His steely eyes displayed his skepticism.

Blair nodded, clutching the sheet against her breasts. "Of course. You have more experience, so it's only right that your decision would prevail. I only ask that my ideas be considered fairly."

"I can live with that," he said. "Anything else?"

Blair suddenly realized she was holding her breath. "One more thing," she acknowledged softly. "About our uh, personal relationship..." Her voice faded as she saw the ominous hardening of his jaw.

He crushed out his cigarette. "What about it?"

"I don't think it's good for the morale of the farm if the trainer is sneaking into the owner's bedroom every night. It'll only cause gossip."

Clint pinned her with his gaze, wanting nothing more than to shake her until those gorgeous white teeth rattled. "Since when is the Tigress Woman afraid of a little gossip?"

She remained quiet for a long moment, simply looking into his darkening gray eyes. "I'm not thinking of me," she said firmly. "I'm thinking of the children."

"Children?" he reached out, taking her by her shoulders, but not to shake her. His gaze searched her solemn face.

"Children," she answered calmly.

"Blair, are you telling me you're pregnant?"

"Probably not yet, although nothing would make me happier.... I love you, Clint. I want to stay here with you and raise lots of winning horses, and beautiful children who look just like their father. But I refuse to allow people to brand our children illegitimate just because their father didn't see fit to propose to their mother properly."

"Blair, I don't think you know what you're saying," he answered unevenly.

She pressed her palm against his bare chest, feeling the rapid-fire beat of his heartbeat. "Oh, yes, I do."

Clint shook his head. "I've thought about it a lot, Blair, and I love you too much to ask you to give up your career."

"My career is here. With you." Blair's smile was so breath-takingly beautiful that Clint felt as if he were drowning in it. "If you want me to stay."

"You know I do."

"Good, because my agent called a couple of days ago. I meant to tell you; then things got a little wild around here and I forgot. They're going to let me buy out the contract." Blair grinned. "Why do you think I finally agreed to Risky Pleasure's match race? We need to make a lot of money, darling. The Tigress Woman didn't come cheap."

Clint drew her into his arms, his kiss gentle, promising. "Believe me, sweetheart," he murmured, nibbling at her lower lip, "she's worth every penny."

Blair sighed happily, settling into his arms for a long, satisfying kiss.

SIX WEEKS LATER, Blair was once again sitting on the edge of Marni's bed, watching her pack. Clint was there, his arm resting comfortingly around Blair's shoulder.

"I'm going to miss you," Blair protested softly.

"I can't believe you won't be glad to get rid of me," Marni said with a grin. "After all, how many people have their roommate living with them after they get married?"

"You'll get no complaints from this quarter," Clint stated firmly. "You're family, Marni. There'll always be a room waiting for you here."

Marni's eyes grew suspiciously moist, and she laughed shakily, then wiped at them with her knuckles. "Hey, if you two keep up like this, you're going to make me cry and ruin my mascara."

"I wish you could stay longer," Blair said, changing the subject as she felt herself near tears, as well. "It'd be nice if you could be here to cheer Risky Pleasure on."

"My God, Blair, you'd both be sick to death of me by September. And not only will I be cheering her on in spirit but, believe me, I'm placing a bundle on that filly's sweet little nose. But it really is time for me to get on with my own life. And as much as I adore this place, I really don't feel right breathing air I can't see."

"So live in L.A.," Blair argued. "It's closer than New York."

"Can't," Marni objected, carefully folding a rainbow-hued chiffon caftan. "Kyle Williams was sweet enough to pull those strings to get me into the Fashion Institute of Technology, so I'd better show up for classes."

"Sweet," Blair muttered, thinking of the brash young designer. "I'd say he owed you one. After all, you did help make him famous. I don't know many people who can carry off his wild designs." She grinned. "I still shudder to think how many wealthy matrons purchased those out-rageously expensive dresses, believing they'd help them look like you."

Marni ran her fingers over one of Williams's dresses, the brilliant purple silk shot with strands of twenty-four-karat gold. "I don't know," she said. "I like his stuff."

Blair shrugged, glancing down at her own jeans and cotton blouse. "To each his own."

Clint's hands closed over hers. "You're both knock-outs," he professed. "I've been the envy of all San Diego County, living with two gorgeous women." He grinned wickedly. "There are rumors that I'm starting my own harem."

"Don't you dare even think about it," Blair ordered, punching her husband lightly on his arm.

They all laughed, but as Marni closed the suitcase, her expression became serious. "Honestly, I don't know what

I would have done without you both. I was kind of a mess after that fiasco with Matt."

Clint heaved a sigh. "Don't feel like the Lone Ranger," he said grimly. "You know, it's ironic. I always considered Matt a pretty good friend, and look at all the grief he caused. And while Blackwood will never be one of my favorite people, it turns out that he wasn't really as rotten as I thought." He shrugged. "Just goes to show, you can never tell."

The trio fell silent for a moment; then Marni smiled. "Well, that's all behind us now," she stated brightly. "And thanks to both of you, I've had a nice, peaceful vacation and plenty of time to think. My mother was wrong, you know," she said to Blair.

"I've always told you that," Blair reminded her friend with a warm smile.

Marni nodded her blond head. "I know you have. I just never believed it before. But I'm a nifty person and I'm going to be a very successful designer someday."

"I'll buy every outfit," Blair promised.

Clint groaned good-naturedly. "I sure hope you'll give discounts to your old friends when you're rich and famous, Marni."

"Of course," Marni assured him. "Far be it from me to bankrupt this lovely farm. Where would I go on vacations to unwind?" Then she glanced down at her watch. "As much as I hate to, I'd better be getting to the airport."

Clint tucked two suitcases under one arm and grabbed the third before walking out to the car. Blair and Marni followed with a garment bag, two hatboxes and a makeup case.

"You'll come visit," Blair said later as they stood at the American Airlines departure gate.

"Of course," Marni agreed. "And you'll stay with me whenever you're in New York."

"It's a date," Clint and Blair answered in unison.

There was a great deal of heartfelt hugging and kissing. When Marni finally turned to board the plane, Blair watched her through a mist of tears.

"Come on, sweetheart," Clint murmured, putting his arm around his wife. "Let's go home."

She smiled up at him. "Do you have any idea how good that sounds?"

He dropped a quick kiss on her lips. "I never did, until I married you," he admitted. "Now I can't think of any place on earth I'd rather be."

Still holding hands, they left the airport to return to their farm.

IT WAS HARD for Blair to believe it was September. The California sun shone as brightly as it had all summer, the temperature was mild and the crowds jamming the stands at Del Mar racetrack were dressed in short sleeves, as she had been only this morning when she'd watched the Thoroughbred splash blithely along the strand.

Her heart was pounding as the recording of Bing Crosby crooning "where the turf meets the surf" signaled post time.

"There she is!" Blair jumped up, pointing at the big chestnut filly drawing cheers as she trotted past the stands.

Clint's attention was not drawn to his favorite horse, but remained on his wife instead. "Damn it, Blair, take it easy. All that jumping up and down can't be good for you!"

She tried to temper her enthusiasm, knowing Clint was only interested in her welfare. But ever since the doctor had confirmed her pregnancy, he'd been treating her like a piece of fine crystal. He supervised every bit of food that went into her mouth, insisted on her daily naps, and had steadfastly refused to allow her to ride.

"I'm fine," she insisted, waving wildly to Risky Pleasure as the filly passed their box. "Healthy as a horse."

"And as stubborn as a mule," he grunted, putting his arm about her. "You better thank your lucky stars you're so beautiful, sweetheart, or I might not keep you around."

"Speaking of round..." She patted her blossoming body, inordinately proud of her pregnancy.

"You're gorgeous. And I still love you even if you do take up more and more room in bed every night."

She laughed, punching him lightly on the shoulder. "Hey, mister, I didn't get this way by myself, you know."

Clint grinned down at her. "Don't I know it," he agreed. "Talk about your risky pleasures."

They shared a brilliant smile, then fell silent as both Risky Pleasure and Cimarron were led into the starting gates. When the loudspeaker announced the upcoming race, all eyes turned to the gate.

There was a long moment of collective silence; then a bell sounded, shattering the intense concentration of the spectators.

"They're off!"

Cimarron leaped forward the instant the gates sprang open and was a full neck in front just two jumps out of the gate. Blair's breath caught in her throat as Risky Pleasure broke indifferently, and she prayed Clint had known what he was doing by refusing to increase the filly's workouts to hype her up for the race.

She squeezed his hand, holding on for dear life as the filly strode choppily through the first hundred yards. The roar of the crowd was deafening when Cimarron raced out ahead, easily holding the lead going into the first turn.

But Annie, astride Risky Pleasure, refused to rush the horse, giving her time to make this her race. As they rounded the bend, Risky Pleasure pulled herself together, striding smoothly, ranging up to assume the lead.

Blair was screaming at the top of her lungs, and Clint gave up on keeping her calm while he added his own encouragement to the horse and rider. When they turned into the backstretch, Cimarron drew even with Risky Pleasure, getting a nose in front, but when they drove down the straightaway, the filly surged forward and regained her lead. Cimarron tried to go inside her, but she whizzed back across and shut him off.

Suddenly, as they raced that way, Risky Pleasure in front, Cimarron right behind, Annie's saddle slipped. Realizing his opportunity, Cimarron's jockey drew his stick, whipping the horse past Risky Pleasure to regain the lead.

"I can't watch." Blair buried her head into Clint's shirt, only to peek up again a moment later, her curiosity getting the better of her.

"She's going to be okay," Clint assured her, his voice harsh from yelling.

Blair breathed a silent prayer while watching the young jockey, halfway up the filly's neck. Risky Pleasure obviously hadn't given up; her ears were upright as she regained her momentum, coming within a half length of Cimarron at the far turn. The crowd was apoplectic when Annie and Risky Pleasure tucked in and made their move. The young jockey flicked her only twice, lightly, on the shoulder; from then on, the filly seemed to fly. She came charging ahead as the two horses raced past the eighth pole.

Cimarron battled back, hanging on tenaciously, but it was too late. Risky Pleasure stretched out and drove for the wire. She pulled away in the final one hundred yards to win by three-quarters of a length, creating pandemonium in the stands. Even Annie brandished her whip in the air in exultation.

Blair kissed Clint wildly, then some strangers sitting behind her, then a nonplussed photographer who dropped his Nikon in the commotion. Then she kissed Clint again. After this exchange they made their way through the congratulatory throng to the winner's circle.

Blair threw her arms around the filly's damp neck, kissing the velvety dark nose. Then she turned to Clint, her eyes sparkling like precious gems. "She won, darling! Risky Pleasure really won!"

Clint drew her into his arms, wondering if he'd ever get over his amazement that Blair MacKenzie was his wife. How could any one man be so lucky? He remembered when this race had seemed the most important thing in his life. Now it paled in significance beside Blair and the child they'd made together.

"Risky Pleasure only won a race.... We're the real winners, sweetheart," he said, brushing his knuckles against her cheek.

"Oh, Clint." She sighed blissfully, wondering if she'd ever grow accustomed to the fact that this wonderful man was her husband. How could any one woman be so fortunate?

Clint lowered his head to kiss her. Blair met his lips eagerly, oblivious to the whirring sound of camera motor drives freezing the kiss onto film.

When the tender scene graced the cover of *Sports Illustrated* the following week, Risky Pleasure appeared over their shoulders, her large teeth flashing in a broad, self-satisfied smile. There were even those readers who swore one of the filly's brown eyes was shut in a knowing wink, as if she had something to do with the lovers' happiness, but other readers insisted that idea was preposterous.

Or was it?

Harlequin Temptation

Duskfire

The sizzling new Temptation by JoAnn Ross, best-selling author of *Risky Pleasure*.

Duskfire is the story of Brandy, a romance novelist, and Ryan, a mystery writer, who join forces to create a book of love and intrigue entitled—you guessed it!—Risky Pleasure.

At first, Brandy hotly resists the idea of working with Ryan, a former cop. But neither can deny the physical attraction that flares between them. It doesn't take Ryan long to decide he wants Brandy to be a lot more than a co-author. He wants a wife. She flatly refuses.

Ryan employs every investigative skill he knows to discover the source of her fears. And he won't stop until Brandy says yes.

H·A·R·L·E·Q·U·I·N

FIRST·CLASS
Sweepstakes

OFFICIAL RULES

1. NO PURCHASE NECESSARY. To enter, complete the official entry/order form. Be sure to indicate whether or not you wish to take advantage of our subscription offer.

2. Entry blanks have been preselected for the prizes offered. Your response will be checked to see if you are a winner. In the event that these preselected responses are not claimed, a random drawing will be held from all entries received to award not less than $150,000 in prizes. This is in addition to any free, surprise or mystery gifts which might be offered. Versions of this sweepstakes with different prizes will appear in Preview Service Mailings by Harlequin Books and their affiliates. Winners selected will receive the prize offered in their sweepstakes brochure.

3. This promotion is being conducted under the supervision of Marden-Kane, an independent judging organization. By entering the sweepstakes, each entrant accepts and agrees to be bound by these rules and the decisions of the judges, which shall be final and binding. Odds of winning in the random drawing are dependent upon the total number of entries received. Taxes, if any, are the sole responsibility of the prize winners. Prizes are nontransferable. All entries must be received by August 31, 1986.

4. The following prizes will be awarded:

   (1) Grand Prize: Rolls-Royce™ *or* $100,000 Cash!
   (Rolls-Royce being offered by permission of Rolls-Royce Motors Inc.)

   (1) Second Prize: A trip for two to Paris for 7 days/6 nights. Trip includes air transportation on the Concorde, hotel accommodations…PLUS…$5,000 spending money!

   (1) Third Prize: A luxurious Mink Coat!

5. This offer is open to residents of the U.S. and Canada, 18 years or older, except employees of Harlequin Books, its affiliates, subsidiaries, Marden-Kane and all other agencies and persons connected with conducting this sweepstakes. All Federal, State and local laws apply. Void in the province of Quebec and wherever prohibited or restricted by law. Winners will be notified by mail and may be required to execute an affidavit of eligibility and release, which must be returned within 14 days after notification. Canadian winners will be required to answer a skill-testing question. Winners consent to the use of their name, photograph and/or likeness for advertising and publicity purposes in conjunction with this and similar promotions without additional compensation. One prize per family or household.

6. For a list of our most current prize winners, send a stamped, self-addressed envelope to: WINNERS LIST, c/o Marden-Kane, P.O. Box 10404, Long Island City, New York 11101

Discover the new and unique

Harlequin Gothic and Regency Romance Specials!

Gothic Romance

DOUBLE MASQUERADE
Dulcie Hollyock

LEGACY OF RAVEN'S RISE
Helen B. Hicks

THE FOURTH LETTER
Alison Quinn

Regency Romance

TO CATCH AN EARL
Rosina Pyatt

TRAITOR'S HEIR
Jasmine Cresswell

MAN ABOUT TOWN
Toni Marsh Bruyere

A new and exciting world of romance reading

Harlequin Gothic and Regency Romance Specials!

You're invited to accept
4 books and a
surprise gift *Free!*

#12 HT

Acceptance Card

Mail to: **Harlequin Reader Service®**

In the U.S.
2504 West Southern Ave.
Tempe, AZ 85282

In Canada
P.O. Box 2800, Postal Station A
5170 Yonge Street
Willowdale, Ontario M2N 6J3

YES! Please send me 4 free Harlequin Superromance® novels
and my free surprise gift. Then send me 4 brand new novels every
month as they come off the presses. Bill me at the low price of $2.50
each—a 10% saving off the retail price. There are no shipping,
handling or other hidden costs. There is no minimum number of
books I must purchase. I can always return a shipment and cancel
at any time. Even if I never buy another book from Harlequin, the 4
free novels and the surprise gift are mine to keep forever.

134 BPS-BPGE

Name	(PLEASE PRINT)	

Address		Apt. No.

City	State/Prov.	Zip/Postal Code

This offer is limited to one order per household and not valid to present
subscribers. Price is subject to change.   ACSR-SUB-1